ELIZABETH'S STORY

MORGAN PHENIX

THANK you FOR
your STORY — your
DAD, too.
Morgan Phenix

ISBN-13: 9781542695374
ISBN-10: 1542695376

WITNESS

This is a work of fiction, set in familiar geography and biography. The principal characters in this work do not reflect or portray any actual person, living or dead. However, there is a Kathryn in California, a poet and writer, among many other accomplishments and talents, who has written chapters in the life of another Elizabeth. That Kathryn's *Elizabeth* lived in another century, and fought battles in no way related to *Elizabeth's Story*.

I attended secondary boarding school with the real-life California Kathryn, yet we have never spoken with each other directly. I recall only her quiet beauty and that she was a very private person. Following a class reunion, which Kathryn did not attend, we touched, in writing and through shared and understanding hearts, concerning our Elizabeths.

Our school was in many ways similar to the one briefly portrayed here. The book's cover is a rendering of an actual photo I took at the school many years after our graduation. Again, familiar geography and biography, most particularly regarding the train station and the tracks. And the dreams and fears and futures of young people. And old. Their stories.

I am grateful for the many real and imagined souls who carried this story to a safe conclusion. This is *Elizabeth's Story*. The authors dedicate its telling to *Kathryn*

Note: The original published version of *Elizabeth's Story* is no longer available.
2017

AN ECHO

"For reasons sufficient to the writer, many places, people, observations and impressions have been left out of this book. Some were secrets and some were known by everyone and everyone has written about them and will doubtless write more....

If the reader prefers, this book may be regarded as fiction. But there is always the chance that such a book of fiction may throw some light on what has been written as fact."

Ernest Hemingway
A Moveable Feast, 1964

CONTENTS

Chapter 1

OUR STORY   IF TRUTH BE TOLD (2017)

This is my story. You will also meet others who helped me finish it, and they will speak, so it's partly their story too, if truth be told. The eyes and imaginations of old friends, and strangers we met along the way. And like some of their stories, my story begins nearer to the end than where it actually started. I can still remember when anything and everything seemed possible, except speeding up time. I was impatient. And then suddenly, here I am. Or rather, here we are.

The other day I glanced up from wiping powder off the porcelain edge of my wet sink. There was an old man in the mirror. Or maybe it was a woman. I couldn't really tell, not from the worried wrinkled forehead or tired lines at the eyes and mouth, hair pulled back. I didn't need to know. I never look closely anymore. Seems just yesterday I was really on my way, like I was speeding on a highway. And now I'm on an exit ramp, lanes suddenly crowding and merging, slowing too fast. Stop sign up ahead.

But I still have my story. Or our story. I'm sure the others will remind me if I falter or try to make changes on my own. The chapters are woven together with so many other stories and tales, everyone trying to make sense. Or live forever. The chapters of our stories. The chapters we write. The ones we live. Brief moments between the years. Not flashbacks and memories so much, and we have plenty of them too. But it's the few moments between the many years.

And then the days to come. Maybe those will be the best chapters. Maybe we can write them into the story now, and live them later. I've done a little of that along the way, and some of the moments have never even come to pass, and perhaps never will. Yet they remain part of my story. As it unfolds.

My story. An anxious future begins to dissipate, smoke in the chill night air. I am juggling fewer choices and fewer worries these days. Perhaps I simply have less to lose, as things begin to wind down. Or just the opposite, the few remaining chapters needing the most care. Reverence, each day a precious gift. Choosing the fewest words and images. The important ones. The moments.

So here is the story. I am not sure which one of us will have told or revised or delivered it. In the end. Strings and threads finally woven into warmer fabric. I can't tell whose story it will have been, at that point. Perhaps we have only a whispered invitation to arrive at the truth of the matter. If truth be told.

Chapter 2

KATHRYN THE LETTER.
A KNOT IN TIME (2015)

Elizabeth's letter came as a surprise, as always, as if it were an ordinary thing to receive on a Wednesday afternoon. Kathryn closed the mailbox and pulled the garden gate shut behind her, shading her eyes from the California sun with the envelope. Even at the awkward close angle she could make out the handwriting, but not the return address. It was from Elizabeth, and the stamps did not appear to be from any foreign land. Elizabeth. How many years of letters out of the blue?

"More than fifty years' worth," she reminded herself. "And how many months now, or years? Since the last letter." Kathryn put the envelope on the kitchen table and went to look for her glasses. She smiled to herself. The irony of looking for glasses. She moved slowly through the doorway to the darkened living room. She could barely see in the dim light, dark-green curtains pulled over the windows. But neither could she remember where she might have left her glasses, anyway, knowing not to push at her frailties, adding needless frustration. Failing sight and faltering memory. She rehearsed the likely options. On the stand next to her recliner, where she had slept, or maybe at her desk. She could not remember and returned to the kitchen. Her glasses were on the table, behind the coffee cup and napkin holder, only a few inches from the letter.

Kathryn opened the envelope, careful not to tear the paper, making a neat slit with her thumbnail. She gently pulled the paper from the envelope between two fingers, like searching for a coin or a lost ring between cushions. The paper rustled and smoothed, and the kitchen became silent. Elizabeth's words unfolded tentatively, just as the paper had emerged from the envelope. The greeting and hopes and polite questions cried Elizabeth's need for peace and quiet. She was looking for a small space, some order and integrity. Kathryn brushed at wisps of hair and flipped the loose dark braid away from her face, over her shoulder. She read on, searching for the heart of the message. Was Elizabeth running again? Some problem she couldn't loosen? A knot in time?

Kathryn knew there were several letters from Elizabeth in the woven basket on the wall, letters read and reread, the last one yet unanswered. She and Elizabeth had agreed on a plan in high school, to share their stories, edit and rewrite their lives. Since high school, weighing each other's choices. It had been an exciting plan, to help write each other's story. But now it had been years, maybe ten or more, since the last time they had shared in a decision or a choice. Or truly listened. How many years since she had listened to Elizabeth? Had she ever?

The handwritten return address in Virginia was smudged and stained by a thumbprint and greenish-gray flecks. Perhaps oregano. Or dust? Kathryn decided Elizabeth must have left the sealed envelope on a kitchen windowsill, between a damp draft and the time it took to decide whether to send it, maybe months. Elizabeth's words circled around the news she couldn't say. She told about three books she had bought, books Elizabeth thought might help guide her life toward a better conclusion. She called it her final chapter, her final trip. Kathryn noticed the books weren't novels or collections of stories, and a sad fear welled up in her chest that maybe Elizabeth had strayed from her love of adventure, Hemingway, Europe, trains, and travel. The trains.

Kathryn glanced down the paper and could see the conclusion. Her eyes immediately filled with tears, her heart caught between her long-ago fondness for Elizabeth's story and the complications and distractions that had taken Elizabeth around the world and back and into a hollow obscurity. Elizabeth was a beloved character in a poetic drama. Elizabeth was a book Kathryn had kept in a special place in her soul. Always at a comfortable distance, putting the treasured volume on a high shelf.

Kathryn knew also that they had been distant in other ways. Two decades, Elizabeth married, on the East Coast, and Kathryn where she had always been since high school, in California, busy with responsibility, teaching, meetings, schoolchildren, and school boards. Even so, Kathryn doubted that Elizabeth had ever given up her passion and excited fear, living on impulse and curiosity. And hunger. Elizabeth always had a distant horizon. A life of adventure. And fiction. It could have been so easy, just staying in touch. But this letter was something new. Kathryn pushed her glasses back on the bridge of her nose and forced herself to read carefully to the bottom of the page. A final chapter. And Elizabeth was coming. As if she lived just across town. After all these years. Elizabeth was coming. She was taking the train.

"Soon," the letter said. Kathryn folded the note and put it in the envelope with gentle care. She hoped Elizabeth was safe. Kathryn mouthed the words silently.

"Fifty years."

Chapter 3

BILLY TREES AND LIGHT (2016)

B illy waited until the anxious and relieved passengers had all moved forward toward the plane's exit. The cabin attendants' glances were patient and their words typically polite, yet they were obviously glad the flight was over. Calm Scandinavian accents. The soft green shoulder bag in his lap was all Billy had brought, so he was in no hurry to beat the rush of travelers toward baggage claim or customs, even though his long legs ached from the hours of cramped sitting. His bag contained the barest requirements, toothbrush and razor and socks and underwear, and an extra pullover shirt. And the books. One to deliver, and an extra, just in case. He lifted the bag's flap and pulled out a copy of the book, to take another look. His remarkable project. The shiny green cover, the trees and rusty rails and weeds. The questions and the promises, now part of his own story. One more book to deliver. If he could just find his way to a small town in Jutland. Terndrup.

Billy had also left a copy of the book on his way, under the old woman's pillow, in Western Pennsylvania. Wellsboro. A small-town nursing home. Smell of bleach, frail and inevitable journeys. The busy traffic of care and confusion hurried him along. Raised voices for the hard of hearing. Billy had sat on the side of the bed and read from the book, several of the more touching scenes that related to the old woman. And her daughter. Billy wondered how accurate the words were, translated by time and distance and fear. And frailty, or failure.

And by him, in the end. No indication the woman had heard or understood any of it, but when he finally stopped reading and stood up to leave, she closed her strained, open mouth and tried to wet her lips.

"No," she said, a weak but clear command, and again: "No." She patted the bedcover with her bony hand. Billy sat carefully on the side of the bed and took her hand. Dry fingers, slips of wax paper, brittle cellophane nails, transparent.

"I have to go. I'll leave the book for you. A nurse can read to you," he promised.

"No." Reaching for the book, clenched lips, fear in her eyes, suddenly wide open. He held the book for her to see, the glossy green cover, gentle arching trees over the soft wooded path, abandoned rails barely discernable through weeds and brush on the forest floor, curving out of sight. A dream. Escape.

"Here. The trees," she said, weak arm and a bony finger tapping on the book's cover, then pointing behind her head, to the pillow. Wisps of brittle white hair. She coughed. "Leave the book here. For me."

"Yes. I'll tell them to read to you. They seem nice."

"No. It's my book. My book. My story." Suddenly clear and strong. "My book."

"Yes. I know. Elizabeth told me to bring it to you. To read to you. At bedtime. Before you sleep." he said.

"Elizabeth," the old woman whispered. She drew several shallow breaths. "Tell Elizabeth why I left." She closed her eyes and lowered her arm to the bed. The old woman tapped twice on the blanket, a cadence. "The fear." And again, patting the soft cover twice.

"Her. Fear." She relaxed back into the pillow and closed her eyes. "Always. Her fear."

Billy sat in silence. He waited until the woman's breathing was regular, at ease. He stood and looked at the book, opening and checking the awkward handwritten words inside the front cover, to be sure he was leaving the right copy.

"I will tell her," Billy said. The old woman seemed to have fallen back to sleep, returned to a private place. The sheets barely rose and fell as she breathed. He wondered if she heard.

"I will tell her," he repeated. A soft whisper. He carefully lifted the pillow with the back of his hand and slipped the book into the cool softness. Safe. He leaned close. The old woman's weak smile.

"I will tell her. Now I know the truth. Almost true." He left the room, leaving the door open. Just a crack, for air. The smell of bleach. An indistinct cry at the end of the hall. Muffled words weaving complaint and comfort.

A woman's pleasant voice called. Close by. Billy's focus returned to the plane's nearly empty cabin.

"Excuse me, sir." Smiling cabin attendant. The tall one. "You are the last one to get off the airplane. We are here." She looked at the book he held. "What a beautiful front cover. Is it a good book?"

"Yes. I think so. I hope so. My friend wrote it, and I helped. I'm bringing a copy to someone who's part of the story."

"So we are flying to Denmark to deliver this book?" Her eyes gleamed with enjoyment and disbelief. "That sounds like a very special thing to do." Gray-green eyes laughing.

"Yes. Maybe it is a little unusual. But it's part of the story, I guess. And I have to find my way to Terndrup. A small town in Jutland. Jutland. Is that a county or a region? Or what?"

"No, Jutland is the mainland. That is where my man and I live. But we are on an island in the sea here. Sjælland. And Copenhagen, which of course is the city near to where we are now. The name means something like *market harbor*. København. So you will maybe go to Jutland on a ferryboat. Or take the train over some bridges, the long way around, or on the bus, over another island where Han Christian Andersen lived and wrote some of his stories. You could not pronounce the name of that island, even though it is just three letters. *Fyn*. See? You don't really pronounce the middle letter. It is also on the way to Jutland. Over the bridges." She looked toward the cockpit doors.

"We need to get off now so they can turn the plane around and go back for more funny people." She looked at the book in his hand. "The green and the sunlight on your book's cover are looking very much like Denmark in the springtime. In the woods. The green and the marsh and fields outside the window here in Kastrup are almost the same. And in just a little while in the woods, the beech trees, how do I say it…the trees are springing out with their new buds, and the sunlight comes down through the new leaves. It is so very beautiful, and we are all going for walks in the woods. Just to be in the spring-time green light."

"That sounds beautiful," he said. *And you are beautiful. And look even taller than me.* He caught himself, wondering if he had spoken the thoughts out loud.

Her eyes were somewhere else. "Yes, the green light is clean and fresh, and honest. I like very much your book cover. I wonder where the old train tracks are going. Into the woods." She looked at Billy. The corners of her mouth turned down; a shadow crossed her face. "Did you and your friend write a story that matches the picture on the front of this book?" Her voice did not seem to be asking for the details. Something else, he thought.

"I helped write it. With the person who had written many notes and pieces of the story. I helped to put it all together. Here, on the cover, my name, at the bottom. I was proud that I could help. I have always wanted to…"

She raised a finger. "Yes, yes, but what I mean is, the story inside the book. Is it about this picture on the book's cover? Is it a drawing or a hazy photograph?" She stared closely at the cover. "It is something I feel I have seen before."

"It's from a photograph taken many years ago. In Pennsylvania. An abandoned railroad, where there once was a train station. At a school. The woman who wrote the notes took the picture. Maybe twenty-five years ago."

"Oh. Maybe not, then. Maybe it's just like the beech trees. A memory. Springing out their buds. The light." She sighed. "Well thank you. OK, we must go before they are locking the door and taking off again."

"What?" Billy clutched the bag and started for the front of the plane.

"No. Just kidding. Be careful coming to Jutland," she called after him.

Billy walked quickly into the terminal and along the moving walkways, overtaking the passengers with heavy carry-on luggage and children, or lost in conversation. He wondered about how to get to Jutland. The best or easiest way. Maybe the train. Or the ferryboat, the islands in the sea, and the strange language. He saw unfamiliar letters on advertisements on the walls. At least the people seemed to enjoy speaking English. Friendly, too.

That relaxed thought disappeared at customs, where he showed his passport, the single stamp from New York, where he had boarded after the long and tiring bus rides to Chicago, Buffalo, and Wellsboro, in Pennsylvania. The trip to New York from Wellsboro seemed even farther. Then another tiring bus to get to the airport from the city.

Thank God for the ocean, he thought. *Otherwise I probably would have taken the bus all the way to Denmark, to save a few bucks.* The trip had been Elizabeth's idea. Kathryn had been skeptical and asked what the purpose was, to visit an old woman who wouldn't understand the gesture. Even worse, traveling to Denmark.

"Why bring old ghosts to life?" Kathryn said. But Elizabeth was adamant, and Billy was simply proud of the book, his name on the cover. He had made the Denmark trip a present to himself for his upcoming community college graduation. Serious debt, but worth it. He knew the journey was a clear marker in his life, too important to step outside the flow at this unusual moment in his life. Both Elizabeth's urgency and Kathryn's caution troubled him. Swirling eddies of contradiction and comfort. Like the story. Or stories, he reminded himself. His story too.

The Danish customs agent asked several times about the purpose of his visit, only one small bag, no reservations. A tall, thin American, determined face and shaggy brown hair, denim shirt and heavy wool vest. And no apparent means or reason for the travel.

"Where are you going, then, and for how long, please?" A second officer stood to the side, watchful yet not staring directly at him. Billy was certain there were more watchers nearby. "Jutland is a very large place. Which town, then?" the man asked. "How will you travel there?"

"Terndrup." Billy showed the address on an index card. Kathryn had written it carefully, checking it against the handwritten return address on Elizabeth's letter from Denmark.

"Terndrup," the agent said. "It is a very small town, I believe. Where will you stay there? Do you have friends or family there?"

Billy told them he was simply delivering a book for a friend. He took the book out of the khaki bag and explained he had helped her write the book. He pointed to his name on the cover.

"My name. Here."

The agent took the book, studied the cover, and opened it to the title page. A handwritten inscription. He turned to hold the page under the counter's light. Billy watched the man's finger brush across the words. A scrawled page number. The agent looked at the words closely, then leafed to a page in the book and read for a long moment. He looked away and then back at the page, studying the words. The second agent asked Billy about his bag.

"No suitcase? Where are your clothes for this trip?"

Billy opened the flap and began to pull out socks and underwear, and the spare book.

"And how will you be traveling to Terndrup?" Stern eyes.

The first agent interrupted the questions and handed the book back to Billy. "Very well, Mr. William Starr Johnson. Yes, I see this is your book. But mostly it is someone else's story. Correct?" Billy nodded. "Thank you very much, Mr. Johnson." He stamped Billy's passport and handed it to him. "I wish you a safe travel. If you need to stay in Denmark longer than ninety days, you must visit to your consulate or the Danish authorities."

The second agent protested, beginning another question. A quick raised finger from the first agent brought silence. He tore a piece of paper from his notebook and began to write as he talked.

"Mr. Johnson. If you do not have plans for someone to pick you up, and I am certain you do not, please travel by train or bus to Kalundborg or Sjællands Odde, and take the ferryboat to Arhus, or perhaps Ebeltoft, and from either of those places a bus, or perhaps better a taxi, will take you to Terndrup. It may be a little complicated because everything in Denmark is so close, yet tricky to get to. Just ask, and people will help. Take the ferryboat. *Mols-Linien*. The Mols Line. I think maybe you are not in a great hurry, and the ferry it is a very beautiful way to travel. I see your passport is brand new. I wish you a good trip and much luck on delivering this book. And the story."

Billy gathered his things and thanked the agent, avoiding the second agent's glare. The second agent looked closely at his partner and asked what Billy could tell was an accusing question. The agent held up his hand, snapped two clear words, and looked away. Billy offered thanks and turned to go. He wondered what story the inscription told. What secret. He recalled how Elizabeth had labored long and hard over so few words. He had guessed it was Danish and now was certain. Something which had softened a busy and suspicious man's heart.

Billy stepped onto the wide sidewalk in front of the terminal. The cabstand. It reminded him of Sacramento and the Amtrak station. He smiled. "Not quite." Lines of Mercedes-Benz cabs, a familiar diesel rattle.

Mercedes. Sweet, he thought, wondering what he could tell a cabbie, where he needed to go. Copenhagen first? Or how far to Kalundborg? Or Sjællands Odde? What a strange name.

"Mister Book Man!" A clear woman's voice from behind, coming from the terminal doors. He turned. The cabin attendant from the plane, striding toward him. The book cover. Green sunlight in the woods. She was fresh and athletic. Beautiful and trim. She had changed to jeans and a sweatshirt, and running shoes. Even in the flat shoes she was still almost as tall as his own six feet. Billy was certain she could both outrun him and knock him to the ground if she had to.

"Hello," he said, and she hooked her arm under his, surprising strength, almost a shock.

"Come on. I will drive you to Copenhagen, only a few miles over Amager, if you are not having a ride from someone. Is there someone here to pick you up?"

"Well, no, I wasn't sure what I would do."

She continued without waiting. "And if you like, we can keep on driving to Jutland, or to where you have told me you are going, Terndrup? That is not too far from where we are living, and I am taking the ferryboat to Ebeltoft this afternoon. Come on, then. My name, it is Bodil. On the way you are telling me about the train tracks in the sunlight. The green woods. And you can tell me the story." She stopped and turned toward him, a surprised look. "Or is it your story?" She steered Billy away from the taxicab lane in front of the terminal toward a walkway to the parking lot.

"I will buy you a nice coffee and a piece of bread on the ferryboat." Her step was strong, and she did not let go of his arm. He was suddenly a leaf on a swift rushing stream, surprised at the tumbling twist of events.

"And what is your name, then?" She looked at Billy as they hurried toward the crosswalk to the parking area. Her steps were surprisingly long, and he had to skip and hop once or twice to keep up with her. He was certain they looked like a young couple, maybe late for an appointment. He wasn't used to such walking speed, and before he knew it he was out of breath. His life as a cabbie. The stewardess had asked his name. "Your name?" His name. *Billy!* His mother's voice. A voice echoed in a darkened hallway, almost a decade ago. Calling. His name? *Billy!* His mother's scolding tone. His name. It was time. And he had the book. He had proof. On the cover.

"William. My name is William." He paused. It sounded like a foreign place. Only a moment and he gathered a quick breath. "William Starr Johnson. Starr was my gramma's—my grandmother's family name, with two *R*'s in Starr. William Starr Johnson."

"My man will enjoy meeting you, Mr. William Starr with two *R*'s Johnson. In our little house in Jutland. Kærby. Between Randers and Hadsund. Then we can take you to where you are going. And in Terndrup you are maybe needing a translator." She pressed his arm to her side. "William Starr Johnson. This is a very nice name." She stopped suddenly, took his arm, and looked at him. Anxious gray-green eyes. *More gray than green.* "William. You are OK with this trip to Jutland with me?"

Billy knew he had never in his life felt as confident as he did at that moment. The name confirmed it. *William.*

"Yes. This is OK. I am fine with this," he said, embarrassed that he had already forgotten the woman's name. He decided he would try to ask later. "I feel very lucky. No. It's not luck. I feel very fortunate today. Blessed."

"Bodil," she said. "My name is Bodil, since you have forgotten already. But there are many things about our little land that you will not forget so easily. How we are always close to the sea, and there is no mountain or river. And today we will drive to the ferryboat, which you will not forget. We drive right onto the ship and drive off again in Jutland. Yes. We are very, what do you say, fortunate. Every day, very fortunate." She pulled his arm and they stepped into the busy crosswalk. A cab skidded to a stop, horn blaring. Bodil waved and smiled to the cab and strode toward the parking lot, Billy in tow.

"Do you trust me to drive, William?" she asked, grinning.

He waited until they were safely at the car, an old and spotless Alfa Romeo. He recognized the model, an Alfetta. Perhaps from the 1980s. Or older. "I trust you, Bodil. But I can drive, if you like. An Alfetta. Nice. Well kept. I'm a cab driver anyway. If you tell me the directions, I can drive."

"No." She smiled. "I drive every week, seven days working, seven off. Besides, on the way you will tell me the story and read from this book you have written. I imagine a cab driver could have many stories to tell. Take out your book, William!"

"No, it's not my story, but I did help write it. I drive a cab at night, while I study at the community college. English and literature. Maybe to teach one day."

She nodded, eyebrows showing interest. "In Denmark, when studying, you would have a pension. To pay the rent. And for food."

They settled into the car, Billy's khaki green carry-on in the back seat. He reached for his bag and pulled out the spare copy of Elizabeth's book. "Where should I begin? Or I can give you a summary."

"At the very beginning. Read to me a few pages, so I can get the feel of it." She shifted smoothly through the five speeds, and before long they were on a highway circling toward the north and west, the city and suburban sprawl giving way surprisingly quickly to green fields, patches of forest, and small towns on either side of the road.

"We will drive to Sjællands Odde. The last miles of the *motorvej* we have the ocean on each side, and then the ship will eat us up, and we will sail!" She looked over at Billy. "William. Read me the first sentence or two."

He started, clearing his throat. He was nervous. An audience. He had always read it in proud silence. He began to explain that to Bodil.

She waved at him. "Read to me a little bit, more than two sentences. And then you will tell me the story."

He began.

"This is my story. You will also meet others who helped me finish it, and they will speak, so it's partly their story too. The eyes and imaginations of old friends. And strangers we met along the way. And like some of their stories, my story begins nearer to the end than where it actually started. I can still remember when anything and everything seemed possible, except speeding up time. I was impatient. And then suddenly, here I am. Or, rather, here we are."

He stopped, wondering how he could go on. He had cried with Elizabeth as they'd shared the words. She'd said they were some of the last words she had written. Not long before she had left Virginia. They had weighed each pause and thought, each comma and unclear reference point, a couple hundred pages. He repeated, "And then suddenly, here I am," and stopped again, and closed his eyes. "Here we are."

"Go on, William. Tell me in your own words. Or read to me. I don't care. Yes, suddenly, here we are. I think when you are reading this, you are writing new chapters in your own next book. Maybe? Go on."

"All right. I'll read the rest of the introduction. The first chapter is about Elizabeth's letter to her old high school friend Kathryn, telling her she's coming to visit. We then meet them as teenagers. A boarding school. They each speak, the girls, and it's a conversation almost. Telling about each other." Billy spread the book's pages open. He began again. The beginning. When he had finished the introduction, he explained once again.

"This is where Elizabeth and Kathryn meet. You will see that they are very different."

Chapter 4

ELIZABETH   OUR LONELINESS (1963)

I knew Kathryn in high school. She was quiet, and at first it seemed to be shyness. She was usually missing in gatherings and pictures and at dances. She arrived at school in September and left in June, spent only one year at the school, our senior year, a coed Quaker boarding school in Pennsylvania. She brushed off my first attempts to get to know something about her, said there were problems at home, and she needed a safe and easy place to gather her thoughts. The school was perfect for that.

Neither Kathryn nor I was raised in the Quaker faith or tradition, and it seemed as if a majority of the boarding students were like me anyway, from New Jersey, or from New York or Florida, lots of Jewish and international students, all sorts of boys and girls. They must have been from families wealthy or connected enough to be able to secure a place there. The school setting was beautiful. Rolling acres, lawns and woods and fields, not far from the Neshaminy Creek. The school was thirty or forty miles north of Philadelphia. A Reading Railroad spur line cut through the forest at the school's edge, and the school had its own small turn-of-the-century train station. Originally, for coal deliveries, they told us. The one daily train to and from Philadelphia did not stop at the station.

I had been at the school for three years already when Kathryn arrived. We roomed together my senior year. My own solitary ways had resulted in no ready takers for a final year's companionship at the school. What I mean is no one wanted to room with me. I guessed the dean for the girls and the admissions officer would pick a roommate, shuffled from a few leftovers and latecomers like Kathryn. It was like arriving as a stranger in the ninth grade all over again, getting a roommate by pure chance. It should have felt like a senior year to remember, friends for life, but Kathryn's newness on campus and my own private ways ensured we would be instant strangers.

She arrived without fuss or fanfare, two plain suitcases and some books. Even in our similarities, we were strangers. Kathryn was new and shy, with a distant edge, maybe a bit of anger. Or despair. But she was beautiful, long, dark hair and the kindest eyes I had ever seen, warm and brown. And accepting. I was just lonely, incomplete, and always in a rush. We never did become close friends, as one usually imagines it could be, never shared secrets and laughter and pranks, but in the second month of our rooming together, a coincidental and momentary brush of our fingertips at the light switch, a startled glance of recognition; we laughed out loud and, in that moment, discovered that our loneliness was mutual. We soon learned that holding hands and talking and sharing words and thoughts and ideas provided comfort. Usually it was me talking, but she was patient and kind, in a businesslike way. It was peaceful, though. I can't say how things went from conversation to a deeper closeness, but eventually we discovered that the nights could pass without dramatic dreams or fears if we slept in each other's arms, quietly and gently. Kathryn's arms were the strong ones, encompassing my usual fears.

We never thought of our relationship as sexual or romantic or quirky or rebellious, as the children seem to do today. We were just walking a quiet path together, and when the year turned toward graduation, college plans dominated the conversations. Kathryn's plan was to return to the West Coast, and for me that seemed adventuresome, though for her it was just going home. I was going to attend a state college near my New Jersey home, to prepare for a life of work, teaching perhaps, and a family one day. But college turned out to be silence once again, transparent in the busy tangles and crowds of animated college students. I went cool and quiet through the years that followed, and thought of Kathryn's clear words, her stern advice from time to time, wondering when she might write to me. I was not lonely, just solitary. Only at night did the comfortable dream of Kathryn's regular breathing bathe me in release. Warmth, and peace.

I waited to hear from her, because she was part of my story. No, it was more than that. In the years since school, Kathryn was supposed to be the co-author of my story. I am not sure she was even aware of that special responsibility, though we agreed she would supply advice and good counsel. She was good at that, confident. My own silence, as I aged, became frightening, sometimes a soundless scream, usually in the quietest hours of the night. I think it was my story. My book. We had called it the Elizabeth Book. I would panic when I felt as though my story was slipping away or that I wouldn't finish it. Rather, that she wouldn't help me finish it. I needed her strength. On the darkest nights I prayed in silence.

"Kathryn, please write to me."

Chapter 5

KATHRYN   ALLOWED TO BECOME INVISIBLE (1963)

Elizabeth was more fragile and uncertain than I was, or at least she seemed so in high school. I was the newcomer in the senior class, but I quickly learned that both Elizabeth and I were strangers on the dormitory hall, visitors, almost, among a comfortable membership. I didn't mind at all walking past people who didn't care about my being there. Elizabeth had lived at the school for three years when I arrived, and they didn't seem to know her. It was as if we both were learning new names and faces.

As a latecomer, I wasn't really trying anyway, and didn't care, I guess. I felt no real surprise that no one ever asked what had brought me from California to an East Coast boarding school for my final year of high school. We weren't excluded, just allowed to become invisible. Unassuming guests. And roommates. And then more. We shared a common understanding of words that comforted. And then that chance moment, the touch. I remember the shock on Elizabeth's face, the unexpected moment of surprise. I told her it was the light switch that must have done it. She laughed. But she didn't let go. Anxious, slender fingers. They matched her face, her entire body, actually. A slender coiled spring. I was surprised she wasn't a star in some sport or another. A tidy ash-blond pony-tail. Ready to run. But hesitant at the same time. Worried. Alone in the middle of activities.

Our relationship seemed to be enough for each of us, and any loneliness or separation I felt from my family and the awful troubles at home, or other girls in the dorm, or boys I might have dated, was satisfied by the special closeness that developed between Elizabeth and me. We spent quiet evenings and weekends, low music while she read, or sometimes reciting a passage aloud, from Gibran or St. Exupéry, but most often from Hemingway. I enjoyed simply resting and letting her words flow over me, while she was deeply involved in her authors and their worlds. I had enough struggle with my own world, thinking about my mom.

Elizabeth's favorite book was Hemingway's Paris memoir, *A Moveable Feast*. She returned again and again to the part about the young wife who lost her husband's manuscript on the train. Hadley Hemingway. She got off the train and then remembered the manuscript. In a suitcase she had left on the train, gone, forever. Poor Elizabeth seemed to live in Hadley Hemingway's shoes. If I was Hemingway's wife, I would have just asked him to gather his own papers and things next time, rather than making me his messenger.

But Elizabeth shared Hadley's Hemingway's loss, more than mistake or catastrophe. I could hear it in her voice, straining as she read, holding back the pain, shadows of sharp guilt and shame. Her voice would crack, and she said it made her feel helpless. She referred to the lost books every time she read Hemingway, about how responsible Hadley must have felt. Losing his manuscripts. The tales and characters and lives lost, like an awful shipwreck in dark icy seas.

Then it happened, a small mirror of Hadley. It was in March of our year together, my one year at the school. I'm glad I was there, because I really liked Elizabeth, and she might have crashed if I hadn't been there.

Elizabeth arrived back at the room early from class or study hall, went to her desk, and slumped in her chair. She was silent and looked really troubled, held her chin in the palms of her hands, fingers pressing in on her ears, like she was trying to keep out any sound. Then I saw her tears reflecting the light from the desk lamp. She breathed in deeply and sighed, shaking her head. Then she started crying, softly at first, and I could see her clenched eyes and mouth, holding her breath. She made a little moaning sound.

I knew not to ask anything right away, so I sat on the edge of the bed and waited. It was hard not to say anything, and I could have laughed even, tried to make a joke out of it. Then I got a small sideways glance from Elizabeth, sort of pathetic, so I nodded at her and tried to smile. I wondered what had happened. If it was some person who had made her this miserable, there would be trouble, and it started welling up in me.

"I'm here," I said, solid. Like everything was going to be OK. "It'll be OK."

Chapter 6

ELIZABETH WRITING
OUR BOOKS (1963)

I was so mad. Partly that Kathryn was in the room, and I wanted to cry and couldn't with her there, and then I just wanted to be alone. Hell, I *was* alone. I was always alone. It was so unfair, and so stupid. Stupid me. And stupid Mr. Johnson, with his stupid ideas, as if he had ever written a book, just a high-school English teacher and a yearbook coach. I had not meant to lose the papers. In fact I had not lost them, just put the folder down. And then I walked away. Didn't remember until hours later. And they were gone. Everyone's work that week on the yearbook, and the special surveys, and clips of favorite memories, and tallies of who would be most likely to succeed or who would be the most this or most that. And even if they found the papers, I would still be the most stupid of them all. The most likely to lose a manuscript on a train. The school's own Hadley Hemingway. Stupid me.

Kathryn was just sitting there, and I knew she was waiting. She said that everything would be OK.

"No, it won't. I'm so stupid."

"So what happened? Did someone do something? Who called you stupid?" Kathryn asked, like she was protecting me.

"It's the yearbook. I lost some yearbook files, or at least I put them down. I don't know where they are. They're gone. How could I be so dumb?"

"OK, so it's just papers. Nobody's dumb. Let's go look. Do you want to go look? Did you tell Mr. Johnson?" Kathryn asked.

"Yes. I told him. I looked all over, and then I went down and told him, and we went back out to the commons where I had been, and they were finished cleaning up, and it was too late, I guess, and we looked in the trash bins and the plastic bags they had put out back. Nowhere. Nothing. Stupid."

"So, was he mad? Did he yell at you?

"No. He was nice, as usual. Probably because I was so upset. I was crying. He said the papers will probably turn up anyway. He said they have copies of most of it. But he's so dumb, he makes me so mad sometimes. Even when he's nice. And I was just stupid. I guess he was just being nice."

"What did he do?" Kathryn asked, a tone of alarm.

"No. It's nothing he did, just the way he talks. Ideas, advice. About the future, as if he knows how you could get there from here. I don't know. I can't even figure out about tomorrow. Or today!"

"What did he tell you?" Kathryn closed her eyes, and I could see a hint of a smile on her face. It softened her.

"And he looks at you like he knew. Like he knows."

"Knows what?" Kathryn asked. She was still smiling. "What was it he told you?"

"Like he knows when you're unhappy, or scared, and you don't know what to do, or how to be happy, or how to make plans, or anything. Everything. Like he knows everything, and that it should be so easy."

"I bet I know what he told you," Kathryn said, "but tell me what he said."

"Did he tell you something about me?"

"No, no, silly," Kathryn said. "Not about you. It was about me, about us all, in English class. The kids were freaking out about SATs and being seniors and applications and having to make so many plans and choices. A lot of them were confused, and a couple of them were actually scared, it seemed. That's how the conversation started. One girl was crying about something, a scholarship she didn't get, I think. Some of them have it so easy here at school. But I know what he told you. Same thing he told us. He's right. I think about it a lot."

"Oh?"

"But tell me anyway, Elizabeth. I want to hear how you tell it," Kathryn said.

So I told Kathryn what Mr. Johnson said after we had looked for the papers, that he asked if I was doing all right otherwise, and was I happy about things, and what was I planning to do after graduation.

"And he asked if, how did he put it, if *things were working out*, if I *felt good about things*, if I was *confident about my future*. So I told him I didn't really know, and then I told him about how sometimes I feel like a loner but not lonely, and alone. Except for my one best friend, you. I told him I felt like I could just quit. Quit everything. Like it was all over. Like it felt like the end."

Kathryn was watching me now. She wasn't smiling, but showing me her strong side, looking right at me, nodding a little, so I went on.

"He said life is like a ten chapter book, a really good book. The best book ever written, or one of the best, he said. And when things are not going so well, or if we are afraid, or we make a big mistake, or just don't know, or like I felt today, how it seems like it's the end of chapter ten in a really bad book, and that it's all over. A really bad book with a really bad ending."

"OK," said Kathryn. "That's it?"

"No," I said and I went on, telling Kathryn how Mr. Johnson had leaned forward, real close, looking me right in the eyes, which were getting tears in them again, and told me we write the chapters of our books. We write our chapters ourselves, and he knew for a fact that I was only up to chapter two right now, maybe chapter three of my book. My book. The Elizabeth Book, he called it. My book. Chapter three, probably, he said, and the rest was going to be great, whatever way I chose to write how the story would unfold. My book. But he said I had to write it. The Elizabeth Book.

"Right." Kathryn said. "Your book." She pulled her desk chair out and put it right in front of me. Then she sat down. Kathryn picked up my hands in hers, real firm, and smiled. "The Elizabeth Book," she said, and then put my hands down solid, right on her knees, and took my face in her hands. I could feel her energy. Her hands were warm, and they were a firm cradle. Her hands. My face. "Yes, it's about the Elizabeth Book," she said.

Kathryn was looking at me, real serious, and then she let go of my face and lowered her hands, touching my lips so lightly with one finger on the way, and took my hands in hers again, kneading my fingers, like she was going to warm them up. Someone turned on a vacuum cleaner down the hall. A door slammed, dimming the sound of the machine, and our room was quiet. Still. Kathryn swallowed. We were alone.

And then she said, like a verdict, "Yes, it's your Elizabeth Book. And you are in my book too. My book is the Kathryn Book." She whispered, almost angry, eyes wide, "You know, I thought I was in chapter ten in a really, really bad book. Until I got here. But I have learned it's only chapter two. Or maybe three. And I have to do the rest." She waited. And then Kathryn said to me, "Elizabeth. I have an idea. About how we could write our books."

Billy lowered the book and looked out the window. Rolling fields and borders of trees, gray glimpses of water in the distance.

"How much longer? To the ferry?"

"A while," she answered, soft words. "So, did their friendship last?"

"Their friendship has been for a lifetime, in a distant sort of way. But that spring was the last time they saw each other. For more than fifty years." Billy watched the green stretch of fields and trees.

Bodil was silent for a minute, watching the road. She sighed. "Fifty years." She sighed again. "Read to me a little more. Is there more about the two of them? I think they are more than friends. And much more than lovers."

Billy raised the book and turned a page. "Yes. I think so too," he said. "Elizabeth longed for many things. She still does. This next part is where they are looking back at leaving the school. Leaving each other."

Chapter 7

ELIZABETH TRAINS AND HADLEY HEMINGWAY (1964)

We were just eighteen, or Kathryn was, and my birthday was coming up, almost eighteen. Graduation was coming too, and I got a chilling tightness in my stomach each time the thought crossed my mind. I didn't really like the school that much, but it had been most of what I could call home for almost four years. My dad visited me from time to time on his business travels, and we had vacations at Christmas and Easter. And summer, of course.

We were allowed six weekends home each school year, but it was far enough away for me to make those visits infrequent. Vacations at home were so quiet without Mom. Dad tried to be my pal but really didn't know how, and his work kept him busy, and even when he wasn't working, his mind seemed elsewhere, preoccupied. It must have been a distraction, or some guilt, I guess, to have me there and not really know who I was. Or what I needed.

What I needed. I never thought in those terms, but when I found something that caught my attention, usually a story or a song, it captured my very being, my heart. I told Kathryn about that, how I could feel it way down inside, like fear, but happy. Kathryn laughed at that.

"Fear. But happy!" She laughed so seldom, and when she did laugh I would get a really big rush of that scary excitement, in my stomach. All over, really.

"You are so beautiful," I would say. "You are so beautiful when you laugh, and I can feel what you're laughing about way down inside, and it makes me so…I don't know what. Deep inside."

"If I'm laughing, it's probably about you," she would say. She would look at me directly and say it again, almost like she was trying to make me take some of that seldom happiness inside, deeper than just a smile, like she thought I was unhappy inside. "If I'm laughing, it's probably about you." She was stronger than I was. I knew that. She would then come and sit beside me, or pull her desk chair over beside mine, and take my hand or stroke my hair back behind my shoulder. My hair was longer then. And we were closer. And it was ending. It was ending. A hollow tunnel in my stomach. A dark corner. Next to the memories of my mom.

We would graduate in June. I was going home, or what was left of home. I applied to Montclair State and had no trouble getting in. My dad could afford it, because I had decided to live at home, in Maplewood. I had been away long enough, but living at home was more than that; mostly it was because I couldn't imagine living with another roommate. I couldn't imagine finding another Kathryn to live with.

"To live with," I thought, saying the words out loud.

"What?" Kathryn asked.

"Oh, nothing, really. Just thinking out loud." I didn't want to talk about this.

"Something you can live with? Is that what you said?"

"Have you decided on a major yet? For college?" I asked, to change the subject.

"Yes, I told you. Art and maybe teaching." Kathryn was looking at me. "But what's the matter, Elizabeth? Tell me what it is, something you could live with. Or was it live without?" She wasn't going to let it go, so I told her what had been on my mind for days, really. No, for months. Or more.

"It's that I just don't know about next year, college and all. I just don't know what life is going to be like. Classes, and living at home, and, well, who my friends will be. I've been away so long."

"Well, you'll find out, and you're ready." She pulled at the plastic clip holding her hair, letting the braid loosen. She had thick, dark-brown hair, always drawn back from her face. I used to tell her she looked Native American, and she would always say, "Yes, part Native American, part Scotch fur trader, I think, so look out. I'll scalp you and sell it!"

"No, it's more than being ready. It's that I'll really miss you," I said. I wanted to get it out. "In fact I don't know how to imagine it at all. I've really counted on you for so much, and for smoothing things out when I get frustrated. Like when I lost the yearbook files."

"But they found them. And wasn't it Mr. Johnson who smoothed things out? About making plans? And about your book? Writing your chapters? The Elizabeth Book?"

"No!" I said, loud, almost angry. Then softly, "No. It was you. You stayed close." The room was suddenly quiet. Every sound seemed to freeze for a moment; the hum in the wall disappeared, the window fan turned in slow motion. A bird trilling in the courtyard cut its song midnote. "You stayed close," I said again, and I began to weep, no sound, just a tightness and clenching fingernails in my palms.

"Oh my," Kathryn said. "Oh my." She waited for a minute, maybe not that long, but I started breathing more easily, shaking my head, a couple of deep breaths. She said, "Let's go for a walk, just to freshen up before supper. Come on. We have time. Lots of time. Bring a book. Let's go down to the creek, the station. You can read me a chapter or two. Bring Hemingway along."

I pulled on the worn back of *A Moveable Feast* and slid it from the ranks of books on the shelf above my bed. We left the room and went down the stairs and out the door to the path that led to our favorite spot. We followed the sloping drive toward the train station, easy downhill steps, Hemingway in my hand.

Holding the book gave me courage. A sketch of a lifetime in a comfortable, familiar grasp, like holding hands with a friend. A lover. I must have smiled at the thought, cradling Paris in my hand, the mysteries of Europe after the war, Americans venturing into unexpected and rich and foreign pleasures, romantic. Living on a Bohemian shoestring. Trains and cafés and wine and lovers and novels and bullfights. Disappointments and tragedies, romantic and forbidden.

Distant. Far away. It was in my hand, yet rich and warm in my stomach. Hemingway.

Kathryn suddenly grabbed my free hand, pulling me to a stop, and then around to face her.

"What? Where were you? Just now! I've been watching your face. Have you been to some magic mountain or something? Or somewhere? An island in the sea? Where were you?"

I looked at the path and the trees on either side of the road. We had walked a couple hundred yards, or more, down the long drive through the woods. The school's old spur line train station stood just ahead, the pond beyond that, and the Neshaminy Creek in the distance. Quiet edge of the school grounds. We walked this way often, and perhaps that was part of Kathryn's surprise.

She asked again, "Where were you?"

"I think I know," I said, and then, "Let's sit down. On the bench at the station. We can watch the pond, there will be birds and things, and it will come alive after we stop walking. I think I know." We circled our arms and slowed to an ambling embrace, made our way to the far side of the station, sat down on the station's old wooden slat bench, facing the tracks and the pond beyond, another hundred feet down the slope.

Kathryn waited while I gathered my tumbling thoughts, like jays in a tree, all calling at once, too many voices, too many books, too many authors. So I started.

"Imagine, we go to a school that has its own train station. I mean, the train doesn't stop here, but it runs past, into Philadelphia, every morning and returns in the afternoon, then on to the end of the line, Newtown, a couple more miles. But I could just get on a train some morning, and I would almost be like Hadley Hemingway."

"OK," Kathryn said. "But you'd be going to Philadelphia. Not Paris. Not Marseille, or Madrid."

"That's not what I mean. What I mean is that we, or I, could go anywhere. I mean, if I read something in this book, I'm just reading. But what if I want to be there? What if I want to be in the book? In the story. Why can't I be in the book? Or be like them? In the book? This isn't fiction." I held up *A Moveable Feast*. "This book is as real as us sitting here at the train station. Hadley Hemingway was there. With Hemingway. And when she lost the manuscripts, she was alone. She was on the train. She was in Europe, she was in a foreign country, riding through the night. Carrying manuscripts and all the copies of the manuscripts. In a suitcase. She was enchanted, like a princess. Like flying on a magic carpet, on the train, like, I mean…"

And Kathryn, so softly and so gently, whispered low shushing words in my ear, holding me close. "OK, OK, OK…" And I don't know how many times, or how long we sat there, in a knot of rocking back and forth and then laughing a little. And then, quiet.

"OK," Kathryn said. "I think I see what you're saying. You're in love with your books, and they're mostly real books, memoir and biography and novels about real places and times, right?"

"Yes," I said. "They are real, and I want them. I want the stories for me. I want a story."

"OK, then. How did Hemingway get them? Or Hadley Hemingway?" Kathryn asked.

"Or St. Exupéry, *Wind, Sand and Stars*, North Africa, Morocco. How did he get there?" I asked.

"Well, he was French. And it was all about flying planes and mail service after the first big war."

"But he wrote other books and was a writer, a philosopher almost, a poet," I said. "And don't forget *The Little Prince*. And the fox! What about the fox and the Little Prince?" I almost shouted this, and Kathryn pushed away from me.

"What?" she said. "The fox? I know about the fox, but why are you shouting? Are you shouting at me?"

"Yes, I think so," I said, "because you have to listen." I stopped and tried to think, and went on. "The fox tells the little prince their relationship is about trust and responsibility. The little prince tamed the fox, noticed him, and the fox depended on him, waited for him, was connected with him!"

Kathryn looked at me and said quietly, "The quote was 'if you tame me, then we shall need each other,' and he said it was them being 'unique in all the world.' Elizabeth, let's talk about this later."

So we sat for a long time, looking at the pond. Water and woods and grass sounds welled up in bits and pieces from the silence, the birds and small moving things forgetting we were there. Sounds, rustling at the water's edge, a splash, birds competing for space, calling out territory. Invitations, everything in balance. I opened my book to the usual chapter, about Hadley and Hemingway finding out she had lost his fiction manuscripts, copies and all.

The book's pages were so familiar and worn, and I typically stopped at that point, halfway through the chapter on an expatriate writer's hunger and discipline. My eyes fell on the opposite page. I read it to myself and then, bringing nature's silence to the edges of the pond again, "Here it is, Kathryn, right after he's talking about Hadley and the lost fiction, Hemingway says, 'I knew I must write a novel. But it seemed an impossible thing to do when I had been trying with great difficulty to write paragraphs.' Kathryn, do you remember your idea?"

"What, that you want to write? A novel?"

"No, no, doesn't matter what, just the Elizabeth Book. I need you to, well, help me write it. I really need you to write it for me, but I guess that's asking too much."

Kathryn said, "Maybe we can help each other. But let's go. It's time, it's getting late. Supper. Aren't you hungry?"

I said, "It's too late to be hungry. The train is coming."

"Nonsense, what train? Paris?" Kathryn said, grinning, and then shock as the sound grew, a low and distant rolling bass hum, then pinging and aching rails, and two short whistles at the trestle over the creek. The sound grew to a roaring rumble, a worn diesel with faded "Reading Railroad" on the side skidding on screaming steel, past the station and our two motionless statues in rippling hair and clothing, then two nearly empty passenger cars barging through the silence and into the woods. Last stop a mile away, at the edge of town. Ticking steel. Distant thunder. And silence.

"Let's go," Kathryn said again.

"I'm ready."

Billy closed the book and leaned back in the seat, the book open in his lap. The Alfetta purred an Italian choral tone, harmonies and waves of refreshment. He glanced at Bodil. She was intent on the road ahead. Her mouth tense, a shadow of worry. He closed his eyes. The sound of the tires and wind carried the story's tune. Its song. Stories and tunes. Billy's mind drifted to his mother's nightly gift, words gently hummed. And sleep.

"Billy. You will not want to miss this." Bodil prodded at his arm. "Here is the ship."

"Where do we park?" he asked, startled, unsure where he was.

"In the ship, silly. We drive the car up into the ship," she said. "And you did miss the motorvej in the middle of the ocean. The last miles were very beautiful, distant dark water and silvery waves on both sides of the road, and the blue sky, and the sun coming out from the clouds." They slowed at a checkpoint, and Bodil scanned her pass, then drove up a broad ramp and into the wide steel cavern. Billy wondered how so much steel could sit so high above the waterline.

"*Odde*," he murmured. "Something to do with the end of the world?"

Bodil continued, "No, it just means a narrow piece of land out into the sea. In the old days, on some of the boats the whole nose of the ship opened up, and we drove in like little fish into a whale. Or at the side or back of the ship. Now it is a very fast catamaran boat. We are losing some of the charm, like dining on white tablecloths. But we come quicker to the other side. This used to be three or four hours. But now the voyage is about an hour and a half. Then we will be driving again."

Billy asked how much his fare was, realizing he had not exchanged dollars for Danish currency. "I can give you dollars for now," he said as Bodil maneuvered the car into a parking slot. Low ceiling, steel echoes. Distant shouts and a bell.

"Nonsense," she protested. "I am coming on the boat anyway. Let's go. You must be hungry, and you will need me to help you order a piece of bread."

Billy began to protest.

"Just bring your book," Bodil said. "You must read more to me. And no hamburger today, William. You could get one here, but I think they still serve a real Danish piece of bread. Even at a counter." She shook her head. "In the old days, not so long ago, on the big, slow ship, it was fine dining and waiters. Today we are just hoping for a nice piece of bread."

"Can I get anything on the bread?" he asked.

Bodil laughed. "Come on, William. And the book!"

They left the car, and Bodil took his arm in hers for the second time, comrades or lovers or carefree strangers for the day. The woman obviously in charge. The ship's interior parking deck was dimly lit, and they followed passengers up a steel stairway that opened onto a bright lobby lined by windows and walkways, a refreshment counter on one of the inner walls. Bodil steered him away, toward a small table near the windows, the North Sea's distant horizon in misty haze.

"Let's have a beer," she said. "Plenty of time for a couple to wear off, or then you can drive, and they will put you in the jail instead of me. The menu is on the wall, but I can order for you." He saw a long list of choices. "All you have to choose today is *franskbrød* or *rugbrød*, white or rye," she explained. "I will do the rest. The Danish rye bread is very thin but, how do you say, dense, with strong flavor, and the French bread is fresh white bread. Usually one orders two or three, usually fish and then some meat and maybe cheese. What do you think?"

He raised his hands and shook his head. "What do you think? What's good?"

"William, it's all good. Do you like fish?"

He nodded, unsure. "Yes, but maybe not the herring. At least not right away. I've heard about the pickled herring. Not my first taste of Denmark, please."

"OK, no *sild*," she said. laughing, "How about if they have a fried fish filet, very nice, with a little garnish on top? I will see if they are serving this today." She got up from the table.

"That sounds good, Bodil, but I need to get some Danish money."

She was gone. Billy sat and looked at the people who took the ferryboat. He wondered if they were commuters or simply tourists. A ferryboat. It didn't look like a river or a bay. He realized he did not know what ocean they were crossing. When Bodil returned, balancing two beers and several small plates, Billy reminded her he could perhaps change some money on the other side. She smiled and waved his words aside.

"Tomorrow, William. Today you are my guest, and I am a working woman. Later, when your book is a famous movie, which maybe you and I will star in, you will come back and take me out in your big, long Cadillac." She placed a green bottle in front of Billy.

"Tuborg," Billy said, turning the beer bottle around. "We wrote about this in the book. A scene in Copenhagen." He laughed at her joke. "No Cadillac, Bodil. I would get a new Alfetta for you, if they still made them."

"No, you would not be able to afford it. That's why we drive the old one, even though it costs a lot to fix and keep it running. My man works at home and takes the train only if he must go to København, or he rides one of the ways with me when I am going to work or coming home. My schedule makes it very convenient to have a car, to ride from Jutland to the airport and back each second week. No, the taxes on a new car are too much, even for a famous author or a stewardess on SAS. We found a nice older car and had it fixed up. So no taxes."

"Taxes?" he asked. "Are they that high?"

"Yes. Everybody isn't earning the same amount, but the distance between the most and the least is not so bad. And the people who earn the most pay the most in taxes." She smiled. "And hospital is paid for, and university. And if I am laid off or sick, I have my income the same as when I am working."

"That sounds expensive and generous, all at the same time," Billy said.

"No, it makes sense. It makes it secure and equal and pays for the things we say we need. But still freedom, like in your country. We are all in the same boat. Like on this ship. But let's eat." She lined up the three plates and pushed one forward, toward Billy. On one of Bodil's plates he saw the marinated herring and onions on thin dark bread; on the other, simple slices of bright-white cheese on French bread, a plain green pepper garnish. Billy's plate held a fillet of fish in golden deep-fried batter, garnished with a yellow sauce he guessed might be some kind of mayonnaise, and a generous portion of tiny shrimp and some caviar and dill sprigs on top. He couldn't see what kind of bread it was.

"*Stjerneskud*," Bodil said. "A shooting star. A special today. It's like twisting golden fish and shrimp falling from the sky. Remoulade sauce." She smiled. "*Stjerneskud*. No. Before you ask. I don't know why they call it that. And I asked for it on French bread, in case you might not like the taste of the dark rye." She lifted her bottle of beer and held it out to Billy. *"Skål, du!"*

"Skal, Bodil. I know that much Danish." Billy felt a distant tremor, and the scene outside the window moved silently, and then began to wheel slowly on a far-off pivot point. The vibration ceased, and they drifted until the gray sea seemed to open toward what he thought must be the front of the ship. The tremble returned, more urgent. Then silence for a long moment and a deep distant rumble. They began to move forward.

"To Jutland, Bodil." Billy raised his bottle. The rumble increased and smoothed as the ship gained speed. It seemed to rise in the water.

"Til Jylland, William! *Værsgo*! Let's eat, and then you will tell me about how Elizabeth is traveling from Virginia to California. Kathryn has the letter, and she is not so sure. Right? Did Elizabeth fly or drive? Or you will read it to me? I would like that. I think your voice sounds like you wrote this. Each of the pieces. So. Is this your story too?"

Billy laughed at Bodil's enthusiasm for Elizabeth's first travel in twenty-five years. "And remember, she is almost seventy years old here. And fifty years since she saw Kathryn. No, she takes the train. She always did, whenever she could. You'll see that all through the book. Are you sure you want to hear more?"

"You will read, William. But first eat!" The ship purred energy and gathered momentum. A shooting star, wide sky, and dim horizon. They ate. Polite knives and forks.

"A piece of bread." Billy chuckled and shook his head at Bodil. "You are very strong, and you are a beautiful person, Bodil. I am proud you asked me to tell you about the book. The story. I have never read this story aloud. It…" He hesitated. "It takes on a life of its own when it is read aloud, I think." A gentle silence. And expectation. Strangers become sojourners, circling the truth. And Elizabeth's story.

Bodil folded her napkin, stood up, and went for two more beers. When she returned, Billy was almost finished eating.

"We have time for another beer, William. And I want to know if Elizabeth was traveling to California just to see Kathryn after all the years, or if she had another reason. Maybe she was running away from something?" Bodil sat back in her chair and held her beer up, a salute to the storyteller.

Billy took a last bite of the crisp fish filet and moved his plate to the side. He spread the book open on the tablecloth, took a sip of beer, and began. "OK, Bodil. Elizabeth is coming to California. To see Kathryn, but also for more than that, I think. Some of the answer is here."

Chapter 8

ELIZABETH MOMENTS BETWEEN THE YEARS (2015)

Elizabeth sat at the kitchen table. She cradled the saucer under her coffee cup. It was Saturday, and she had only one or two things left to do. One was to tell Donner. She picked up the spoon and stirred in the cup, the only sound in the kitchen, muffled by her hand on the cup and the cold coffee. The coffee had been untouched for an hour or more, while she weighed the decision she had arrived at days before. Weeks. As she stirred, the thin scum of cream dissolved into flecks and then into a smooth gray-brown. She thought of warming the coffee in the microwave but was not interested.

"Never mind," she said, speaking to herself. The kitchen was quiet. Her husband, Donner, and Michelle, his daughter by his first marriage, were at home. A faint hum of urgent conversation in the den downstairs, television, a critical basketball game, seeds of anticipation planted and watered for an hour or two, blooming into satisfaction or a disappointing harvest in the end. Every now and then father and daughter would erupt in excitement or fury, muted cries from the basement, fouls or missed shots, bad calls, television commentary, and lousy referees.

Elizabeth glanced out the window at the backyard. The day was uncommonly warm for January. Bluebirds circled the wooden birdhouse and post. Usually only sparrows or swifts this time of year. Bluebirds? In January? The birds chattered, diving from the low chain link fence to the grass and back, as if it were a bright summer day, May or June. They were wheeling and playing at mating, or searching for bugs, four or five of them. One bird clutched at the small wooden cross already weathering between two evergreen shrubs. The bird's tiny claws gripped the first of the inscribed words, "My Little Dog." Elizabeth ran that piece of history across her heart's horizon, and her decision. A gray Thursday the previous October.

Donner had taken her aging and always grateful and trusting little dog to the veterinary clinic, to see if there were any options left. Rear haunches weak, legs that wavered and collapsed as the tiny dog struggled to run or relieve itself. She knew there were likely no good solutions. Donner returned several hours later, and his look confirmed the sorrowful news.

"Where is she, Donner? My little dog."

"At the vet's office." His eyes were bleak.

"Oh? They can do something? They're keeping her overnight?"

"No. No, honey. She's gone. The vet put her down."

"Oh." Her heart sank. "When will they bring her, so we can bury her?"

"I didn't think you would want the painful reminder. They'll dispose of the little girl."

She hadn't responded, simply told him to drive her to the vet's office so she could retrieve the little dog. Black and brown, tan mask and boots. The dog lay wrapped in her clean blanket, but they had left the lonely package in a dusty plastic bag on the floor. A back room. Elizabeth held up her hand for the assistant not to help. To stay away. She discarded the plastic bag and cradled the blanket, the dog's familiar angled legs like silverware enfolded in a dish towel. She went to the car where Donner waited. Silent. Elizabeth parted the soft folds of the blanket. Another look, to be sure. Maybe her little girl had escaped. The dog's shiny coat was wet and matted. Her eyes were open. Vacant shock.

Disbelief, thought Elizabeth. The wide eyes, still glistening. *Disbelief. My little girl.* They drove home, and Elizabeth shoveled a grave in the generous loam Donner had long cultivated at the property line. The cross. *"My Little Dog."* The birds.

Her thoughts returned to the kitchen and her decision. The birds. Searching for spring. Maybe they were confused. Or maybe they hadn't been able to make up their minds to fly south. Was that a sign? An omen? Confirmation? She used to ask Kathryn what to do. She could have done that instead of sending the letter. That she was coming.

Elizabeth had made up her mind. In steps, but now she was certain. She put the spoon on the table. One last trip. One way. Or round trip, if it had to be. But it was the last trip. When she looked up, the bluebirds were gone, and Donner was in the kitchen. Her husband. Twenty-two years. It felt like more. A lot more. Maybe a hundred. It was halftime in the ballgame. Her husband, Donner, quiet and comfortable. Competent. Average. A square box with softened corners.

"Zip up, Donner," she said. He must have been to the bathroom before coming out to the kitchen to look for something to eat. Or drink.

"What's for supper tonight?" he asked, and then, "You want me to call for pizza?" He searched in the fridge, and she knew he would not find much. She had not made any plans to find a ride to the store or plan a cozy meal or evening. And pizza never tempted her fit 121 pounds. Elizabeth seldom stepped on the scale and walked rather than hitching rides with Donner or Michelle or neighbors. Age and eyesight and a sleep disturbance had converged to take her driver's license. She wondered if that was part of her need to escape, fuel for her travel, at any cost. Maybe, but she had passed that point.

"Donner. I'm going to visit Kathryn," Elizabeth said, getting it out before she could hide it. No more hiding. "I'm going to visit Kathryn," she said again, louder, and grasped the table edge to stop from repeating it again. Or screaming it out loud, like she had been doing inside for days, shouts of joy or fury, she wasn't sure.

"OK," Donner said, still looking in the refrigerator. "Will you be back by supper? What're we having? Michelle's staying over, since Jimmie's working the weekend shift." Elizabeth's stepdaughter often spent the night with her father and Elizabeth when her boyfriend was away.

"No. That's not it. I'll be here for supper, but I'm going to visit Kathryn. In California. You and Michelle can manage."

"California?" He stood at the open fridge, plastic package of cheese slices in hand. "Kathryn?"

"From high school. My friend Kathryn. I've told you about her. The books. The chapters. You know, all the chapters. Of my life's book." She could feel her face flush, the foolishness, as the words fell and landed, chapters and books, silencing the kitchen, like ice cubes tumbling from the refrigerator door ice dispenser, skittering on the floor. Her treasures, these words, but foolish when spoken. At least to Donner.

"California? Which Kathryn are you talking about? Is she in some sort of trouble? When are you going? Where are you flying out from?"

"No, Kathryn's fine. I just need to see her. I wrote her I was coming."

"OK, but…"

"I'm going Monday morning, and I'm taking the train."

"The train?" Donner sat down. He and the chair groaned. "What's going on? The train to California? Are you crazy? That would take days, a week. How long?"

Elizabeth stood and picked up her coffee cup. She opened the microwave door and put the cup in, punched in her lucky thirty-three seconds, squinting hard to see the numbers, then thought it might need more and pushed forty-four seconds. Lucky elevens. The kitchen was filled with the winding down of the microwave numbers, and she counted eleven, then twenty-two, married twenty-two years. She rehearsed the countdown silently.

"More lucky elevens," she said to no one. The microwave beeped, and it was quiet. Elizabeth reached in for the cup, put it down on the table, and sat. Then she lifted herself and scratched her chair a foot or two closer to Donner. She tucked her hair behind her ears, both hands, looking down, gathering her courage from an incoming tide of adamant resolve. It wasn't an argument or an ultimatum; suddenly it was just a moment in time. Or maybe she wouldn't go after all, think it over one more time. But she had written Kathryn and told her she was coming. She filled her chest with a long breath and closed her eyes.

"What's going on? How long will you be out there?" Donner asked.

She knew he would pick at his left thumbnail with his right middle finger. She noticed long ago that he did that when trying to make sense of something that was escaping him. She wondered again why he didn't pick with his index finger.

"Tell me what this is about. Please," he asked again. His right eye twitched. Donner was seven years younger than Elizabeth. Maybe that was part of it. She would be seventy this year, but he was young and full of his daily job at the pharmaceutical plant, a manager, production. Or he had been promoted to something in shipping. She did not remember. Or care. He was kind and careful and kept the house supplied with appliances and fresh paint. He mowed the lawn and paid most of the bills without ever mentioning anything about money. Elizabeth's former income as a substitute teacher and then as an aide in the county schools had been replaced by a tiny Social Security check, a result of living abroad for so many years, travel and part-time jobs, and a few years in which she had simply lived off the generosity or patience of friends.

"Tell me," he said again. A resigned demand, unusual for Donner, she thought.

Elizabeth sighed and began. "I was thinking I need to visit Kathryn and try to remember some things we used to talk about and take some time to think it all through and just make sense of the few years I have left, and try to remember how I used to feel about some things. I don't know, really, but I need one chance to find out and maybe make a new plan."

"A new plan?" Donner asked. "What kind of a new plan?"

"I don't know, really, at least not yet, and we never talk about things like this anyway, Donner, and I don't really want to talk it over here. We've never talked about things like this, at least not the last ten years, and why now? It's sometimes like we are guests in two different rooms in a hotel, and we each just go about our business, which makes no difference to either of us, really. Well, you have your job, but, I mean, it's just too lonely and quiet, and I feel like I'm alive, but like I'm dying!"

She went on, catching her breath, "You know, it's like each day, it's like holding up a sheet of paper and tearing off little pieces, and it's a sheet of crisp paper, little pieces of paper falling to the floor, tearing off one little piece, holding it up and letting it go, and then another and another, and then one day there's nothing left. Just little pieces. Sweep 'em up. Gone! A lifetime!"

She could hear her voice, shrill and small and scared, the words sticking and repeating.

Donner dug at his thumbnail, opened his mouth and closed it again, looking away. "Well, what can we do about it?" he said, to the wall. "Is it too late? I know we don't spend too much time doing fun stuff, but then we talked about that once or twice. Been a while since we talked about it. I guess I never knew you weren't happy with me." He leaned back in his chair and looked toward the basement stairs to see if Michelle was coming. "I sort of knew you weren't real interested, but you even said one time you weren't really interested. Anymore, at least. Is that what this is about?"

Elizabeth let out a long breath, slowly. Suddenly it was all clear to her. She stood up and went to the counter under the kitchen window. She caught a reflection in the glass, a young girl, a teenager maybe, bright and fierce eyes and face, a wispy traveler and explorer and gypsy and nomad. Her eyes focused into the afternoon yard, on the birdhouse. The post. And the cross. She saw two birds. Patches of springtime blue, motionless confirmation between the bushes, one on each of the outstretched wooden arms next to their migratory home. Elizabeth swallowed. One bird darted from its clutch on "My," a single splash of icy blue and dusty peach underside, flying straight at her, through the window's reflection and the girl's sudden astonishment.

"No!" Elizabeth shouted before she could move. The tiny bird wheeled, only a faint and dusty rustling brush against the glass.

"No," she said, "it was a little bird, almost hit the window." Her thoughts numbed, needing no more defense. "No, Donner. It's not about sex or sleeping together or going to movies or ballgames, and we don't do any of those things anyway. For the sex part, how long? Ten years? But that's not it. It's just I have to try to remember some things that seemed so important so many years ago, and I've lost them. I have lost them. I wrote Kathryn and told her I was coming."

"Well, let's talk about it first. We can talk."

"Donner, I'm leaving Monday morning. The train is cheaper on the first days of the week. Monday. Missy's driving me over to Charlottesville. To the station. Amtrak."

"I could drive you. We can talk," Donner pleaded.

"No. And if I still had my license, I'd drive myself to the station, or rent a car, but it's only an hour's drive. I'm leaving. Donner, you haven't missed a day of work in years anyway. One of your good points, I suppose. You always tell me how proud you are, haven't missed a full day of work in years."

Donner cleared his throat. "Forty years this June," he said quietly. To the ceiling.

Elizabeth stared at him. "Donner. I'm going up to pack. I hear Michelle down there, complaining to the refs. Go on down and comfort your little girl."

"What'll I tell her?" Donner asked, leaning back, worry spreading across his face.

"Tell her I'm taking the train to California to visit my high-school friend Kathryn. That's mostly what I'm doing. Or don't tell her anything. I don't think she'll even notice I'm gone." Elizabeth put her hand on Donner's shoulder. "I will be fine, Donner. The train will give me time to think. You'll be fine. Monday."

⚬⚬⚬

The train rolled into the station, almost silent. It was there before she noticed. For the size of the engine and shiny metal cars, the sheer mass of metal and motion, there was no clanking or whistles or creaking rails. No shouts or bells or laughter. Maybe it was her thoughts drowning out the noise. Only when the train stopped was there a brief shudder of brakes and wheels, doors opening and steps revealed, escaping compressed air, a final sigh.

The small crowd boarding in Charlottesville for Cincinnati and Chicago seemed pleased the train was only an hour late. Only an hour late. It didn't matter to Elizabeth either, but she remembered the trains in Switzerland, an angry train master when she asked a question on the platform as the black second hand on a huge white clock face counted toward the top of the dial.

"On the train now, miss!" he had shouted. Polite, but a clear shout. "Yes, Luzern. Please get on this very moment!" The trains left exactly on schedule and arrived and departed each stop along the way with the same tense punctuality. She was glad the train was only an hour late. She shouldered her small bag.

"Only fifteen years late," she whispered. "Let's go."

Elizabeth had left Missy at the curb, thanking her for offering to wait until the train arrived, no need to wait. She assured her friend it would be on time. Elizabeth knew it didn't matter when the train came. She would have stayed in a motel in Charlottesville overnight, or for as many days or weeks it might take until a train arrived, rather than retrace her steps home. She was leaving.

Elizabeth stepped up into the train and found her seat, two cars forward. The upholstery cradled her slender frame. She needed nothing. It was comfort and safety, her own space. The train's loving arms. On the train, recalling Geneva and Luzern, and then so many more miles.

Forty years ago, leaving Geneva, she thought. *Probably the same day Donner last missed a day of his precious work.* She settled into the cushions and pulled the worn khaki canvas shoulder bag onto her lap. It was her only piece of luggage. It still had Rita's name and their inked address in Denmark inside the flap. Donner had protested, no way of knowing how much the bag meant. A trip around the world, years and lost dreams, thousands of miles ago. She pulled a book from between socks and underwear and T-shirts.

"No luggage? Where's your luggage?" Donner's fearful echo, now fading. "That can't be enough for a week or two in California, and days on a train! What are you doing?"

"Donner, this bag took me around the world thirty years ago. Two months, around the world. And when my jeans got too ratty, I cut 'em into shorts. I'll manage."

The train rocked as it crossed a switch to a siding. Mainline tracks. They headed south, and then circled toward the west.

"I'm already halfway there, Kathryn," Elizabeth said aloud. She opened the book she had chosen to take from among the three that had settled her heart at home. She had written about the three books in her last letter to Kathryn. Elizabeth had discarded the one she knew held no more use for her, by a Japanese woman, about tidying up clutter. No more need. There had also been a popular self-help book about trust, and she smiled. The one she had brought with her was the one she thought might be useful, a smart-living expert's story about a tiny house he had built. Something about turning daydreams into small and personal places.

Elizabeth noticed the well-dressed man in the seat next to her was looking at the book, then at her, a friendly smile.

"You said you are already halfway there?" he asked. "And you have just boarded the train? We have just left the station. That is funny."

"It's a long story," she said, glancing at him and then beyond, out the window. He asked if she would like to sit by the window.

"If you prefer," he said, "instead of your seat next to where, where the people walk." Gentle foreign accent. Swiss? Danish? German? She noticed he couldn't find the word *aisle,* just briefly. He glanced at the book in her lap, and his smile widened. He pointed at the book. Long hands and fingernails. "I see maybe you are building a safe cabin? It is a good book on the subject. I know it well." She noticed his nails were manicured. Perhaps polished.

The train picked up speed. Elizabeth thought for a moment and answered. "No, I've been writing about it. Sort of. Making my way to a better place. Or escaping. Ideas for a better life. My own space."

"You are a writer, then?" he asked.

"No. I just write in my spare time, trying to make sense of things. I was thinking about that when I heard the train coming into the station. In Charlottesville. Quite some time ago, maybe ten years, I wrote about the same scene but in Luzern. In Switzerland. The trainmaster. His whistle. The sound of the train's wheels on the rails. I was leaving but did not understand yet where I was going."

"And you have been writing very privately, yes?" he said with certainty.

"Yes, but not just writing. I think I am working my way back. To my story."

"Yes," the man said. "We are all doing that. In one way or another." He looked more closely at Elizabeth. "Do I know you from somewhere? I mean, I apologize for being too direct, but there is something I recognize. No, something I remember. About stories." He smiled. "It will come back to me. I am sure. But tell me about your writing."

Elizabeth thought for a moment. "It began as a mood, an atmosphere in my home and a need to find a private place. Quiet and safe and secure. It was something I couldn't share with anyone I knew, so I hid it. Fifteen years. Pieces of my story. I brought them with me."

He watched her with polite interest, nodding. "And?"

"And? I have pieces of my story."

"Tell me. We have time perhaps. How far are you traveling?"

"Sacramento," she said. "California."

He smiled broadly. "Yes. It is in California. That is where I am going, too. Chicago, and then to Sacramento. A conference. I will represent my company. I am giving a presentation. We are designing technologies for certain rail-road cars, recreational vehicles, mobile homes. Space and convenience. And comfort."

"So that's how you knew this book?" She held up the paperback.

"Yes, that is true, but tell me some of what you have written. Maybe it will help me in designing comfortable space for a person. Maybe especially for a woman."

"That would be interesting. You design RVs and mobile homes?" she asked. "You are an engineer?"

"Well, it is part engineering and part psychology."

"That sounds interesting. Yes, I will be glad to share some pieces of my writing. But let me get settled first. I have to be sure I'm well on my way. Once we're past Staunton or Roanoke, maybe I'll feel better. Feel that I'm safe, if you know what I mean."

"Yes, maybe I do." His clothes were tailored and expensive. Sandy thin hair well-groomed, and an unusual hint of a complex cologne. Elizabeth knew she would not have to look to confirm the quality of his shoes. She smiled at the thought. And he was intelligent and friendly. She was grateful for the good for-tune of traveling companion, even as she worried about the uncertainty of her venture westward.

The train gathered speed as it headed southwest, the sun high in the sky, a bright day. Elizabeth felt urgency, as if she were escaping someone who might be following her. A tall, dark figure, long, loping strides in the woods at a field's far perimeter. Out of sight. A grinning giant. Long strides. Laughing. Beyond the trees. Following. Or leading. Knowing the way she was going.

"This should be smoother," she whispered, sensing hesitancy in the train's momentum, as if the rails or wheels were uncertain, for just a moment uncommitted to a clear and easy path westward. She reminded herself that the blue-green valley and ridges of Virginia funneled her toward her reunion with Kathryn. And with her former self. This should have been the most hopeful piece of her journey. Her story. She knew she had been negligent along the way, careless, and she wondered now how Kathryn might greet her. What if they turned out to be awkward strangers? What if the visit timed out after a half hour of polite exchanges? The terrors of pleasantries. And silence.

Elizabeth fidgeted in her seat, suddenly uncomfortable and nervous. It reminded her of a feeling that had clouded her days as a teen, and at stagnant times in her retirement. She opened the flap on her khaki bag. Her trusted companion through so many miles and years. She pulled the book from beneath her manila manuscript folder, the two sheaves of legal pad paper showing at the edge. White and yellow sheets of evidence. The factual. And the plausible or possible. Her life. Her stories.

The book's cover had offered hope for her plan to build a work shed or study in her large backyard. Near to the bird feeders and the small wooden cross. The private study and writing space remained only a hopeful dream. Donner then suggested converting the guest bedroom instead. The idea of writing in the house cemented her resolve to get away, at least for a while. Then the moment of clear realization. That she would leave. The house had become silent and hostile foreign territory. Expectant normalcy.

The man commented once again on the book. "Yes. I know this book. It is very good, but in some ways it does not join the technical and the psychological dynamics of comfort and ease in small spaces." He smiled at Elizabeth and went on without encouragement. "He is maybe telling us that the small private structure itself is the source of peace and tranquility. And he thinks by putting the cabin or tiny house in the forest or by the creek or in a quiet yard, one will feel at peace. Like Thoreau. *Walden*." He angled his head and looked at Elizabeth. His eyes asked if she understood. If she agreed.

"It sounds as though you've studied this. So it wasn't just a hobby?" she asked.

"No, no. This is my work, my business. I have studied for a long time about engineering for manufactured homes, modular homes and workplaces. And then I got involved more specifically with the large motor homes and even railroad cars. Like this one. Particularly the different configurations of sleeping compartments. It's a big business."

"Yes. It must be," she agreed politely. "But this book is just about a connection between daydreams and architecture, it says. It interested me because I felt I needed a comfortable and quiet place. My own place. It was my dream."

He smiled broadly. "And so now you are maybe going to Sacramento to find that dream? Leaving these beautiful valleys and mountains?" He held his hands out and then clasped them in apology. "I did not mean to offend you. I am sorry. Sometimes I get carried away. But I sense maybe you are on a special journey." He squinted and pursed his lips, studying her face. "There is something," he said.

Elizabeth shook her head and smiled. "No. I'm going to visit a friend. She lives near Sacramento. An old friend. I haven't seen her in fifty years. Excuse me," she said. "My name is Elizabeth. It sounds as though we're going a long way together."

"Yes, the conference I'm attending is about this business of personal space engineering. It's mostly about the motor homes and large campers, but also about trains." He reached in his jacket pocket and produced a card. He showed it to Elizabeth. Arthur Newcomb, consultant. Air-Ride Design & Engineering. Elkhart, Indiana. Newcomb put the card back in his pocket. "I am returning from a conference in Philadelphia. I never fly. Taking the train gives me a chance to see if we're learning anything, or if there are things we need to learn. On an airplane it doesn't matter so much, because the trips are relatively quick. And with cruise ships, lots of chance to move about and eat and exercise. Trains and buses are right in the middle. Cramped and relatively slow, for longer trips. See what I mean?"

"Did you ever design or make anything for a train like this one?" she asked.

"Well, yes, but of course as a team. I'm presenting some new findings at the conference in Sacramento. A very big step for me. For my career. Because of our study and work, some railway sleeping compartments now are connected, so there is a feeling of more room. And for families. And we have found it was very easy to widen the lower bunks just a little bit, so two people can sleep together in a little bit of comfort. The people would do so anyway, so why make it cramped? Or why not let them have their children in the next room, with an easy way to move between the compartments? And wash basin and toilets. Privacy and security and keeping clean and fresh." He beamed with satisfaction.

"But you said something about psychology of the space. What does that mean?" she asked.

"No. The psychology is not of the space, really. What I meant was that one carries his or her psychological baggage into this small compartment or cabin, and we want to maximize the space to not add to the special and often troubling dynamics of close quarters or travel to unfamiliar places. Or maybe the traveler has a heavy heart. Whatever it might be. See what I mean? The traveler, just like the hermit in the cabin by the lake, has a dream or a worry or a unique way of seeing the world, right? Whatever is on his or her mind or heart. This is the new and exciting thing I will talk about in Sacramento."

"What about a story?" Elizabeth asked. "What if the baggage is a story? What if the travel itself is the story?"

He blinked and took a short breath. "What is your name again? I mean, Elizabeth, I know you. From somewhere." Newcomb scratched the side of his head and stared at Elizabeth. "I am certain we have met before." He shook his head. "It will come to me."

"I don't think so. Yes, my name is Elizabeth, and I have lived in Virginia for the past twenty-some years, not too far from Charlottesville. I lived in Europe for eight years, and New Jersey before that. Born there." She smiled. "My life on a three-by-five-inch index card."

"There you go. The psychology of it all." Newcomb beamed.

"What do you mean?"

"Well, for one, you have reduced your life to three places you have lived and the many years. Add a headstone, and that would be it." He chuckled at the thought and then softened. "I didn't mean to insult you again. Life is so unrepeatable. Yes, it sounded like an insult. I am sorry if I offended you."

"No. It's correct, in a way, especially the past twenty-five years. In many ways the years were wasted. Because I didn't pay attention to the important moments. Not at the time. The moments between the years."

"Never wasted," Newcomb said. "There certainly are the moments. Between the years. The defining moments. Aaaah, now I have it! Have you ever been in Bethlehem? The one in Pennsylvania, I mean. It was there. A young woman said something to me about 'moments between the years.' In Bethlehem. Maybe this was you?"

"No. I have never lived there, though I had a friend who attended a college near there. I visited a couple of times. It was only an hour from my home in New Jersey."

Newcomb nodded. "It was a going-away party," he said. "For a young college faculty guy who was leaving for study abroad. Or for a job. Overseas. A surprise party, and he was trying to be polite, but he wanted to get away. I think he was running away from something. Or someone." He studied Elizabeth's face. "Or from himself. You were there, weren't you?"

Elizabeth turned toward the window and scanned the horizon. The immensity of the land, yet coincidences that captured such tiny, improbable corners of the universe. She turned back to face Newcomb. She shook her head and closed her eyes briefly, her escape marred by sudden fatigue. "Yes. I remember the party, though I didn't know who it was for. But I remember it for a different reason. I was visiting my friend, and we went to the party, and I didn't know anyone there. I was tired and bored. I wanted to go home. To New Jersey and to my dad. I went into one of the bedrooms and sat on the bed. There was music playing in the living room, and the guy who the party was for came into the room and closed and locked the door and just stood there, looking at the door. He didn't know I was there. It was dark, just light from the street. Through the blinds. In the dark. He stepped carefully to the bed and sat down." She laughed. "Chekhov."

"His name was Chekhov?"

Elizabeth grinned. "No, Chekhov the writer, a short story he wrote. One of the finest short stories ever written. 'The Kiss.' A soldier is invited to a house party in the town where his unit is stationed for the night, just passing through. At the party the soldier wanders about and goes into a darkened room.

A woman who is in the room suddenly embraces him and kisses him once, and then she realizes it's not who she thought would be there, and she flees from the room. The soldier comes back into the party and has no way of knowing which woman it had been, and he never forgets the kiss or the moment but never pursues it either, not even when his unit returns to that town and is invited to the same home for another party. He doesn't attend. The question is, why didn't he search for her? Or did he know reality might ruin the moment? Or is there some other answer? Another question, maybe?"

"In Bethlehem? You kissed this man?" Newcomb asked.

"No. No. Or I don't remember. Or maybe we could talk about something else, Mr. Newcomb. But yes, if you and I talked that evening before I left, I might have said something about moments between the many years. It was something that happened, or something he said. The man. I have never forgotten it, and now it seems I am paying the price. Too many years lived, and too few moments noticed. But the man certainly was surprised that a woman was sitting on the bed. In the dark room. Let's skip this, please."

"Well, then," Newcomb said, "back to the psychology of small spaces." He stopped and stared at Elizabeth, then shook his head. "Well. Never mind. So, into that space we transport our dilemma or our joy. Like the man coming into the darkened room. The space barely matters, but if we design the train compartment or the camper or mobile home properly, it can enhance the good or reduce the bad which people may bring into the room. And whether they settle in or whether they escape, they still have the baggage."

Elizabeth sighed and shook her head. "OK, Mr. Newcomb. I think you're probably right, and I'm glad you're not simply designing aluminum boxes to squeeze in the most people for the least cost. Not just about profit margins. I'm finding out very quickly that our lives are too precious a commodity to waste. Maybe there is a mathematical equation, a special relationship, maybe something like, moments divided by years equals happiness." She laughed at the thought, a mathematician with a slide rule. She wondered if Newcomb used one. "Maybe I should write about scientists with slide rules, figuring the happiness quotient to any situation. Or space." She smiled at the thought and looked out the window. "Moments," she said to the glass.

"So you are actually a writer," he said. A statement of fact.

"No. A housewife. Twenty-plus years. Hiding from the truth. And the inevitable outcome." She shook her head. "I'm sorry. That sounded pretty grim. I was always interested in books and stories. And I've been writing about some things that have happened along the way. That's all."

"Interesting. Have you divided it into moments and years?"

"I never thought about that, but yes, I guess so. Writing about the years would take too long and would be way too boring. The moments are easy. They jump out at you once you start paying attention. And if you write them down, then you can't ignore them, and they get harder and harder to dismiss."

"You have been keeping track of them?" Newcomb asked.

"Yes. Sort of a journal. Or what could be a memoir. But then something happened, and I lost track. Or, rather, I started to imagine the other persons involved, and the choices. Or what lives might be like, or what mine would be like if I changed some of the hard facts."

"That's called fiction, isn't it?" Newcomb said, smiling.

"No, not always. Sometimes it's just what might have happened, you know, what could have happened. Or what did happen, but I didn't know or understand it at the time." She paused and looked at the horizon, moving so slowly, or not at all, while the underbrush and gravel along the tracks were an invisible blur. Both part of the visible landscape, actually moving at the same speed. Joined by a thread. It occurred to Elizabeth that Newcomb was either genuinely interested or simply being polite. A coincidental marker in her life. Or a con man. She went on.

"Just like today. I don't know the truth of the matter. But I am very interested in each and every moment. Before they slip away."

"Yes. Interesting. I would very much like to hear some of your writing. Did you bring any? I didn't see that you had much luggage. Just the shoulder bag."

"Right. This is all I've brought. But I brought the things I've been writing. Much of it is just notes, but some is completed chapters. Chapters of my story. The Elizabeth Book, I used to call it when I was a teenager, and in the years after. But I didn't start writing it until maybe fifteen years ago. Maybe not that long, but it's all here." Elizabeth patted the bag on her lap.

Newcomb smiled and leaned closer. "Would you be willing to read some of it to me? Your writing? Or tell me about your notes. The stories. We have a long trip to Sacramento and, if we are on time, a pretty long layover in Chicago."

"That's kind of you, Mr. Newcomb. I'm not sure how interesting they would be. But sure, I can read from one or two of the chapters. And I have notes on some trips I took. One trip was around the world. From Denmark to Jordan and Thailand and then New Jersey." She laughed.

"Oh. I haven't been to New Jersey," Newcomb said, laughing. "I'm just kidding, of course." He smiled. "And call me Arthur, please. And after we get more acquainted, maybe Art." He stood up in the aisle and leaned over. "I am pleased to make your acquaintance, Elizabeth. And I am looking forward to hearing something of the Elizabeth Story. Or you said the Elizabeth Book?"

"Yes. Either one will do. Thanks, Arthur. I think this will be a nice trip. Just don't let me get carried away telling you my stories. I have a way of going on and on once I get started."

He excused himself politely, touching his forehead. "I will be back shortly." He smiled again and walked forward. Elizabeth saw that he stopped and spoke briefly with the conductor at the door to the next car. The conductor nodded and smiled, looking her way. Elizabeth could interpret the conductor's answer. A pantomime.

"Yes sir. Yes sir."

Newcomb returned after an hour or so. Elizabeth had rested her head on the coach's flat window. Gentle vibration. The sounds of wheels and rushing wind and steel combined to a chorus of tones that rose and fell. It reminded Elizabeth of long drives with her father as a child. Summer vacations, a trip out west, naps in the backseat, and the comforting soft crescendo of untuned blended sounds. Wind and tires and the car's symphony of inertia and friction. As they combined, a distinct choir of voices would develop, if she allowed. And she found she could modulate the chorus, willing it up and down, tone and intensity and harmony. Turning the choir into a choral arrangement. Flowing hymns and psalms. A female conductor in a white formal dress beamed, tapping the podium and the music with her baton. Elizabeth startled awake and sat up.

"I'm sorry, I was just asking. Did I wake you? Did you get a nap?" Newcomb asked.

"Not really, but it's been restful. At least I'm feeling free. I was holding my breath until we were safely out of Virginia. We are, aren't we?"

"Well, not quite yet, but certainly far enough. I was asking if you would like to get something to eat or freshen up?" he asked.

"No. I'm fine. I went to the bathroom and then got a snack."

"Well, let me know. I have a connection with the railroad. Through my company. I can arrange for a compartment for you. On the train from Chicago to Sacramento. We change trains in Chicago. A cab to another station, for the West. The trip will start getting very tiring, and in a compartment you can get some rest or sleep, and you can get cleaned up in private." He shrugged and held up his hands. "If you like. I'll trade for you reading me some of your story along the way. Or telling me. From your notes. No pressure."

"I'll be fine as is. I might feel otherwise after ten hours sitting, but thank you for the kind offer." She felt comfortable enough, no alarm in her stomach. Arthur Newcomb. Air-Ride Design. Design and something. She knew also that the trip had to be her own, even if it meant sitting wide awake all the way to Sacramento.

She smiled at Newcomb. "What sort of thing would you like to hear? Maybe something from when I started writing, about fifteen years ago? Or when I came back to the States and then moved with my dad from New Jersey to Virginia? That would have been more than thirty years ago. Nineteen eighty-six." Elizabeth thought about how hard it had been to find the time and space to write. She closed her eyes and recalled the aching need for privacy. And something more. Escape perhaps.

"Tell me about when you started writing," he said. "It will tell a lot about who you are. Or who you wanted to become."

"All right, Arthur. I wrote only when there was no one in the house. Weekdays, during the day. I loved the weekdays." She pulled reading glasses from her bag, and a legal pad, loose yellow sheets bunched on top. She shuffled them, took a deep breath, and began. A whisper at first.

Chapter 9

ELIZABETH — FACT AND FICTION (2001)

The house was quiet. Elizabeth went into her bedroom and closed the door, even though she knew she was alone. Donner had left for work, another twelve-hour shift, and she felt the relief. It was her impatience with him, just for being nearby. Annoying, especially when she had something she wanted to focus on, something all her own. Michelle, Donner's daughter, was at school. She was in her senior year, independent, and wouldn't make her way home until bedtime. She would spend the evening with her boyfriend, at someone's house, doing whatever they did. Mostly watching television, she guessed. Michelle seldom brought the boy home. Perhaps it was just too quiet, and Donner was usually at work.

Elizabeth felt the luxurious cloak of silence and privacy. Her barefoot steps on carpet, soundless, a scout on a dark forest path. She caught a glimpse of her face in the dresser mirror, flushed cheeks. Expectant eyes. She opened the closet door and stepped in. She knew the closet's threshold marked a clear boundary. Her comfort and sense of well-being increased in the private space, even when she already had the house to herself. She pulled the string to a single-bulb light fixture in the closet ceiling. Simultaneously the phone rang, echoes from several extensions, the living room and kitchen and den. She breathed in a low curse, barely audible. It seemed interruptions were timed specifically to her private moments, or when she had a project of her own. Like today. Her story. A chapter. Today, a chapter. She knew she had to make a fresh start.

The phone continued to ring, three tones, then four. Insistent. She had disconnected her bedroom extension as she'd begun to realize there were so few calls for her, or if a voice happened to ask for a Mrs. Wade, it would likely be a bothersome solicitation. Or something that would send her on a detour or throw an obstacle in her way. Especially on the special days of comfortable loneliness. And hope.

The ringing stopped, and she heard the answering machine click on in the kitchen. No voice or message called out into the silence of the house. Just an extended complaining beep. The caller had hung up. Elizabeth was relieved. She needed the morning.

Elizabeth had planned to gather old thoughts, years past, concerning a critical turn in her story. *Elizabeth's Story*. She needed to recreate how it had happened. She had no sources of reliable or accurate information, only her memory, and she wasn't sure about that anymore. She couldn't explain, even to herself, why she had done one thing or another. It seemed as though she had often just tumbled forward, without a plan. But now her memory, the only key left to twist in the locked moments, a strongbox of concrete facts wrapped in dreams and regret and a growing wonder. The outlandish possibility of regaining lost ground. The chapters already written, so easily spent. Handwriting in the air. A brief sparkler in a backyard night sky. But at least the remembering, figuring what had happened. Or what might have happened, if only. And writing it. Elizabeth had made a bold turn in her story, or at least she had drawn a parallel tale. She was rewriting pieces of it as fiction, because she was less and less confident in her memory and in her estimation of other persons' roles. Or intent. It was hard enough to even begin to know herself, but she knew that was why she was writing. Her buried treasure.

Elizabeth reached to the closet's upper shelf, where she kept the carefully folded sweaters and blouses she rarely wore. She lifted and slid out the portfolio, a slim reddish-brown manila accordion, gathering a slim breath, its song. Words and years. Her story. The chapters, and she had already neared the end of the chronology, several times in fact. But so much was missing along the way. It wasn't just about years and people and jobs and the familiar milestones or churchyard cemeteries that lined the road. Or the dust and ashes. That shock still visited her, surprising her calm. She would never forget the moment she wrote the words. Ashes. And silence. She had promised herself this day, to face one more of the inexplicable turning points, one of the chapters she had avoided. Some were just so hard, this one because it led to Rita. But for this chapter, that was not the difficult part. She simply did not know what exactly had conspired to carry her forward, or alter her journey. One of the fateful detours.

"How the hell in God's name, ever?" she whispered to herself. She knew there was no answer, at least no reasonable excuse or logic. It was like leaving a comfortable and clear and well-trod trail in a peaceful meadow, to forge a path into wilderness underbrush, obstacles hidden in brambles, gnarly roots of young trees trying to reach the canopy. Such freshly blazed searches seldom returned anyone to the smooth path, it seemed. If ever.

Maybe the path shouldn't be smooth, she thought. She wondered if ordinary comforts were the problem. The house and work and the yard and laundry and supper. She hated supper, where anything would do, as long as it was hot and on time, regular schedules, and no surprises. Not today, which was her own. Today was about her story, and a difficult chapter. She stood in the closet. The lightbulb fixture hummed, barely audible. A loose wire. Tired filament. The chapter.

"How the hell in God's name, Dan?" she intoned, several times, varying the cadence. Old rage deflating toward mild disbelief. She opened the portfolio, checking to see if her marker had been disturbed, a special intricate twist in the binding twine clasp, in case someone was following her journey into the pages. Spies or a fearful companion, wondering if she was slipping away. She smiled.

"I'm already gone. I've been gone." She could see she was safe, and she could meet Dan again on paper, without worry or having to explain. She knew it was the chapter that contained the seed of her special treasure. And guilt. Rita. But for today, more fiction, and she loved the freedom it afforded. Dan and Elizabeth, and Geneva and Luzern, Hemingway and the train, the many miles, knitting a loose weave. Dan and Elizabeth, for a time. A time, now worlds and universes spinning apart, the end of everything in sight. She had to hurry, before it was too late.

Elizabeth pulled the light switch string and went back through her bedroom toward the kitchen.

My bedroom, she thought. *Imagine. My bedroom. The place where I sleep. The comfort and embrace and love and safety and rescue, somewhere down a hallway. Somewhere dark*, and she escaped the howling thoughts of her mother. And her daughter. There were also the other careful enfolding arms, once or twice in her life, missing names and faces. She had recaptured a few of those moments already. The darkened rooms.

In the kitchen Elizabeth opened the portfolio and spread papers on the table. Smooth white plastic surface. Legal pad sheets, thin paper-clipped packets, some yellow, some white. Handwritten chapters. Gathering into a story. A lifetime.

OK, Dan. She remembered the train's whistle and the impatient trainmaster. Geneva. Twenty years. She began to write, and her thoughts touched upon Kathryn. A chapter. *This one I will send to Kathryn. Or a postcard, just tell her I'm writing again.* Elizabeth closed her eyes and drew in a long breath. She had not written to Kathryn in months.

"Or years, perhaps?" she wondered out loud. She felt the smooth scratch of her pen on the paper. Fiction today, but she was there. No, Elizabeth was there.

⸺⌾⸺

Elizabeth stopped. Newcomb studied her face.

"So this is where you began writing?" he asked.

Elizabeth rested the legal pad on her lap and looked up. Bashful pursed lips. She looked down at the pages and then out the window. Her right index finger tapped on the pages.

No. She had been writing for a while. Looking back on things that had happened. But the details and facts began to grow on their own.

"It's a story," Newcomb said. "Sounds true to me. Fiction, maybe, but it sounds true." He cleared his throat. "A woman's prison." He waited. "So who's Dan? She sure sounds upset with him."

"She?" Elizabeth laughed, the self-conscious pressure released. "Yes. She's me. Sort of." Elizabeth shook her head. "Dan was a son of a bitch in the end. Or maybe that was me. Dan was my Danish husband. I lived in Demark. Years ago, the seventies. Or the eighties. I have to think twice anymore to come up with the dates. But I remember the day we met."

"Have you written about that? Can I read any of that? If you're tired of reading."

"Are you sure you want to hear more? It's all here, either written or in notes. Meeting Dan, that's on the white pages." She pulled another legal pad from the khaki shoulder bag.

"Are the white pages about Dan?" Newcomb asked.

Elizabeth smiled. "No. The white pages were supposed to be the memoir, the factual stuff. If one knows what's true."

"Well. Read to me about Dan, and I will tell you whether it seems more factual than Elizabeth writing at home."

"OK. This is where I'm leaving Geneva for Luzern. I had finished a job, or more like a study vacation from teaching, and I was going to take a European cooking course. In Luzern." She thumbed through white pages. "Are you sure you want to hear this? I have some more interesting things, I think."

"No, let's take it in order. Tell me about you and Dan." Elizabeth started to explain Dan's work, but Newcomb interrupted. "No, I didn't mean that. Read what you have written."

Elizabeth sorted some pages and squared them into a neat sheaf. "OK. This is in Geneva. The train station. Leaving for Luzern."

"Read," Newcomb said.

She pushed her glasses to the bridge of her nose.

Chapter 10

ELIZABETH RIBBON OF BLUE STEEL (1978)

Elizabeth went through the gates and onto the platform, carrying her single small suitcase. She approached the trainmaster. He was waving toward the front of the train.

"Is this the train to Luzern?" She showed the trainmaster her ticket, and he blew into his whistle, his focus toward the front of the train and then the rear, toward the gate to the station, and then toward the large round clock hanging above the platform. The second hand passed the top of the dial. Twelve. There were no latecomers. Switzerland. No one would be left behind.

"On the train, please, miss. Please, now!" He looked at his watch and then back along the platform as the train began to glide, inches at first, no sound other than the trainmaster's urgent command. "Yes, now! Luzern. On the train, please!" He urged Elizabeth into the train and then waved toward the front of the train. He took her suitcase and pulled the door shut behind them. Onboard. Safe.

"Now, miss. Let's look at your ticket to Luzern. Yes. Your seat is in the next car forward, please. Still on time, Lausanne. And Bern and Luzern too." He smiled broadly, clipped her ticket, returned it to her, and waved her forward, carrying her bag.

They made their way past the compartments, along the windows, the eastern end of Geneva's deep-blue lake still visible to the south. Two men smoked at an open window, the wide window glass pulled down. Fresh air mixed with the strong smell of the unfiltered smoke and their laughter. The train seemed to glide, accelerating, a smooth flowing noise she could not quite place, a stream becoming a river. Steel and the sound of water flowing, a heavy current. She could feel the train gaining speed, but no swaying or jerking or clacking. A smooth and steady wind, gathering its force.

In the next car, the trainmaster slid open the door to her compartment. Two rows of three seats facing each other, only two passengers in the compartment, both facing forward, a man and a woman, an empty seat between them. The woman was in business attire, a trim blue suit jacket and skirt, and the man balanced a thin aluminum attaché opened on his lap. He looked up at Elizabeth and smiled, then turned his attention back to his briefcase. The trainmaster placed Elizabeth's suitcase on the rack above the rear-facing seats, and Elizabeth sat in the middle seat, facing her compartment companions. To no one in particular, the trainmaster announced breakfast, well-practiced English.

"If you like, breakfast served in dining car, one car forward. Ready now or when you like to go." He repeated it in French, and the woman nodded. The man looked up and thanked the trainmaster, who tipped his hat and left, sliding the compartment door shut, a solid and soundless latch. The compartment and the train's smooth motion enfolded Elizabeth's senses, and she closed her eyes. Lausanne and Bern, and then Luzern. Three hours. A new chapter, cooking school. A real European cooking school. A dream and a treasured private chapter, separate from the burden she had just completed.

Elizabeth's four months in Geneva had been a mixture of enchantment and boredom. Research and writing and language lessons, but evenings of food and sights and cafés. And walking. The streets were unlike anything she had ever experienced, a luxury of sound and smell and sight, shops and vendors for specialty or need, bakers and greengrocers, windows displaying cheese and chocolates and wine, everything so clean and fresh. She had finished the writing project that had justified her grant to travel and study. The weekends had been hers, and she had even taken a few days off and rode the train to Paris, just to walk the streets.

In Paris Elizabeth learned her French was of no use, as the people seemed uninterested in helping her through questions or small talk or directions. She tried to picture Hemingway in that place. And Hadley Hemingway, gathering his manuscripts. And the carbon copies. Packing them all in a suitcase. Elizabeth wondered if she was measuring up to Hadley on the Paris trip. Or in Geneva. But Hemingway had always seemed to have English or American friends with him, and lovers, and wine and whiskey. Elizabeth had savored the strong coffee and a glass of wine or two, just to sit on the edge of a Parisian boulevard and watch.

Imagine, she thought. *A boulevard*, and she rolled the familiar word perfectly in French, the practiced and sophisticated tongue of her fancy, soundless to anyone nearby.

"*Boulevard. Merci. S'il vous plaît.*" She smiled at her perfect pronunciation. And her remarkable good fortune. Just to be there. Paris cafés, the waiters disdainful and busy. Paris.

Geneva was another world, a tapestry of international agency workers. Everyone seemed willing to try their English or help her with her French, and no one was in a hurry, a wealth of time doing the world's business. Europe. Her dream. She had wondered about keeping notes, then noticed that nothing terribly exciting had happened. She settled on the atmosphere and the European air. Just being there was enough.

"Would you like to get a cup of coffee? Or some breakfast?" The words startled her thoughts, and it was so seldom that anyone approached her. Elizabeth looked up as the man slid his briefcase onto the rack above his seat and asked again, smiling at her.

"Coffee?" The man's eyes were the clearest blue she had ever seen. She stared at him. Coffee. She wondered if this was an unusual request or if he was going to bring paper cups of coffee back to the compartment. Blue eyes. Smiling. Coffee.

"You're getting some coffee?" she asked, thinking at once how the words sounded like a foolish puzzle. His blue eyes. She wondered if she had responded in her bad French. His face reflected her confusion, but he smiled even more broadly. His eyes. He laughed and shook his head.

"No. Come on. I'll buy us cups of coffee and croissants. Swiss Rail is the best croissant anywhere in the world. The coffee too. Swiss Rail dining car is three stars, maybe. In Michelin. Come and see." His English was clear.

Perhaps Swiss German. From Luzern or Zurich, she thought.

"Coffee?" He held out his hand.

"What?" Elizabeth knew she was smiling. She did not know whether she should stand up. The businesswoman was looking at her magazine, ignoring the conversation, clearly not part of the invitation. Elizabeth stood up and reached for the rack above her head, for balance. She could see the countryside flashing by the windows, but she did not sense any swaying or inertia. Solid footing. She wondered about the dining car and how they poured coffee, or if she should ask the woman if she wanted some, and the Michelin three stars. The man slid the compartment door open and waved her into the aisle.

"Come on. You will like this very much. My name is Dan." The morning sky to the south and east flashed in his eyes. Sunlight through the trees. He turned, and Elizabeth followed him to the end of the aisle and through the doors to the next car. On New Jersey's Lackawanna rails, the noise in the vestibules between cars would be deafening, a crashing cascade of steel and couplings and brakes and rails and drafty wind. Here there was a muffled bass rumble, wheels beneath their feet, but smooth and reassuring, the train confident, at work.

Once in the dining car, Elizabeth stared. Gleaming white tablecloths at the windows, stainless steel panels and fittings. The light. Bright silverware and crystal water glasses. The sound of ice and glass. A waiter bowed quiet French assurances of seats and led them to a table, placing menus in front of Elizabeth and Dan, heavy card stock, linen napkins. Dan pointed to the card, and the waiter disappeared. Elizabeth tried to catch up to the unfolding scenery.

"This is like a restaurant. New York or I don't know where. Thank you. My name is Elizabeth. I am from America. Maybe you could tell." She knew she sounded like a girl from New Jersey and regretted she had no smooth introduction ready. "I've been studying and writing and working in Geneva for several months. Now I'm going to a cooking school. In Luzern. Before I go home. This is beautiful. I didn't know." Her words felt brittle and awkward.

He seemed unconcerned with her nervousness. "Yes. I just thought you might like this, but then maybe you would fall asleep two hours and just go on and miss it. We never know what we have missed. While we slept. Maybe a moment that would live in our heart for a lifetime. I am working in Switzerland for these days. I am coming from Denmark and will go back soon, after I am visiting with some people in Zurich."

The waiter brought a silver tray of croissants, curls of butter, thin slices of cheese, shaved ham, and deep-red preserves in a tiny crystal bowl. He placed the tray carefully between them, a solemn gift, retreated, and was back at the table with coffee. Elizabeth froze. The scene was so unexpected. Commonplace luxury, a tray reflecting windows and a gleaming silver sun, and the man's blue eyes. She realized suddenly that she could not remember his name. The waiter's careful motion and respectful glance at each of them painted the obvious picture: lovers, an early-morning train. Somewhere in Switzerland. Hemingway and Hadley.

Elizabeth pushed her seat back from the table. She couldn't retrieve his name from her swirling pool of thoughts. She searched for something to say or ask. Anything. The rushing sound in her head. She wondered if it was the train's wheels. Smooth liquid steel. She poured heavy cream into her coffee, too much. It would be good. Rich. He was talking, asking her something.

"*Hotelfachschule Luzern?* The school you are attending in Luzern?" he asked, as if anyone might know the school.

"Yes. You know it? I'm going because my high-school and college German might be good enough to manage. A school in French, I couldn't do it. I wanted to go to a cooking school in Paris."

"No, in Luzern is a good school. Many hotel and restaurant owners are sending their kids there when they want to start their working. To get their papers. Their licenses." He searched her face. "Elizabeth, are you OK?"

"Yes. I mean, no. I forgot your name, and this is so very nice here. The train and the dining car. Nothing like this in America. Everybody in a hurry. Maybe a paper cup of coffee. Spilling coffee. And this train is making no noise, no clickety-clack wheels. The sound. Why is there no sound of the rails and the wheels? No clickety and clacking? This train just swishes in my head, like a river." Elizabeth lifted her cup and drank in the rich European roast. It tasted of

Paris and Geneva and Hemingway and Hadley and years of yearning. For something. She felt tears clouding her eyes.

She could see he was studying her face. She went on. "I know. It's just that it's so beautiful here. I always dreamed of it. For so many years. And I love trains. But this one is like a dream. And then I forgot your name, I'm sorry."

He waited until she paused. "Yes. And my name is Dan. Here is how you remember. Danmark is how my land is spelled and pronounced. Danmark. My name is Dan, and it is a very ordinary name anyone could forget, so don't worry if you do. I am working for the Danish newspapers. But I can tell you about the sound of the wheels. It is very simple. The Swiss have made it work for the fast trains. Everywhere else in the world, they bring in the heavy rails and nail them in place on the wooden ties, big heavy nails, right?"

She nodded, relieved he was talking, and he went on.

"And so of course at the end of each long rail, there is a small gap, and so your clicky-clack, right? But the very smart Swiss make the steel rails very strong and hard, so they don't stretch too much in the sun and the heat, and they place the rails on the ties and then weld the ends to each other and make it like a perfect smooth ribbon of steel. No clicky-clack, as you say."

A ribbon of blue steel. Elizabeth studied his face. It was his eyes. "Blue steel," she said and caught herself. "The Swiss seem to be very smart. All the international organizations in Geneva. And the banks." She realized she didn't know much about the country. "But it's so nice and clean here. Everything is clean. And peaceful."

He shook his head, smiling. "Well, the Swiss are maybe looking very clean. But the Swiss, their laundry is dirty, like everywhere else. Or maybe worse. And peace, I don't know. Look in any beautiful country town here. Go to the elementary school or to the church. In the basement are the machine guns all lined up, hanging on the wall. One for every citizen of age in the town. Everyone is in the army, you know. In the summertime the jets are practicing flying through the mountain passes. Lots of noise. So the German tourists can remember them when they go home."

Dan's face was intense, serious. He went on. "And in Geneva, where you have been, and where I sometimes make my report for the Danish newspaper, all the agencies are counting up the numbers of the poor and the starving and displaced and diseased children and people of the world, making lists and graphs and scientific studies. And the money and power stays right in Geneva. But that is the way it is doing everywhere, maybe? What do you think?"

"I don't know, Dan. I never thought about those things. In Geneva and in Paris, there are so many simple things that make me feel rich. Like the coffee and even the simplest food, and it seems it's made with care and love. And it feels like Switzerland is a puzzle with three pieces. The French heart, food and wine; the German order, the trains and being on time and being so tidy and in charge; the Italian soul, poetry and passion, music and religion. And here we are on the train. I feel rich, croissant and butter and coffee, even though I'm going to have to tighten my belt to get through the cooking school and home again."

Elizabeth knew she needed to stop talking. She reached and broke off a piece of the last croissant. She glanced at Dan and realized he was watching her, and she continued, wondering where she might stop.

"Until I go back to work. I teach school. I'm on a study and travel grant, half of the year off, sort of like a sabbatical. No one applied for the grant, probably because they had obligations and families to look after. I'm still living with my dad and have no bills or kids, so I could just take off. Like I said, I feel rich. I'm finished with the study and writing and have enough time to take the cooking course." She brought the piece of croissant to her lips. His eyes followed her hand. Her eyes met his. Blue. The air was silent.

"Maybe you will visit me in Denmark? Before you go home?" He took Elizabeth's hand and held the tips of her fingers loosely for a moment, then released them with a gentle squeeze.

"Is there a train to your Danmark? I am rereading my favorite Hemingway. He always took the train." The words sounded foolish, something she might have said in her high-school English class. "And he loved Europe and being in the middle of important ideas and events. The war." She gave up, out of breath, it seemed.

Dan smiled. "Yes, there is a train. But I am thinking Hemingway didn't always have important things on his mind. Except maybe about his next bottle of wine. Or his next woman."

"Well, maybe it's that simple, Dan. But I think Hemingway also knew that so often people were broken, searching for what was missing. Something in themselves." Elizabeth looked out the broad window, a framed portrait, an expanse of green valley, reaching south, toward the sun. The sound of a river, of rushing water and wind. A ribbon of blue steel.

"Yes, Dan. I think I would love to see your Danmark. Since you say there is a train."

⁂

Newcomb interrupted Elizabeth as she read. "So you went to Denmark? To visit him?

Elizabeth looked at her notes and repeated the final words, slowing as she read them, as if she were laying losing cards on a poker table.

"*Since you say. There is. A train.*" Newcomb studied her face. He waited. "So. You went to Denmark."

"Well, yes," she said. "I went. I took the train."

Chapter 11

BILLY — A LITTLE GIRL TO SPOIL (2016)

Bodil stirred her coffee and waited for Billy to find his place in the book. She pointed toward the windows.

"We have a little more time. You can see the coast in the distance, a dark shadow. It is always a little surprising, coming home on the ferryboat."

Billy pressed the pages flat and looked up. "But it must be nice, after flying around the world for a week. Does your husband know you're coming this evening?"

"Yes. My man. I keep in touch, though I think he does not worry about me. And when I get here, there I am!" She beamed.

"Do you have children? I imagine they would miss you."

A shadow crossed her face, a brief twitch of her mouth. "No. We have tried for many years. Maybe the traveling keeps my body out of balance. I think my man is very disappointed that he has no little girl to spoil. Other than me." A weak smile.

"Well, maybe. You never know. You're still young and healthy. I could barely keep up when we walked to the car."

"I noticed." She laughed. "And we were almost run over by that taxi. Tell me, William. How did Elizabeth ever come to Denmark? I mean, why?"

"She met a guy on the train. In Switzerland. A Danish guy. He worked for the newspapers. He invited her, and she came to visit. They met when she was traveling, to begin a cooking course in Luzern."

"So she fell in love with a Danish man on a train. I don't know if they are that exciting, really. The Danish men," she said. "But falling in love isn't always a choice, is it, William?"

He thought for a long moment. "I'm not sure it was about falling in love. I mean, I think there were other reasons." He turned the pages forward in the book, looking for another place to read. "Here we are. You want to hear some more? This is all about Denmark. Elizabeth coming to Denmark. It's sort of how I feel right now. There might be lots of different emotions tugging at a person."

"Yes. Read to me about some different tugging emotions, William." He was afraid to look up, and she laughed. "I too have different tugging emotions as I am getting nearer to my home. And my man. He will like you very much, and you will read to us a nighttime story, or what do you call it, a bed story?"

Billy smiled and shook his head. "You are very beautiful, Bodil, and I feel very lucky. I can't wait to see your home and your man. Does he have a name?"

"He is my man. Read, William," she said.

Chapter 12

ELIZABETH CAFÉ SOMMERSKO. PARISERBØF. HVA' HEDDER DU? (1978)

A gray sun receded behind rows of identical five-story concrete apartment buildings as Elizabeth's train slowed toward the main station. Copenhagen. The suburbs had extended for miles, framed by the names on local station marquees, Hedehusene, Albertslund, Dybbølsbro. She wondered how the language might sound. Dybbølsbro? She stood at a window in the narrow walkway that extended the length of the passenger car, sliding doors to the compartments, two sets of three seats facing each other, special racks and curtains and hooks for converting the space to sleeper berths. The heavy glass window felt cold to her touch. Winter soon. No snow, just a darkening of the pavement, glistening wet shadows on concrete. Perhaps it had rained, an icy drizzle.

Elizabeth wondered if she had made a mistake coming to Copenhagen. A long way to go to visit a stranger. Dan. She could have just returned to the States once the cooking class was over. The experience had been uneventful, without much flair or romance, but it was part of her European adventure. Switzerland. Luzern, the lake and the daily view of the mountains. The thought was a pleasant satisfaction. Perhaps Copenhagen and Dan would be an interesting side trip before heading home. Home. She exhaled and shook her head.

"Home." What a thought. She mouthed the word silently at her reflection in the darkening window. A regretful kiss. "Home."

Elizabeth looked at the skyline and wondered why the train was so late, the arrival scheduled for midafternoon, and the sun was setting. She checked her watch as the train slowed past nearly empty commuter platforms. It was only three thirty in the afternoon. They were ahead of schedule. A paper bag skidded, twisting across a vacant parking lot. A stiff wind. She wondered how cold the northern evenings might be. It would soon be December. She warmed at the thought that she had a full twenty-four hours to wander and get her bearings before meeting up with Dan. And now she had an evening in the dark mirror side of the summer's almost midnight sun. Dan. The thought of him made her nervous. A chance meeting on a Swiss train, his casual offer and her offhand agreement, now two months ago.

Elizabeth had written to him three weeks before, then called to make sure he would be in Copenhagen, and that it was still OK to come. She had told him she would meet him at the train station, the daily afternoon arrival from the German border. She smiled in relief. It would be the same train, but tomorrow. She planned to find an inexpensive hotel or hostel somewhere near the station, get a room for the night. No, for the next two nights, to be sure everything felt right about Dan. This evening would be on her own, a cup of coffee or a glass of wine, and something to eat. She hoped people would be friendly and welcoming. Pedestrians on the streets were bundled up, bending forward in the wind and gathering shadows. Hurrying toward warmth. Maybe this little country had some cozy answers to the northern cold. She hoped so, and she suddenly felt eager. And curious. Europe.

The train eased into the cavernous main station, the high arched ceiling a reminder of bygone days of steam and diesel. The end of the line, Copenhagen, its back to the North Sea and the shadow of Sweden. She looked at her guidebook map of the city. She would walk toward the front of the train and out the doors. Across a main street, Bernstorffsgade, would be the Tivoli Gardens. "Closed in October, reopening in May," the book said.

The map showed a labyrinth of small streets and squares in the center of town. Another exotic and romantic chapter. She was certain her life's book would unfold through exciting days like this one. The moments between the many years. Stickpins along a map's trail. And here she was again, trains and rails, rolling into a station. Blood running through veins, Hemingway reporting her odyssey. Peacetime news.

Elizabeth guessed the hotels in the center of town would be expensive, so she walked to the station's main doors, took a good look at the sky, and then went back through the station, stopping to exchange Swiss francs for Danish kroner, bright pictures on various sizes and colors of crisp paper. She found the exit to a darker side street, the opposite side of the station from Tivoli Gardens and the main town square. Istedgade. There was a small Chinese restaurant with a bright and steamy window at the sidewalk's edge halfway down the block. She went in, welcome warmth and spicy air. She asked a young waiter if there were any hostels or inexpensive hotels nearby. He looked at her small travel bag and smiled.

"Yah, sure. Clean hostel this block, share room and walk up many stairs. Also little hotel next block, not too expensive. Street here safe. Nighttime maybe people out after drinking. OK, but be care." She thanked him and went out onto the sidewalk, confident. She walked past the hostel to the next block, reassured by the people she passed, simply making their way purposefully toward home or shops or some clear destination, a few on bicycles in the street, leaning into the chill.

The hotel was in an old and narrow brick building. Elizabeth asked the lone clerk behind the desk how much a single room would be, with bath if possible. Two nights. He told her, and she did the conversion of kroner into dollars, dividing by six, close enough. It was expensive for a night's stay, though not as much as hotels in Geneva or Luzern, or the larger hotels in Copenhagen's center. She guessed they would be twice or three times as much. She reserved the second-floor room, reminding the clerk she wanted it for two nights. He smiled and told her he had quoted the total for two nights' stay. She counted her good luck, the nightly cost now half what she had thought it would be. She also felt assured with the freedom to come and go, regardless of Dan's schedule or plans. Or how it all might turn out.

Elizabeth went up the flight of stairs two steps at a time. Her room was small and neat, and spare of any luxury. She hung her jacket in the wardrobe and put her things on the bed. She sat on the bed for a moment, deciding if she wanted to make it an early night after the long train ride, to be fresh in the morning. And for Dan, tomorrow afternoon back at the train station. She stood and went to the small bathroom, no tub, simply a terrazzo floor with a wide brass drain, and a fabric curtain separating the shower from the toilet and sink area. Elizabeth looked in the mirror. She was surprised by the smile, mild satisfaction showing in her eyes. Denmark. Copenhagen. Her story.

"Who would have thought?" she said out loud. The young woman in the mirror was confident and fresh. Intelligent and pretty. She looked more closely, her hair a little stringy, but strangely made her look younger than her thirty-two years. She ran her fingers through the ash-blond strands. Shoulder length now. Clean enough. It would do for a European traveler, and for an evening alone.

"What do you think?" she said to the mirror. "Plenty of time to rest later. Let's go." The town felt safe, and she decided to make a quick trip back to the small Chinese restaurant for supper, or perhaps ask the hotel clerk if he had a suggestion. Even a cup of coffee would do, she thought. She splashed water on her face and brushed her teeth, ready now for a quick walk and a bite to eat. She took her jacket from its hanger, hoping it would keep her warm in the chilly darkness, looped her soft fabric passport and money holder over her neck and under her light sweater, safely folded the documents between her breasts. She went into the quiet hallway, pulled the door shut, and returned down the stairs. She asked the clerk where she could get a cup of coffee, maybe a sandwich. Somewhere nearby, maybe a place he would go. An interesting part of town, but not too far.

"Café Sommersko," he answered, no hesitation. "Newer place, couple years. Sit and read a book or newspaper, folks come and go. You will like it. Good food, sometimes live music at night. Not too far. You go down the Walking Street, which is nice. *Strøget.*"

"Stroll?" she asked, repeating the word. He laughed.

"No, Strøget. It means something like 'shopping street,' and it has no traffic allowed, so you can walk the length of the city center. No cars in street, except some crossing. So we call it the Walking Street. Yes, the name does sound a little like *stroll*. You learning Danish maybe?"

"No. In Switzerland and also in Paris, my French was not good. I took a cooking course in Luzern, in German. It was hard. I am not so good with languages. Your English is very good."

"Thank you. I am studying at the university, what you might call social philosophy. You are just traveling here? Or on business?"

"No, I'm visiting someone. I met him on the train in Switzerland. A Danish journalist. He lives here, in Copenhagen."

"And you are staying in a hotel? So, not a close friend, then?" His voice hinted offended wonder, as if a Dane had compromised the country's welcome to a stranger.

"No. I don't really know him, just met him on the train. I told him I would be coming tomorrow, so I could spend a little time on my own. I'm glad people speak English. Friendly, I think. But it's very dark at four o'clock in the afternoon."

"Yes," he said. "Danish winter. They say the suicide rate goes up in wintertime. Dark very early. And if the sun shines bright in December, everyone is turning their faces toward the sun in the middle of the day, like when they are waiting at the bus stop. People even have little tin foil reflectors, catching sun in their faces while they wait on the sunny days. It is very funny, all turned the same way, eyes closed. Of course in the summer it is the opposite, very light outside until nine or ten o'clock at night."

"I would love that," she said. "Midnight sun."

"No, not quite midnight, but almost. But go enjoy Café Sommersko. And if someone is very drunk there, or on the street, probably don't go with them. Usually they are harmless but very loud. Big, loud voices. Too much beer."

"Thank you. What is your name, please?"

"I am Torbjørn. That is an old Viking name."

"Well, thanks, uh, Torburn. I think I got it, almost. Which way to Sommersko?"

"Yes, the *bjørn* part is hard to get right. It means 'bear.' OK, you just go back past train station and front gates of Tivoli, and then the Walking Street is over on far side of big square. You walk down Strøget five blocks to Amager Square and then walk up two blocks to the left, to Crown Prince Street, and Sommersko is there, on right-hand side of street. Or just ask anyone. Café Sommersko. That's *summer shoe*. I don't know where that name comes from, but they have pictures of a shoe everywhere."

"Thanks, Tor*bjurn*." She tried to make the word sound like what he had said.

"That's close. At least you are trying."

Elizabeth walked out onto the pavement and turned back toward the station. In the next block, she hesitated for a moment in front of the welcoming brightness of the Chinese restaurant's window. The warmth and rich spiciness almost drew her in, but she knew she had traveled too far to go no further than a block from her hotel room. She skirted the front of the main train station, its tall arched roof echoing sounds of steel wheels and rails, brakes and compressed air, a muffled announcement from a loudspeaker. She couldn't remember anything in Hemingway about this northern corner of Europe. Elizabeth liked that it was her own fresh adventure.

She walked past the Tivoli Gardens, lights strung across the front gates, the park otherwise darkened for the winter. An amusement park and restaurants and concerts and flowers in the middle of the city, right next to the town hall. Her mind filled with her future.

"Maybe one summer I could visit again. Copenhagen. Maybe visit Dan on summer vacation. See the midnight sun," she wondered.

Across the main square, it was easy to see the entrance to the Walking Street, as people funneled into the passageway or fanned out across the square. The smell of hot dogs wafted from a street vendor's cart. She had seen the stainless steel carts outside the station too, and at some of the street corners she had passed, men and women standing at a shallow chest-high ledge on the cart, dipping hot dogs into puddles of mustard and ketchup on waxed paper squares. No buns, just thin bright-red or dull-brown hot dogs held between fingertips. She thought she might try one before she left the city. Not a red one, though. They seemed much too red.

The Walking Street was lined with every kind of shop imaginable, special offers hanging in the windows or on street displays. T-shirts and souvenirs, restaurants, bars, and upscale shops, ceramics and glass and jewelry. Elizabeth walked briskly with the flow of shoppers and tourists and children. Several streets that crossed the Walking Street had slowly moving automobile traffic, but otherwise it was remarkably easy to walk, and well lit. She saw a street sign she thought must be where Torbjørn had meant for her to turn off the Walking Street, though the spelling of *Amager* on the street sign didn't look like what he had said. There had been no *G* in the middle of his halting, shuffled words.

She walked two blocks and came to Crown Prince Street, but it was spelled in one long word that didn't have anything that looked like "street" in it, as in German. The passageway was narrow and dark, but the café was right where Torbjørn had said it would be.

Elizabeth pushed open the glass door to Café Sommersko. The room was large and busy, though not crowded. On her right a bar ran the length of the room. She found a small square table with two empty chairs along the wall, newspapers on a rack next to the table. She took down a copy of the *International Herald Tribune*. World news, in English. She sat for a minute or two, looking to see if there were waiters or waitresses. At the table next to hers, there were several young men and two women. One of the women smiled, catching her eye, and pointed toward the bar. Elizabeth nodded, returning the smile, folded the newspaper, and put it on the table. She went to the bar and asked for a coffee, pointing at the espresso machine.

"Espresso? Café au lait?" the bartender asked. Elizabeth pointed at him as he named her choice. Café au lait. The bar had sandwiches on crusty French bread under wide glass covers. They reminded her that she was hungry from her trip, but she decided to wait, maybe stop somewhere on the way back to the hotel later. Or the Chinese restaurant on Istedgade. She put a blue fifty-kroner bill on the counter, to be sure she wouldn't have to exchange questions with the bartender about how much the coffee cost. The language sounded truly foreign, not laced with faintly recognizable words, as in Italian or Spanish. Here the sounds were down in their throats, swallowed, and halting. It wasn't really very pretty. Not romantic at all, and very foreign. She felt certain Hemingway never spoke any Danish. Perhaps never even heard any. She felt a special privilege. The tiny country. An obscure language.

Elizabeth took the change and coffee and returned to her table. She opened the newspaper and watched the people come and go, earnest conversations and humor, several silent lovers. The two women at the table next to hers glanced at Elizabeth from time to time, obviously curious. They were not engaged in talking with the three young men at the table, who seemed to be involved in a friendly argument. Elizabeth watched and listened closely over the edge of her paper but could not sift any sense of the discussion from their words. Sounds too difficult to decipher.

One of the women leaned toward Elizabeth, smiling. "Football. They are arguing about a football player who is leaving his Danish team and going to play in England. We don't care. Let him go." And she laughed.

"Ah. I couldn't tell a word they said. It's a difficult language. Are you all friends?"

"Yes. We are working together in the summertime. In Tivoli. My name is Hanne. And this is Lise. The boys are cooks. Steen, the very quick funny one, they call him Speedy. Bruno is the good-looking one with the curly black hair and cigarette, and Fleming, the serious one, is doing most of the talking. They don't speak English, only a little bit. Lise is a server, and I work in the cold kitchen, *smørrebrød* and salads and desserts. Now we are all without our work since October, and maybe we will go to classes. We meet here sometimes, and then we go out to eat and drink a beer or two."

"I am sorry. I hope you find a job," Elizabeth said. "I just finished a cooking class. In Switzerland. And I hope the cooks will find jobs soon."

The women stared at Elizabeth.

"No, we are fine," said Hanne. "The union will give us a job, or we are paid to go to a class. Or the kommune pays our usual wages."

"Is that for Tivoli workers only?" Elizabeth asked. "It sounds like it would cost a lot. It's maybe half the year for Tivoli?"

The women smiled and shook their heads.

"No. That is for everyone in Denmark. It does cost a lot, so we have the high taxes. So when we lose the job or get sick, then we still have our income to live. I think it means if someone is having troubles or getting old or sick, then we are all sharing that. Something like that." She smiled. "I am thinking my English is not the best."

The three young men began to gather their jackets and papers, and the women stood up to go.

"We are going for a quick supper, to Laurits Betjent, for *Pariserbøf.* The best anywhere. On a weekday when they are open at all, they close early, so we will hurry. It was nice meeting you, and practicing my English." She smiled warmly and then turned back.

"Hey, are you waiting for someone? Why don't you come along with us? It's not far. Maybe we will have time for a beer or two." One of the young men smiled and waved for Elizabeth to come as he went toward the door.

"Pariserbøf?" Elizabeth tried to sound out the word. "I don't want to be a bother. Or a fifth wheel."

"*Fift* wheel?" the woman asked, puzzled. Elizabeth laughed.

"Fifth. Fifth wheel. A car doesn't need five wheels. Never mind."

Hanne still looked puzzled, and Elizabeth surprised herself. "Yes, I would love to go with you all. And then you tell me about Pariserbøf. Maybe I will cook in Tivoli one day."

Hanne glowed with satisfaction.

They went out to the street and retraced Elizabeth's path from Amager Square, crossed the Walking Street, and continued down a narrower and darker street. Elizabeth saw glinting water between parked cars. Boats. An inlet between the streets. The young Danes were athletic and walked at a quick pace. Elizabeth had noted that pedestrians in the city moved easily and with confident steps, as if to get somewhere without delay. For a time the two women locked their arms under Elizabeth's, and they strode as if they were comrades, best of friends. Elizabeth rode on an unexpected tide of good fellowship, and even though she realized she could barely recall their names, she floated on the energy and the friendly invitation. And the safety.

Several blocks beyond Amager Square, they came to the restaurant. Laurits Betjent. The women held the door for the young cooks and then for Elizabeth. It was dark inside, shades of brown and black, signs for disco music and weekend late-night events, open until five in the morning on Fridays and Saturdays. This weekday evening the restaurant would close at seven, within the hour, so they placed their order as they took their seats at a comfortably large round table. Six Pariserbøf and beer. Carlsberg or Tuborg?

There were disagreements among the cooks as to which beer they liked or was more suited to the food, and the women said it didn't matter, they were the same. They all laughed. It appeared to be a regular debate, and Elizabeth shrugged. Hanne translated Bruno's idea that Elizabeth could supply an unbiased decision, and that they had ordered a Tuborg and a Carlsberg for her. She beamed with feigned pride and agreed, but only if they would accept her ruling once and for all. Hanne translated for the others, and they howled in agreement.

"Once and for all." Elizabeth could hear the words repeated, and their agreement, without translation. Elizabeth still had her question about the food and needed to hear their names again. "I need your names again. I am sorry, everything is new. My name is Elizabeth. And what is a Pariserbøf? Is it a steak? Or a hamburger? We have walked a mile for a hamburger?"

Hanne translated, and they laughed. Elizabeth said she remembered Hanne, because she had introduced them all, so the other woman had to be Lise. One of the men was smoking another cigarette, so that must be Bruno. She pointed, and he nodded and winked at her. Steen said his name was actually Speedy, and Fleming admitted he was the last one.

"I am Fleming," he said. Hanne held up her hand and told them all Fleming would describe the making of the meal, and he wanted her to translate for Elizabeth.

"Fleming says he is the only one of the cooks who could give a proper professional description of ingredients and process." Hanne pointed and sternly told Elizabeth to listen carefully.

Fleming cleared his throat and began, a solemn glance at Elizabeth. "The Pariserbøf is best quality beef, no fat or gristle, shaved or minced, as if we were to be making steak tartare. You are a trained cook, Elizabeth, they tell me. You understand tartare?" Hanne translated, and Elizabeth nodded.

"Two hundred grams, best quality shaved beef, as I have said, formed into a ball and then spread on the cutting board with the flat side of a very experienced cook's knife, back and forth, until maybe twenty-five centimeters by fifteen centimeters and maybe one centimeter thick. Four angles, what do you call it, a rectangle? So, a piece of French bread, and this is the only reason for calling it the Paris steak, as it is a Danish specialty." He minced the word with pinched fingers for emphasis.

"Specialitet." He went on, "And that is even though the bread is baked right here in our little Denmark. So! The bread is fried in nice Danish butter until

golden brown on both sides and placed on the serving platter. More butter is put in the hot pan, and once the butter is frothing the beef is placed in the pan for thirty seconds only, and then carefully, carefully, mind you"—Fleming raised a cautionary finger and stopped, and they all laughed as Hanne translated— "carefully you turn the beef over and cook for an additional thirty seconds on the other side, so it is nicely browned and hot, but very rare inside. OK, Elizabeth? Eh?"

"Yes." She was transfixed, or perhaps she was playing along.

Fleming continued. "A little salt and pepper, and we take the beef out of the pan and place it on the grilled French bread. On the serving platter."

He stopped and took a sip of the beer that had been placed before him. Elizabeth reached for one of her two beers, and they all stopped her.

"No, no, no! You must wait for our taste test," Hanne cautioned.

Fleming continued his explanation, clearly enjoying the drama. "So we have the platter, the grilled French bread, and the lightly cooked top-quality shaved beef. Little salt and pepper. Right, Elizabeth?" She nodded again. "Now the garnish, which of course, Elizabeth, you know is the most important thing. Besides the quality of the beef and the butter. And the careful cook's skills, which you are hearing from me, who is Fleming. Plus, we need the correct pan and heat. But, OK, the garnish." He took another sip of beer and pointed and then wagged his finger at Elizabeth, that she should not touch her beer yet. "Almost, but not yet, Elizabeth. We have four or five special pieces of garnish to add on top of the finished beef. The garnish is for taste, but only in combination, as any one alone is too harsh. In combination they are a delicate symphony. And I am the symphony conductor. OK?" She nodded.

"In separate quadrants surrounding one nice fresh raw sweet onion ring, the cook places a teaspoon of capers, then medium-chopped onion, diced pickled red beets, and the special Danish pickle relish, which is sweet mustard with finely diced carrots, pickling cucumbers, cauliflower, and onion. OK?" He swiped at his brow and took a swallow of beer. Elizabeth stared. "And now…" His outstretched hands indicated the final suspense. "And now, into the raw onion ring on top of the beef." He waited. "We place one very fresh raw egg yolk, careful not to break open, except by our guest customer. If it breaks and spoils the presentation, we must start all over. Then we finish this with lots of freshly grated raw horseradish. And there you have it!"

Everyone clapped. When they stopped, Elizabeth reached for one of her beers. They stopped her again.

"OK, Elizabeth," Hanne said. "Before the food comes. And once and for all." She stopped and looked sternly at the cooks. "Once and for all, we will take your expert judgment. Close your eyes, and I will hand you one beer and then the other, and you will tell us if you can taste any difference. Ready?"

She nodded and noticed they had all finished their beer, and a second round was being placed on the table. She was ready.

"OK, Hanne. My eyes are closed."

"Not so quick," Hanne said, and drew a linen napkin over Elizabeth's eyes. Lise held the ends behind her head.

"OK, Hanne. I would not cheat you. I need to be the once-and-for-all expert. Go ahead."

Hanne placed the first bottle in Elizabeth's hand, and she lifted it to her lips. It was cold and clear and tart. Liquid dreams of Copenhagen and the lights of Tivoli Gardens, and midnight sun. Surrounded by friends. Her story, gaining strength. Strange words and food. The beer was fresh and delicate. And very cold.

"And the other?" Closed eyes behind the napkin. Elizabeth grasped the next cold bottle Hanne touched to her fingers. She took a sip. And then another. It had a slightly creamier texture. Rich. The bottle was cold, but the beer didn't taste as chilled as the first one. No. It was thicker, almost mellow. She hoped they were not playing a trick on her. They took the beer from her hand, and she heard the clink of shuffling bottles. She removed the napkin blindfold.

"It's easy, unless you are pulling my leg," she said. She waited for Hanne to translate. They all looked puzzled. "OK, never mind my leg. The first one was clear and tart, cold and fresh, like the sea. The second one, the bottle was cold, but the beer was smoother. Creamy, as if the beer was not as cold as the bottle. I like the first one lots better." She paused, holding up her finger, for silence. "I think the second one would give me a headache in the morning." They howled with laughter and complaint, and she knew the argument would never be settled. So she asked, "Which one was the first one? I would like another one of those. The first one."

Hanne pushed the two bottles toward her. Fleming's serious face. Hanne translated for him. "Take another drink, and tell us which one is still your favorite."

Elizabeth took a long sip of each. The server brought their food. Elizabeth held up the Tuborg. "One more of these, please." She was warmed by the cold beer and the delight of her unexpected part in the gathering. Her heart filled with thanks for her good fortune on this evening, alone in Copenhagen. A good omen. She was certain the evening could not be improved upon.

The server placed oval porcelain platters before Elizabeth, the women, the cooks. The plate was exactly as Fleming had described, though she could see that Steen's egg yolk had broken. He did not seem to even notice, and she was glad it had not been served to Fleming. She wondered if he might have sent it back. Fleming caught her eye and winked, shaking his head.

Elizabeth asked the group, to no one in particular, "So this is the hamburger Fleming has described? Fleming? Can I get a bun? And some ketchup?" Hanne translated, and they erupted in laughter. Elizabeth broke the egg yolk with her fork and wondered how the flavors would join, white slivers of horseradish, finely chopped onions, and a yellow mustard relish, cubed beets. And capers. She had never tasted capers, nor raw horseradish. The minced beef glistened, rich and buttery, the crispness of French bread. Strangers around a table, new friends.

She cut a piece with the fork and knife. She lifted her fork with her left hand, as she had learned to do in Switzerland, and took a bite. She lowered her fork and closed her eyes. The evening was complete, gathering Elizabeth in warmth and gratitude. Such a distance from the train and the rails and the journey and the hotel room. And tomorrow and Dan. She wondered what the new day would bring. How could she return home? Home? She swallowed her fear and excitement. Capers and horseradish and butter.

Hanne broke the silence. "Elizabeth. Are you OK?"

Elizabeth could not find the right words. "Wonderful. And you too. All of you. I have never tasted anything like this. And this evening." She stopped.

It was her adventure. A gift, from strangers. To not let it get away. Never. She blurted out, "I just don't know. I don't know how." She wiped a tear at the corner of her eye. She lifted her fork and knife and took another bite. Richness and surprise again. Even richer. Capers and horseradish and butter and toasted French bread.

An hour later Elizabeth hugged Steen and Bruno and Lise good-bye in front of the restaurant. Hanne and Fleming said they would walk Elizabeth back to her hotel. She told them she would be fine if they just took her to the Walking Street and pointed her in the right direction. She told them she felt like walking alone. They walked toward Amager Square, and there they said good-bye.

"You will come back and visit us? In the summer?" Hanne asked. "We can show you our kitchens, and we can drink some Tuborg out in Tivoli. It was so good to meet you. And just by chance."

"Yes. That's what I was thinking about, Hanne. How to come back. Maybe it wasn't by chance."

"This Danish man you are meeting tomorrow, Elizabeth. Maybe you will come to visit him again too?"

Elizabeth thought for a moment, trying to reconnect with her memory of Dan on the Swiss train. Her thoughts strayed to horseradish and capers. Fleming's story about making something just right, perfect. A cook's gift. A chance in time. Dark shiny pavements, a slight chill mist, strange muffled words. Safe and friendly mysteries. Clear, cold beer. Or two. One fresher than the other. By chance?

"Elizabeth? Visit him too?" Hanne asked again.

"Oh. Dan? I wasn't really thinking about him, Hanne."

The walk back to the hotel seemed to take only minutes, while the evening at Café Sommersko and Laurits Betjent had held a lifetime of wishes, easygoing company, enchantments of taste and friendship and welcome. Elizabeth passed up a brief thought of getting a cup of coffee along the way. She went straight up the stairs to her room, saying good night to a new young clerk behind the hotel's front desk. Her room was the perfect safe haven. She washed her face and brushed her teeth and went straight to bed. The few minutes before sleep enfolded her were warmed with the evening's adventure. The night was thankfully dreamless.

Elizabeth woke early, though slowly, and to a growing awkward feeling about meeting with Dan. She showered and dressed and went out to walk and clear her mind, hoping to reclaim her sense of well-being from the evening before. She found a coffee shop on a street near a busy commuter train station, underground in that part of town. She ordered coffee and cream and an open-face cheese sandwich on thickly buttered yeasty French bread. A young Pakistani man, she guessed, behind the counter. He answered her request in English.

She found a small table and sat, thinking how the day might turn out. The buttered bread and cheese were rich and creamy, and she wondered what kind of cheese it was, realizing she didn't really know anything, and she was simply on a silent excursion, hoping for enjoyment. Or rescue. She knew a repeat of the good fortune of Café Sommersko and the restaurant the night before was unlikely, and even there she had been at the mercy of another person's command of English. It would be the same with Dan, she was sure. Suddenly she just wanted to go, to run, to leave Copenhagen before the spell was broken. A fleeting dream better than confirmed disappointment. And knowing her careful conversation sounded less than intelligent. It certainly was not smooth. Elizabeth finished her coffee and got up to leave. She thanked the counterman, and out of curiosity she asked him what sort of cheese was on the sandwich.

"Mild Danbo. I think," he said. "Let me ask the kitchen." She tried to stop him from the bother, but he had stepped away quickly, and she heard him call out to the kitchen worker, a stream of what sounded like perfect Danish. He returned.

"I am wrong," he said. "It is Havarti. I have not been here very long in Denmark. But I should have known. Sorry. It is Havarti."

"No, that's no problem. It was very good. Thank you." She turned to go and hesitated, then returned to the counter.

The man smiled, ready to serve or help. "Yes?" he said, then bit at his lip.

Fear and excitement rose in her. "You said you were not in Denmark very long? How long? I am just curious. I heard you speak in Danish to the kitchen. It sounded as though you speak Danish very well."

"Ah yes, six month here, nearly finish with K.I.S.S. course." He beamed with pride.

"Kiss? What kind of course is that?"

"No, it is name of the school. Københavns Intensive Sprogskole, K.I.S.S. Just around corner from Nørreport Station. Two, three blocks from here. Intensive program, maybe stress, but very easy, really. Very cheap, very fast. Nice people."

"Ah. Where exactly?"

"Go out door to left, two blocks along main street here, turn left on Nørrebrogade, go one block. See sign there. Small door, stair up to second floor."

"Thank you. And what is your name?" she asked.

He looked carefully at her. "*Jeg hedder*, Sam." His words sounded as though he was swallowing while he spoke.

"What?"

"I answer your question. You ask, *'Hvad hedder du?'* and I answer, *'Jeg hedder Sam.'*" He pointed at her and at himself in rhythm with the exchange. He repeated, "You ask, 'Hvad hedder du?' and I answer, 'Jeg hedder, Sam.'" He waited, and then repeated it again. And then again. She understood easily, but the words were muffled, brushing off his tongue. He smiled at her. "Go over to KISS and ask how they teach this. All repetition, over and over. You learn a couple hours a day. Okay stress, make a person nervous. But learn very easy."

"Thanks, Sam." She smiled as he beamed.

"Remember how I repeat it to you? Hvad hedder du?" he asked slowly, pointing at her.

"*Ja h'ther* Elizabeth."

"*Tak,* Elizabeth!" he said, touching his heart and then his forehead lightly, two fingers.

"Tak, Sam. Tak."

Elizabeth followed Sam's directions. The street was busier now, people on the way to work, though it was still early. She found the school's narrow doorway and a poster under a plastic cover on the wall: *K.I.S.S. Københavns Intensive Sprogskole.* English translation underneath. *Copenhagen's Intensive Language School.*

Thirteen levels, three weeks each. She went up the flight of stairs to the school's office. A woman at a desk explained the program.

"Yes, new starting class every five or six weeks. One must pass each level to take the next level, and most students have to repeat some levels. Class three days per week, three hours, choose morning or afternoon. Very intense language training method, developed by Israelis. Or Americans. For spies, they say." The secretary shrugged and smiled. "Step one class starting today. Good if a person wants to work here in Copenhagen. Everyday street Danish. Very inexpensive course. Or the kommune pays most of the cost."

"You say a new class is starting today?" Elizabeth asked. "Is there a waiting list? Can anyone take the class? Can someone who doesn't live here take a class?"

"OK, OK. There is time. Relax. Yes, the classes are always full, twelve students only, each class. But today a British businessman and his wife are not coming. He called this morning. He is transferred back home. You want to begin the course? Too late to call for someone to fill in."

"Morning class?" Elizabeth asked, and the woman nodded, looking at the clock.

"Class starts in fifteen minutes. Let me get information. You have passport or identification card? Let's start with your name." Elizabeth looked at the clock. Shock and surprise welled up through her stomach. The woman smiled. "Your name?"

Elizabeth grinned. "*Ja h'ther*, Elizabeth. *Va h'ther du?*"

The woman stared and shook her head, a broad smile spreading. "Jeg hedder Katrina. *Og du er sgu halv skør, lille skat. Ikke?*"

"Tak, Katrina."

Katrina stood and laughed. She hugged Elizabeth, who began to sob.

"Little darling," Katrina crooned, holding Elizabeth close, rocking her gently. "You certainly are a little bit crazy, aren't you? That's what I have said to you, and you have thanked me." Katrina laughed again. "You will be fine, and you will learn what we are saying about you. And you will learn how to answer back. It will all be OK, little darling."

—❧—

"And she begins to learn Danish already?" Bodil asked. "And when do we meet her guy? Dan? Can we hear about Dan, or get a look, before the ferry lands?"

Billy shrugged and smiled. "We didn't write about him. He is one of the important chapters, but the moments are confused and painful. So we put them in. And left him out.

A bell rang. The ferry slowed in the water, its weight gathering as it settled deeper into the green-black surface of the harbor water. Billy closed the book and slid it onto the table. Bodil looked around at passengers who were gathering their things.

"We better pack up, William. Maybe pee before we go back to the car and drive."

He watched her stride off to the lavatory, energy and speed and enthusiasm.

She must be anxious to see her man, Billy thought. *Lucky guy.* He gathered his things and went to the men's room. The mirror reminded him he had been traveling for two days, with only rudimentary attempts to keep himself clean and presentable. He was thankful for the thought he might get a bath or shower at Bodil's before continuing on to meet Rita. He had no assurance she would even be there. And if she was, what would he say? Or ask. Part of his heart hoped she wouldn't be there.

He left the lavatory and returned to the table. Bodil was not there. He looked around, a moment's fear that she might leave without him. He caught sight of her passing through a small gathering of passengers beginning to move toward the stairs. He noticed a tense look of worry, her face suddenly worn. Not older, perhaps just tired. He reminded himself her job must take a toll. Or was it something else? He got up and joined her.

"Are you OK?" he asked. "You look worried about something."

"It's nothing. Not to worry, William."

He sensed it was something private, or perhaps she had been reminded of her fatigue when she looked in the mirror in the women's room. He decided not to dwell on the matter.

"Thanks for the lunch, Bodil. I'll pay you back when I get some dollars changed," he said. He knew what was coming, but he felt he had to at least offer.

"Never mind that, William. Your story has been a wonderful vacation day for me. Maybe you will send me a signed copy of your book when you come home. I want to have something to remember you by. I loved hearing your voice reading it. It is your story, I think." She looked at him, suddenly intent, serious. "Is it your story, William?"

He wondered at such a question. He could not think how to answer. She studied his face. His eyes. He looked away.

"I thought so, William," she said, getting to her feet. "But as I am listening, and thinking about it, and wondering, it becomes mine too, no?" She turned and started for the door. "Let's get going."

The steel superstructure of the ferry's berth and unloading ramps moved slowly past the windows. A last glimpse of the gray horizon and sky. The stairway tunnel to the car deck echoed their steps. A gritty painted walkway across the steel floor led them to Bodil's car. Once inside, they pulled the doors shut, twin sighs of relief. Comfortable small capsule. They waited as the ship's engines reversed, sending rumbles through the steel cavern. Then silence and a slight hint of inertia forward, a soft tilt to one side, a distant shout and rattle of cables and winches.

"We are here," Bodil said. "Only a short drive to my home, William. Kærby. Between Randers and Hadsund. A half hour. Or a little longer."

Billy could hear hesitation in her voice. He glanced carefully, not turning his head. He saw the fatigue again. And something more. *Perhaps fear*, he thought, so he asked. "Did something in the story bother you, Bodil? Worry you, or make you sad?"

"No, not sad." There was a sharp clang of steel, and the daylight flooded a portion of the deck ahead. "OK. I will tell you something personal, just for you and me, please, but also because you have shared so much of yourself. It is that I am always a little afraid coming home. The closer I get. On the ferryboat I always wonder about what would happen if my man was gone when I got there. I think your Elizabeth reminds me how easy it might be for someone just to go here or there. Maybe even leave everything."

She started the engine and followed the line of cars toward the door and the steel ramp.

"And I wonder what it would be like if my man found another woman. Maybe one who had children. Or one who could have a child." She looked away. "Every time I am landing at Ebeltoft, I get the same feeling." She took a deep breath. "I have not asked if you have any children. I see you have no ring, but one never knows."

Billy laughed. "No. I am not married, and I have not had any children." He thought for a moment. "Except for this story. Elizabeth's Story. It's my child." He smiled. "I had it with Elizabeth. We gave it life, and it's growing. That's what this trip is about, I think. Delivering the story. Bringing it to life. Or back to life."

"What do you mean?" she asked.

"The next chapter. It's different. Very troubling, I think. This maybe is a place where I am not sure if Elizabeth is telling her story or making it up."

"How long did Elizabeth stay in Denmark? She learned the language, I am guessing. From where you stopped reading." She studied Billy's face. "And she cooked? Maybe in Tivoli?"

"Those are the years we did not write about. Elizabeth had notes, but they were just years, with good things and bad things, but mostly just day by day. Eight years. So we left all that out and jumped to one of those moments between the years. A terrible moment. And then more. Where things are both very confused but also very clear."

"Like when I come home and my man is gone?"

"No, Bodil. But tell me. When you come home, like today, what's it like? After you have been away for a week?" Billy asked.

"William, I can't tell you about that. It is too much loving and sleeping late. After I am home for ten minutes, I am never worrying."

"Would it be different if you had a child, though?" he asked.

"Oh no. If I had a child, I would take a long time off from this work and then find another job, maybe in a *børnehave*, or school. You know, a kindergarten. I have my education. I would write my new Bodil Story." She laughed.

"So why don't you do that? Why do you fly around the world?

"William, you are very slow to understanding about stories and how they are written. If I did not fly, I would not be meeting you and your story today.

And if so, what about *our* story then?" She beamed with satisfaction. "Read me this new troubling part, and I will be thankful, even if my man is not there when we get home, because Elizabeth is bearing my burdens." She steered the car onto the ramp and toward the highway.

"You are too much, Bodil." Billy shook his head and opened the book.

"Read, William. Make me sad about Elizabeth so anything that might happen to Bodil and her man will seem better."

"OK. It starts right where I met you. In a plane. The airport at Copenhagen. Kastrup. Elizabeth is leaving."

Bodil shifted into fourth gear, and then fifth. "Read, William. I will drive."

Chapter 13

ELIZABETH   THE BLESSING (1986)

The plane wheeled and paused at the end of the runway and waited in line, three planes, and then for permission to take off. Elizabeth had decided to travel from Copenhagen to New York by the longest route possible, taking China Air through Amman, Jordan, to Thailand. In Bangkok she would buy discount tickets to New York, with skips and stepping-stones in Hong Kong and Japan or Hawaii and California, and finally to the East Coast. Her dad's home in New Jersey. Tivoli's winter closing had always allowed quick yearly visits to the States, but this time she wanted to take her time. The restaurant would reopen in May, so she knew she had until early April to make up her mind whether she would cook for another season. Or whether she would return to Denmark at all. But Elizabeth knew in her heart she would never return to Dan. Ashes.

Elizabeth had played the scene over and over in her mind. She rehearsed the horror, unable to erase it from the final week of February. The dark cloak before spring's bloom. She had delayed the trip to see her father when her little Rita's condition worsened. She had waited for the operation. And now it didn't matter. They could have thought it over a bit longer, gained a few precious months, or weeks. Even a moment would have been a treasure. The nightmare had accelerated through February, Rita's operation on a bright Monday morning, confidence evaporating two days later, Wednesday, about noon. Rita slipped away in midafternoon. The winter sun set in disbelief.

Her beautiful daughter had turned four a week before the operation. Rita's condition was serious, but the operation was routine, the doctors assured. A routine repair, a not uncommon childhood condition, explained all, carefully correct English, despite Elizabeth's insistence on speaking her competent but awkward Danish. The University Hospital in Copenhagen was the best in Denmark, Dan promised. Her husband's pale words frightened Elizabeth, even though he had tried to be a good father to the little girl. Rita was his flesh and blood; he certainly knew what was best; the surgeon had assured them it would all be fine.

"Ninety-eight percent, everything is OK. In the rare cases, we go back and have to fix something." That sounded like one hundred percent success to Elizabeth, and Rita's gray lips and labored breath increased the urgency. They operated on a Monday, and Rita came through the operation perfectly. The waiting vigil quickly grew confident, almost relaxed. It was so smooth Dan went to the newspaper office on Wednesday morning, to check mail and meet with the editorial staff. Elizabeth noted her familiar disbelief, and had witnessed his easy connection with women wherever he went. She guessed he was having another affair. It had seemed to become part of the natural order of things in this beautiful and intelligent and tiny land. Everything in its proper place, smart. Convenient. She was sure he was not at the office.

Dan didn't return Elizabeth's call at noon and didn't answer her message that the doctors had sounded concerned about a rattle in Rita's breathing, that they had taken her from the relaxed and safe room on the recovery hall. Tense looks, and few words. They seemed to accelerate, sliding the little bundle onto the gurney, "Here we go, honey." Her lovely little baby, weak blue smile and fluttering eyes, "Mommy," and hurried wheels on tile, one caster rattling. Gone. A faint echo. "Mommy."

Dan was maybe at lunch, his secretary said. He didn't answer his pager either. An hour later Elizabeth called again, but was interrupted by a doctor coming to report there were some complications with Rita. Complications. The doctor studied a clipboard chart while he talked, pointing to lines on the paper, reminders and indications. Complications. They were working on this, and would know more in a bit, the doctor said. He repeated it was going to be fine, but his face said something else, his eyes a distant and unknown language, separate and incomprehensible messages, words or not. Fear. Or confusion. The doctor's clear school English halted, searching for correct words.

"We are doing everything. Perhaps make a call to the father." The doctor turned and was gone, as Elizabeth called Dan again. No answer.

"With some damned bitch," Elizabeth said, too loudly, to no one in particular, and a doctor and an aide at the nurses' station looked up, then back to their reports. A light flashed at the far end of the hallway, in time to a pleasant soft-edged tone. The elevator doors opened and closed with a polite ping. No one left or entered the lift. The doors opened again, and there was laughter from inside the elevator, but no one emerged. Elizabeth looked for an exit, anywhere to run, if she could find her baby. She would find her Rita, and they could think it over again, whether to operate or not, take a week or two to decide. She went to the desk and asked where her Rita was, maybe she could just take her home, please.

"Please," she tried to ask, searching her best Danish for the word. There was no single, easy word for *please* in the obscure and difficult language, and her mind couldn't assemble the several and suddenly too many words needed to beg for her baby. Please. Rita. They would leave the hospital right now, please. Please. If she could just ask someone! She would ask Dan. Elizabeth punched at numbers on the nurses' station phone, starting over twice, and the receiver slipped from her fingers and clattered to the floor, and then swung back on its coiled cord. She kicked at the swinging handset, shouting at Dan, certain he could hear.

"You son of a bitch, where are you? You bastard!" She kicked again at the swinging handset. Pieces of dull plastic skittered across the hall, clacking against the wall.

—⁂—

Bodil put her right hand on the open pages of the book. Billy looked up at her.

"William, this is very sad, and it is happening very often. In Denmark it is sometimes easy to have a lover, and it may seem no one feels it is unusual or something very bad. But it hurts. And a foreigner who lives with a Dane maybe can't understand it at all. Or just the opposite, thinking it is too easy, and just fine. And so they do too much." She shook her head. "I think sometimes we are fooling ourselves. I worry about it. But I would never damage my marriage. And I am hoping always that my man feels the same way. I think I would know."

Billy glanced at Bodil. She bit at her lower lip, smiled at him and shook her head.

"Yes, I know I look worried. When I am chewing on my lip. Go on. Read some more. She was trying to call her man. The phone was on the floor. Maybe broken."

Billy scanned the page. "OK. Here we are. She's trying to call. Rita is maybe not doing well. I think this was a hard part of the story for Elizabeth to write. It does not flow smoothly." He took a deep breath. "Let's see. OK, here." Billy read on, quickly at first, to catch up.

⟨⟩

Elizabeth kicked at the swinging handset, shouting at Dan, certain he could hear.

"You son of a bitch, where are you? You bastard!" She kicked again at the swinging handset. Pieces of dull plastic skittered across the hall, clacking against the wall.

"Damn you, Dan!" she shouted, and sat down on the floor, and tried again, "Please," awkward words trailing on tile. A nurse knelt at her side, lifted her to her feet, and cradled her toward a small waiting room, private. Reserved for solitary agony, she guessed. Elizabeth could not sit, and stood clutching the back of the chair by the door, knowing that sitting would signal surrender. She remained motionless, repeating her demand, her wish. Her prayer. She laughed to herself. In Danish there was one clear and simple word to say thanks yet so many impossible words to remember or imagine to say please. No, to beg. For my child, please, if you would...

If you would be so kind. The Danish words flooded into her mind. Now they could go! *If you would be so kind! We will go as soon as my baby is ready. Tak! Thanks!*

Thank God! She heard the elevator chime, and more laughter, distant joy over-flowing into the hallway. A good sign, she was sure. Relief flooded her soul.

Rita drifted away as the sun set, shortly after three o'clock in the afternoon. The ancient Scandinavian mystery, dusky winter sun, hopeless transparent gray sunset afternoon. An evening of despair. The darkening sky harmonized a chord in Elizabeth's heart. She remembered the first time she heard that suicide spiked in the long winter months without sun. When hope fades to gray. Enough, now. Enough.

Dan returned to the hospital hours later. Rita was gone. Dan gave no expla-nation as to where he had been. He cried when he heard the news. She remem-bered that. He had cried, but so soon after that he began the paperwork and tying up loose ends.

The pilot's voice on the intercom invaded Elizabeth's endless replay of the prior weeks' horror and shock. He was telling the flight attendants to take their seats. Take off. Soon. Not soon enough.

"Son of a bitch," Elizabeth hissed, clenched teeth, pushing back in the plane's seat. The plane's engines whined to power and strained against the brakes. They were ready to take off. She could not shake the terror of her decision to trust her husband's arrangements, mingled like a poisoned drink, explanations in foggy Danish. *De Ukendtes Grav.* The grave of the unknown ones. Anonymous.

"De Ukendtes Grav," he had said. They would bury Rita in Copenhagen. He added there might be a country church cemetery somewhere on the mainland, in Jutland. If they could find a priest who would allow the burial. They did not attend church, and it was a slim chance. No one attended church anyway, he said, even though everyone paid the tax. A tiny coffin was all Elizabeth could imagine. A baby coffin for a baby girl. And she said yes, whatever he could arrange. Dan was good at making arrangements. Paying the light bills. Or refin-ishing furniture, making things fit.

When Elizabeth asked again about a funeral, Dan simply said everything was taken care of. Days passed. It was done. De Ukendte. The unknown souls. The howling comprehension had rushed into her chest and throat.

"The Unknowns?" She had screamed at Dan, "An unmarked grave? Ashes? No, tell me what you have done. No, don't you dare tell me!" Clasping her head, her ears. "Where is she, you bastard, you damned monster, what did you do with our baby? Damn you to hell forever, Dan! My baby!" Ashes and memories. Ashes in the wind, no marker, no quiet churchyard glade. Ashes and January dusk at three in the afternoon. A single clear intercom tone interrupted her nightmare thoughts. Whining engines, straining. Screaming steel.

The brakes released, and the plane accelerated, heavy rumbling, long minutes, it seemed, until the plane lifted from the runway, suddenly silent. Hard hydraulic thuds from beneath Elizabeth's seat as landing gear folded into the silver belly of the plane. Into her belly. Machine madness. Tons of steel lifting into the air. She didn't care if the plane exploded into a billion glowing shards, wishing only the settling dust would join somewhere with the ashes of her dream, the entire world an unmarked grave. The Unknowns. A land with a shallow water line and no room to spread or grow. No frontier. No mountains, no rivers. Gray ocean horizon.

Elizabeth cried softly for leaving her beautiful little girl. And then she cried for the green meadows and woods of this gentle and peaceful land. A smart land. Smart and tidy. Honest and fair and just, and damn you, Dan. You did your own best, and I wasn't paying attention.

"Oh dear God, I am so sorry for being so stupid." Elizabeth pulled her olive-green canvas bag from the floor. It held her passport, two credit cards, loose paper money, and the neck pouch she would wear, two T-shirts and underwear, a toothbrush. She had decided to buy what she needed in Amman when they made the stopover in Jordan on the way to Bangkok. Or wait until Bangkok. She needed nothing. China Air to Thailand. She would purchase tickets in Bangkok for the rest of the flight home to the States. The long way around the world, and less than half the cost of a direct flight to New York, three times the miles and ten times the hours. She didn't care. She could take as many days as she wanted on a beach somewhere before leaving to face her father or anyone who might ask her how she was. And she would use the trip to assemble a letter to Kathryn. She did not know which way to turn. But she knew she had closed another chapter. It wasn't a good one. It felt like the final chapter in an awful book. A book about hell. The final howling hell of a chapter in a book about hell. And how many of the words had she written?

"I need a plan, Kathryn," she said aloud, to no one in particular.

A man in a trim business suit and glasses in the aisle seat opened his brief-case. "Excuse me. A plan?" His polite and careful Danish accent, and she shrugged and smiled, as if she didn't understand. A plan. For now, one night in Amman, a long flight to Bangkok, and a week or two or a month there. Maybe lay over in California on the way east, maybe see Kathryn. It had been more than twenty years. She wondered what Kathryn might be like now, what she might say. Maybe. Thoughts floated on clouds as they broke through the winter haze.

<hr />

Billy looked up from the book as Bodil downshifted several times. They turned onto a road that twisted among smaller patches of farmland, whitewashed or brick farmhouses. There was remarkably little traffic, an occasional moped. A small tractor with an empty hay wagon.

"We're almost there. Our little house on the prairie," she said. "We moved to Kærby from Arhus after studying at the university. We wanted to live where we could have some animals, sheep and goats and chickens. My man has also studied weaving and woodworking. He just wanted a quiet place to work."

She slowed and turned in at a low barn in the shade of a large tree. The building's side wall faced the road, small dark windows. Perhaps stalls. The drive curved around the barn onto a gravel courtyard. The tires pushed waves of crunching stones, and they stopped in front of a small whitewashed house connected at right angles to the barn. A garage and chicken coop and open woodshed formed the third side of the courtyard.

"The house is hundreds of years old, but we have fixed it up. It's old field-stone, and you will see the walls are very thick. It was damp and cold, but we have made a modern insulated wall inside the house, cinderblocks and stucco, also white. You will see."

She honked the horn several times. A small door where the house con-nected to the barn opened, and a man appeared. Billy watched Bodil's face. The anxious worry he had seen on the ferry was replaced with a glowing smile.

Pride and relief. She got out of the car and ran toward the man. He took three or four steps toward the car and then waited, hands on hips, a smile to match Bodil's, his sandy hair blowing in the fresh wind. He opened his arms as wide as his grin and waited. He was almost as tall as Bodil, faded and worn denim jeans and sandals, a pull-over linen shirt with loose tie-strings at the open neck. He was clearly muscular, and had wide and powerful hands. He and Bodil hugged and rocked back and forth. He stroked Bodil's hair and clasped it into a pony-tail in his hand. He gave her a kiss and another hug, then waved at Billy. Billy retrieved his bag and stepped out onto the gravel.

Bodil brushed at her eyes and turned around, then looked back. "This is William. He was on the airplane and is visiting in Terndrup tomorrow to deliver a book." She spoke slowly and carefully.

"Aha!" the man said, smiling and beckoning. He turned back to the house. "I am Søren. *Kom ind!*" he called. Bodil took Billy's hand and pulled him toward the house. He felt swept on a curious tide into the centuries-old house, cluttered furnace and laundry room foyer, rows of wooden clogs and boots and slippers. A door on the left stood open to the kitchen and a large archway leading into dining and living areas, an iron woodstove between the archway and dining table.

The man turned. "I have some work to finish. Go in and be comfortable." The invitation was pleasant, and the man disappeared through a door on the right, down a step into the barn. Billy caught a glimpse of a workbench under bright lights. Wood shavings. Tools on the wall. A large loom in the background. He couldn't place a distinct, clean odor fanned by the workroom door as it closed..

"He will come in when supper is ready. William, since you have no real luggage we need to clean you up. And your clothes too. I will get you some of Søren's pants and a shirt, and then you can relax, while I do the wash and make supper." She led Billy through the kitchen and dining area into the open living room and pointed him to a sofa covered in a loosely knit blanket. Three other large chairs were covered with similar pieces of soft fabric. Bodil disappeared through curtains in an archway at the other end of the living area, matching the one to the kitchen.

She called out to Billy. "This house is really one large room, in a *U* shape. There is one small room upstairs, but you can sleep on the sofa, if that is all right with you." She emerged from the bedroom with a shirt and jeans and a towel, underwear and socks. "Come on. These will fit for one day. I will turn on the gas heater. Hot water for a shower." She led him through the kitchen and back into the entryway. The bathroom was on the back wall of the house, the door between the furnace and a washing machine. Shirts and socks hung on hangers near the furnace. Bodil lit the pilot light inside a small water heater that hung on the wall and showed Billy how turning on the hot water tap lit the burner and gave him hot water when he needed it.

"I think you can manage. Leave your used clothes on the floor here when you come out. I will wash them, and they should be dry by tomorrow. Do you have what you need?"

"Bodil. This is just fine. Thank you for everything. My head is sort of spinning."

"Mine too, William. Let me see what he has put in the refrigerator. This is a game we play. Bodil coming home. What did my man put in the refrigerator?"

"Sounds lots better than Elizabeth leaving home," Billy said. "I think your man told me his name. Your man. But I didn't really get it."

"Yes. I am surprised he told you, just like that. Usually it is just 'hi,' and he goes about his business. This is a good sign." Bodil looked genuinely pleased. "It's Søren, maybe a little hard to pronounce, but it is a common Danish name. Søren. You know, in the comics, *Peanuts?* Charlie Brown in the Danish version is named Søren Brun. Søren in Denmark is as common as Charlie in America!" She laughed and disappeared into the kitchen.

Billy splashed cold water on his face. He looked in the small mirror above the washbasin. He was suddenly ten thousand miles from home. In every way. "*Sir-un,*" the face said. "*Sir-en.*" He shook his head and stepped into the shower area of the bathroom, the smooth cement floor sloping toward a large stainless steel drain. The hot water was refreshing, but the meager flow encouraged him to be quick. He rinsed off the soap, then shaved, washed his hair, and turned off the water.

Two minutes, maybe, he thought, shaking his head in disbelief. He dried off and pulled on the clothes Bodil had borrowed for him to wear. Søren hadn't looked taller than him, but was clearly very muscular, and the clothes fit loosely. Comfortable, but he was glad they weren't going anywhere this evening. He imagined Bodil and Søren might want privacy in the one downstairs room. He would ask to sleep upstairs, right after supper. He could feel the weight of travel and began to look forward to a night's sleep in a regular bed.

"Nonsense, William," Bodil said as they finished supper. Søren had not spoken more than a few words but seemed pleased with Bodil's and Billy's conversation. He watched their eyes, smiling at Billy and murmuring a few words to Bodil. "Nonsense," she repeated. You aren't running off to bed upstairs right away. You can sleep upstairs. Or you can sleep on the sofa, which is more comfortable. But before you sleep, I want to hear more from the book." She looked at Søren. "And my man says he wants to hear some of it too. Elizabeth leaving Denmark. She is in the plane, no? She is going to Thailand?"

"Yes. But she is in Jordan for one night. The flight is cheaper with the lay-over in Amman." Bodil explained the details in quick Danish.

Søren smiled and nodded. "I am understanding just fine. William, you are maybe reading us a bedtime story from your book?" He smiled broadly.

Bodil got up from the table and began to clatter dishes and silverware, gathering things to take to the kitchen sink. Søren reached out and placed his hand gently on her arm and said several soft words. Her shoulders relaxed, and she rested the dishes on the wooden table.

"Yes. OK," she said. "I will get ready. William, if you want to wash up or anything, go ahead, and then find your book, and you will be reading something to us. Let me freshen up first. Søren will do the dishes and then use his washroom in the workshop."

Billy welcomed the cold water and toothbrush, and the promise of sleep. Sofa or upstairs bed didn't matter now. He waited on the sofa, looking at the book's cover. Elizabeth's Story. It was becoming his story, the path leading him to a doorstep in Jutland. "Where fact meets fiction, maybe." His thoughts drifted back to Pennsylvania. The old woman. Her story.

"What was her story? The truth of the matter? Her message for Elizabeth. About the fear." He felt sleep wrapping his thoughts.

"Come on, William," Bodil called from beyond the curtains. "Søren will fall asleep if you don't hurry." Billy heard a chuckle and a few words. "No, he says he is wide awake and wants to hear something from your book." More muffled words. "A chapter or two, he is saying."

Billy went through the curtains. The bed was low and wide, a mattress on a platform, perhaps. He was certain Søren had made it. The wooden skirt below the down comforter glistened like ship's varnish. A matching low wooden nightstand and a light at one side of the bed. Bodil and Søren lay under the covers, close, on one side of the bed. Bodil patted the covers next to the nightstand. The room smelled clean. And familiar. The workroom in the barn. Billy couldn't place the fragrances.

"Read to us about Elizabeth. In Amman. And then going to Thailand. Where you left off in the car. The plane was just taking off, breaking through the clouds. I have told my man a little bit about the story. About Rita and her ashes." Billy heard Søren chuckle and complain, and she blurted a gentle laugh. "OK, OK, my man says he will catch on. No matter what."

Billy propped a pillow against the wall and leaned back. He adjusted the light to illuminate the pages and not shine in their eyes. He took a deep breath, and the fragrance was clear. Wood chips or sawdust. Soap. And salt. Fresh and clean. It was her man's natural fragrance, he bet. Salt and soap. And wood chips.

"Yes," Billy started. "Elizabeth is flying from Copenhagen to Thailand. Layover in Amman, Jordan."

Bodil turned on her side, moving to a comfortable position facing Billy, her left arm on top of the covers. Søren was behind her, his head propped on his folded pillow, his left arm around Bodil. They watched Billy, intent as he prepared to read. As if he might skip a word. Or steal a moment.

Billy found his place. "Yes. Here we are. The plane is breaking through the clouds. The winter haze."

In Amman, the China Air travelers were required to stay one night, to allow the low rates, they were told. International regulations about fares. The plane would leave in the morning, and Elizabeth slept without any tossing or dreams. She was up early, showered, and set out to walk the busy avenue toward an older part of the city she had seen from the shuttle bus the evening before.

Not too far, she knew. She was advised at the hotel's front desk that the airport shuttle would leave in two hours, sharp. Her connecting flight would be on time, just after noon. She walked through the lobby and into the blinding sunlight and clamor, refreshing heat and spiced air, cinnamon and pepper, diesel fumes and noise, buses, and human waste. Human waste.

De Ukendte, maybe, she thought, and noted how briefly the poisonous thought visited her mind, not insistent or rude, dissolving quickly in the bright and noisy street. Motion and traffic. Vendors, their canopies shading tables displaying so many similar wares, beaming men inviting her gaze to identical items. A young boy squatted behind a stall, a scrap of newspaper in his hand, part of the exotic hot breeze. Elizabeth smiled at each invitation from the vendors and shook her head, pointing her way.

"Just walking and looking," her hand said, and they bowed politely. She remembered a long-forgotten warning to wave only with the right hand. Something to do with clean and unclean. She wondered if that were true. She felt welcomed but remembered the desk clerk reminding passengers not to stray onto the street after dark. Poverty just behind the rich and busy and welcoming façade. She could feel the northern mantle shedding, melting coldness and the constant reminder, her memory. Rita and the Unknown.

"Rita, let me buy something sweet for you and for me, sesame bars, maybe something with honey," she prayed as she spoke to a vendor, asking only the two words, "sesame?" and "sweet?" A hopeful look to match, holding up two fingers and nodding at the Arabic labels, bright colors, expectant. Suddenly she was desperately lonely.

The young man studied her face. "Yes, here, miss. Very good. Sesame. Little bit honey. Just right." He pointed to thin bars, bright ruby wrappers and magic Arabic script, a promise of sweetness. He put two in a crisp white paper bag, folding one corner of the bag to a crease with his thumbnail. Elizabeth searched her purse for coins or bills, hoping he would take the dollars she had exchanged for her Danish kroner.

"No, no," the man said. "No pay." His hands completing the translation. "Welcome, Amman, miss. Something for you. I wish for you today something. My wish for you. May you be happy again. Giving thanks to God. Thanking you, miss. No pay." The man bowed, smiled with a shade of sadness, and held his right hand to his heart.

He continued. "Miss. Life more than yesterday. Life today. And tomorrow. For you. Tomorrow, good," as his hand and fingers rolled a small wave into the future. Elizabeth followed the tips of his fingers, and then his eyes, half-closed, a respectful apology for whatever he had guessed.

"Thank you," she said. "These were for my little girl and me. She would have loved this. Yes, she would have loved this. And you. She would have loved to meet you. Thank you."

"Aaah. I see." His face softened further. "I see," as he searched her eyes. He bowed again, saying several quick throaty words, a musical wave of cumin and clove, a blessing, fragrance. The morning held its breath, suddenly silent. Motionless and silent. Streets and air having waited for this moment. This prayer.

"Tomorrow, miss. Yes? Remember. Tomorrow, please?"

"I will, yes. Thank you. Yes."

Søren whispered several low words to Bodil. She asked Billy to stop for a moment.

"He asks if you will reread this scene. He says it has some special meaning." Bodil plumped her pillow and moved about under the covers, settling in to sleep. Søren did the same, adjusting the comforter and holding Bodil close, moving gently, stroking her hair.

"Read again," Søren whispered. Bodil hid her face in her pillow. Sleep.

Billy turned back a page. "Yes. These are good thoughts for good dreams," he said, and began. He read slowly. Measured verses.

"I wish for you today. Something. My wish for you. May you be happy again. Giving thanks to God. Thank you, Miss. No pay." The man bowed. Smiled. With a shade. Of sadness. And held his right hand. To his heart.

"Miss. Life more than yesterday. Life today. And tomorrow. For you. Tomorrow, good," as his hand and fingers rolled a small wave. Into the future. Elizabeth followed the tips of his fingers. And then his eyes. Half-closed. A respectful apology for whatever he had guessed.

"Thank you," she said. "These were for my little girl and me. She would have loved this. Yes, she would have loved this. And you. She would have loved to meet you. Thank you."

"Aaah. I see." His face softened further. *"I see,"* as he searched her eyes. He bowed again, saying several quick throaty words. A musical wave. Of cumin and clove. A blessing. Fragrance. The morning held its breath, suddenly silent. Motionless and silent. Streets and air having waited. For this moment. This prayer.

"Tomorrow, miss. Yes? Remember. Tomorrow. Please?"

Bodil whispered, her voice catching on the words. "William. Please, a moment. Please read this part one more time. Please. The blessing."

Billy turned back again and read. Slowly.

"I wish for you today something. My wish for you. May you be happy again. Giving thanks to God."

Bodil grasped Billy's left wrist between her forefinger and thumb. Her grip tightened. Another finger, and relaxed. Then tightened again. Billy focused on the page and read, holding the book flat with his right hand, spreading the pages at the top.

I wish for you today something. My wish for you. May you be happy again. Giving thanks to God. Thank you, Miss. No pay." The man bowed, smiled with a shade of sadness, and held his right hand to his heart.

"Miss. Life more than yesterday. Life today. And tomorrow. For you. Tomorrow, good," as his hand and fingers rolled a small wave into the future. He bowed again, saying several quick throaty words, a musical wave of cumin and clove, a blessing, fragrance.

Bodil's fingers wrapped around Billy's wrist and pressed his left hand into the mattress. Billy lost his place on the page for a brief moment, found it again and was not sure where to begin. He repeated the street vendor's wish, the words a cadence of hope and thanks.

His hand and fingers rolled a small wave into the future. He bowed again, saying several quick throaty words, a musical wave of cumin and clove, a blessing, fragrance. The morning held its breath, suddenly silent. Motionless and silent. Streets and air having waited for this prayer. The morning held its breath, suddenly silent. Silent.

Bodil's fingers relaxed. A minute passed. The house and countryside and heartbeats. Silence and distant thunder, perhaps a train. Bodil released Billy's hand and tapped his wrist once, lightly, her forefinger. Barely a touch. She pulled her hand back and slid it under her pillow. She breathed evenly, then slid her hand from underneath her pillow and patted his arm.

"*Go' nat*, William."

"Bodil. *Velsignelsen*," Søren whispered.

Billy clicked off the reading lamp. Dim shadows from the lamp next to the sofa in the living room. Billy eased off the edge of the mattress and stepped carefully around the bed to the curtain. Bodil's voice followed him.

"Søren is saying it is the sign of goodness which the man has given to Elizabeth," Bodil said. "The blessing."

Billy brushed the curtain aside and went into the living room. He heard a brief muffled sob and a soft comforting chuckle.

"Yes. The blessing. Tomorrow. And the future," Billy said, and added, "Thanks for today, too, *Su-ren*. And Bodil." He was sure his pronunciation of the names was off-key. He had no idea where steps to the second-floor room might be. He went to the sofa and stretched out. He pulled the wool blanket over his shoulder. It too smelled of salt and soap. Wood chips.

"What a day," he said, his voice muffled through the rough wool. He reached up to the lamp and switched it off. Darkness. Dreams and travel. The stories circled his heart. Months and months of writing the book. His and Elizabeth's nightly embrace of words, lives intertwined and conflicted. And loved. The embrace of words, and sleep. Elizabeth's Story gathered him in the wool's aroma. A promise of safety and warmth. The blessed mystery. He heard Elizabeth's voice in the night.

"The blessing," she said.

"Yes. We'll look at it in the morning. Revise and fix things, if we like. Then we'll move on," he said. An echo.

"Yes. The moments. In the morning," she promised.

"Bangkok, right?" he said.

"Yes. Bangkok. Then Koh Samed," she said. "And remember. I went to Buri Ram. After Koh Samui."

"Sleep now, Elizabeth," Billy whispered.

"Don't forget my story," she said. "You're writing my story. Promise?"

"I promise, Elizabeth. Sleep now." Salt and soap. Wool and wood chips.

Chapter 14

ELIZABETH   DAYS AT THE EDGE OF LIFE (1986)

angkok was hot and crowded, oppressive humid heat, after Amman's dry
and dusty breeze. The city's traffic was deafening. Constant motion and
noise. The airport had warned loudly, signs about drugs, possession and use,
or carrying forbidden items through customs, large posters of naked European
prisoners in caged compounds.

A crowded bus to the city center, diesel and alarm and three-wheeled
motorcycle taxis, shouts and horns warbled a constant din. Elizabeth asked
friendly European travelers where one could go to enjoy the beach and sun and
get away from the noise and traffic and diesel fumes. Many named a common
destination, Koh Samui, an island in the south, eight or ten hours by bus and
ferry, but worth the trip. Koh Samui, lots of fun, beautiful water and beaches,
cheap huts, good food, safe once you get there, they promised. The buses traveled together on the way down. Elizabeth wondered about the bus convoys and
what the danger was. The more experienced tourists told that Burmese rebels
sometimes came from the jungle, over the mountains, smashed the wide bus
windshields, stopped them in the road, robbed the passengers.

"You have to hide your valuables, or leave them in a locker in Bangkok, or
just have some money you are willing to lose. Keep some in a shoe, and your
passport."

Elizabeth didn't feel like Koh Samui was the right plan. She asked at the desk in the small hotel she had picked while walking, not too far from the train and bus stations. She asked where one could go for peace and quiet.

"Visit shrines and elephants, northern mountains. Very beautiful. Chiang Mai."

Elephants. She shook her head. It seemed her trip was accelerating toward home, to the States. She could just continue on to San Francisco, as the heat and noise and bustle seemed to be increasing, nearly unbearable, and the typical destinations weren't for her. Not now, at least. Elizabeth inquired at a travel agency with an American Express poster in the window, asked about reservations for a flight to the States. She told the Thai agent she needed some peace and quiet, and the stories about the island paradise in the south sounded too risky. She wondered if every foreigner looking for a wild time would be meeting up there anyway. No, she did not care to see elephants or shrines. The Thai agent looked disappointed.

"You don't like Thai?" he asked. She told him it was nothing personal, she just needed some time, peace and quiet, a place to write letters, rest up, forget some things. She wondered about this nice young man, polite and concerned that she should appreciate his country.

"So. Where would you go? For your vacation," Elizabeth asked.

"Ah, yes. Always go Koh Samed," he said. "But it mostly for Thai. Not speak good English there, and not many service. Electricity and water only when run generator. Island. Take bus, couple three or four hour. Then get to island by fishing boat taxi. Thai go there, but not too many. You see, Thai working." He smiled broadly. "Thai working all the time. Maybe one or two English there. I don't think American. But safe and friendly. Thai."

"OK, let's make the flight to San Francisco, but maybe in a couple weeks or a month. How do I get to Koh Samed?"

The man beamed at his success. "You like Koh Samed. My uncle have beach huts there, maybe dollar, two dollar each night. Ocean side of island, not bay. Bay, all local Thai. Maybe everything full. But ask for uncle, Mr. Visith. And my cousin. You call him Mr. Tu."

"Yes," Elizabeth said. "This is good."

"OK. I will fix tickets. Get ticket Rayong and then Ban Phe over bus terminal. Boat to island, you pay cash. You come back here for America ticket when you ready. No problem, America ticket. We get right away, same day." He beamed with pride. "Thank you, miss. You very lucky today."

"Yes," Elizabeth agreed. It had been easy in the end.

"Cup tea? You like some tea? Thai tea." The man's smile.

The bus to Rayong, and then another to Ban Phe, across the bay from Koh Samed, were crowded and noisy. Elizabeth noted her fellow riders were ordinary travelers, men and women and children, all sorts of packages and bags, clearly not tourists or workers. She figured they had probably been visiting or shopping, or simply making connections. The bus unloaded its human cargo at the small port, Ban Phe, a confusion of small fishing boats. She asked a woman if there was a boat to Koh Samed.

"Koh Samed?" The woman pointed to the end of the first pier. "Koh Samed!" Her smile, friendly and urgent. "Hurry, boat leaving!" There was a single sign, chalkboard and white scrawled "Koh Samed, 20 Baht." Elizabeth paid a boy on the pier and stepped to the boat, clutching her khaki bag. There were a dozen or so Thai passengers, sitting either on the dry deck or on a shallow bench along the edge of the boat, beneath the gunwale. Crates, bags, and belongings cluttered the deck. Squabbling women, laughing and peering into their bags.

Elizabeth looked at the water, diesel-brown swirls and flotsam in the small port, and then toward the island, turquoise water. The island was a green sprawl of trees, a steep hill in the middle, about a mile distant. The boat's engine rumbled to life, deep, clearing its throat, shouts from the small cabin in the middle of the deck. The boat edged away from the pier and toward the swells and waves, which began to look rougher as they headed toward the open harbor. There was more excited pointing, a large shark on the end of the pier, ten or twelve feet long, freshly landed. Blood. Teeth. An angry grimace.

The boat entered rolling waves, and the older women huddled to the deck with their packages. Several boys and young men sat on the bench or along the gunwale, black or gray knee-length light-fabric pants gathered and tied in a knot at the waist, grinning and shouting, T-shirts or bare chests. Elizabeth was the lone foreigner, she was sure, likely the only person on the boat not tied to the island or the port. She breathed in a promise to be not the tourist but a passenger. A companion traveler, working fishing boat, women bringing supplies to the island, a knot of tough teenage boys. Or grown men, thirty or forty years old. She couldn't tell.

The boat rolled at an unexpected swell, and one of the women's bags spilled, cans and fruit rattling and thumping across the deck, changing direction erratically as the boat rocked. Elizabeth leaned forward from her sitting position on the bench, bending to help retrieve some of the loose items rolling at her feet. She noted the young Thai boys next to her on the gunwale didn't move, not interested in helping. Or maybe they were afraid they might be accused of taking something, she thought. Elizabeth imagined the woman might accuse her of that too, and she straightened quickly and leaned back.

She felt fingers in her rear pocket and a forearm pinned between her back and the gunwale. The boy next to her was trying to pick her pocket, maybe thinking a quick profit from the trip. Rich lady, maybe. There was nothing of value in her pocket, a pen and some papers, which probably had been visible. Elizabeth carried her money and passport in the small pouch hanging by a soft leather neck cord, warm and safe between her breasts. The boy's fingers were firmly pinned in her rear pocket, and she leaned back on his arm, hard, her eyes locked on his, all in surprise. He could not pull his hand or arm free. He didn't know yet if there might be dollars or baht in his grasp, an unexpected chance to celebrate in the island harbor.

Elizabeth weighed her situation. The only foreigner on the boat. Alone. Would they turn back if she fell overboard? Or was pushed? The shark's bloody grin widened in her stomach. Several of the passengers were looking away, toward some distant view, unwilling witnesses, but clearly aware. Elizabeth heard muttered comments to no one. High pitch. They knew. The boy was among male friends, and she could see he was a teen, or older. The women's heads were tucked down, fear rolling with the boat's bow and the cans on the deck.

Elizabeth stared at the young man, finding a hard and neutral face to wear, to deflect her fear and his growing shame. She reached behind and pulled his wrist free, holding his hand up to see only fingers, nothing from her pocket.

She knew there could be only worthless paper or the pen, but the invasion was unwelcome, a blow to her paradise island trip.

She released his hand, and he slid away from her along the gunwale, looking down, tight bitter smile. Elizabeth knew she was defenseless but did not blink or look away, a blank stare at the boy. He muttered words and moved closer to his friends, who looked shocked, afraid. Elizabeth turned her stare to them. She was a fellow passenger on the boat. She smiled, shaking her head, seeming to say how silly this boy here could have been. The boy's friends erupted in laughter, and the guilty young man said two or three words, sharp edges, looking away. His friends erupted again, laughing loudly. One looked at Elizabeth.

"Sorry, lady. Very sorry. No problem."

Elizabeth nodded and smiled. "Yes. Thank you," she said. "Please you tell him, no problem, gentlemen. Please. Tell him. No problem. Tomorrow OK." Elizabeth leaned back against the gunwale and surveyed the green paradise floating toward them on gently rolling blue glass.

She stayed two weeks. Mr. Visith was cordial, surprised at the American visitor who demanded nothing. She slept in one of his six grass thatched huts on raised wooden platforms, an occasional scorpion in the rafters. The tiny resort offered running water once a day when Mr. Tu started the clattering generator, simple meals prepared by Mr. Visith's wife in the open-walled restaurant facing the beach. High and low tide seemed to span no more than a few inches. Thai students from an up-country school celebrated their approaching graduation, locals played cards in the restaurant and traded stories, several barefoot armed guards in shorts and T-shirts patrolled the grounds in the evening, when the chance of a loud argument among locals or drunken Europeans increased. Elizabeth knew from the first day that her paradise by the sea would be short-lived. A pointless and silent repudiation of dreams. Her restful pause turned to impatience.

Elizabeth sat on the boards of her hut's low porch. Restless evening. She had told Mr. Visith she would leave the following morning, thanking him for his generosity and friendliness. He bowed his head and repeated his offer of earlier in the day, that she might stay and enjoy the hospitality in exchange for cooking and helping Mr. Tu. No charge. Elizabeth thanked him again and said she had to go, but she might return before she left Thailand.

Mr. Visith came to the hut as the sun set behind the island's low mountain. He invited her to accompany him to a small gathering on the beach. A farewell campfire. She walked with him in silence, the evening shadows wrapping the beach in a promise of cool breezes and sounds of low waves rolling on the sand. Darkness enveloped the gathering, a handful of men around a small campfire. Mr. Visith's wife brought an oval tray of food.

"Special Thai," she said, and bowed. "Many taste." Elizabeth noted a half dozen or more items at the edges of the serving tray, some obvious, dark boiled egg in quarters, and peanuts, bits of hot peppers and tofu. Maybe fish sauce, shredded ginger? There were subdued sounds around the small fire, the crackle of sticks. A woman sat in a nearby hut's darkened doorway. From time to time, she retreated to the darkness inside. Or a man emerged and disappeared in the night. Elizabeth reached for the tray with the spoon offered by Mr. Visith's wife, scooping a piece of the hard-boiled egg. She raised it to her mouth.

"No, no," the woman said, "little bit each one on spoon. Taste same time. Together one very good taste." Elizabeth dipped her spoon into each of the ingredients on the tray. No single item dominated the unusual harmony.

"Yes. One taste. Hundred-year egg. Days around edge of long life," the woman said.

Elizabeth closed her eyes, savoring the ginger and peanut and chili and spice, the quiet moment, no pressure to go or stay. Safe. The empty spoon tasted of peanut and ginger, a viscous sheen of egg and fish sauce. The low waves breaking on the sand, green-blue phosphorescent edge. She asked Mr. Visith, pointing at the water, "Blue reflections of the moonlight?"

"No, they tiny sea creatures, light up in waves moving. Edge of wave, at top." Thai moonlight and silvery-blue shimmer of waves. Elizabeth's thoughts drifted green-blue to Rita. The widening gulf of time. The night. A young man joined the group, walking up from the water's edge, a shadow in the moon's light. Elizabeth recognized him, a man she had met on the taxi boat to the island, a day's excursion to Rayong two days before. She had felt safer next to him on the boat, and they had talked briefly on the way to the mainland. He camped on Koh Samed's beach.

"Hello," he said to the group, and then to Elizabeth, "Hello again."

"Yes. I remember. From the boat. Asher. I saw you coming up from the beach."

"Yes. My tent is there. Is it OK for me to sit with you? Yes. My name is Asher." Polite. European accent.

She could see the ridge of his tent near the water. "You are not afraid you and your tent will wash out to sea in the storm?"

"Storm?"

"No, I was just kidding. But I wanted to ask you the other day. Is your name by any chance Asher *Lev*?"

"Why do you ask that? Did you know I am from Israel? A Jew? Asher *Lev*? I am thinking you know the tribes of Israel?" He smiled and studied her face in the fire's glow.

"No." Elizabeth laughed. "It's the title of a book I once owned. *My Name is Asher Lev*. I never found the time to read it. I think that cost me a job once, in New York City. I wanted to be a teacher there, and they had tests we had to take, even though I had my teaching license from New Jersey. One of the examiners who would decide on my teaching license I think was Jewish, and the other one African-American. They wanted me to name a book I had read that would show how I would teach about diversity with inner-city high-school kids."

"You taught in New York City?" he asked.

"No. I never read that book, and I couldn't think of any other books. I was interested in Hemingway and Fitzgerald and those writers, and I just drew a blank. I mean, I couldn't think of anything to say at all."

"So you didn't get the job?"

"No. Neither examiner seemed impressed with my knowledge of Hemingway. They gave me a substitute teaching license. So I went and got a job in New Jersey instead. Teaching. For a few years." She looked at Asher. He seemed smart and polite and clean-cut for a man in a tent on a beach in Thailand. He laughed and asked if she would like to go for a walk on the beach. Elizabeth savored the last hint of ginger in her mouth, the fire's smoke. And the moonlight. She thanked Mr. Visith and his wife and said good night. Stars and tiny blue-green creatures on the momentary edges of black waves. She thought of Rita again, as she had each night in the silence of her hut. She did not want to return to her hut.

Elizabeth took Asher's hand, warmth and reassurance. Night shadows. Each carrying hope for the morning. She yearned for warmth. Maybe a gentler memory of leaving her Rita. Or a hope. She was certain she would spend the night with Asher. Or at least near to him. They sat on the beach in front of his tent and watched the phosphorescent swells and the silver runway of moonlight. Elizabeth wondered what it would be like to swim among the tiny creatures in the night's shadows and reflections. She wondered whether they would cling to her for reassurance, grateful passengers. Whether they would illuminate her body as she moved. Her wings and her mane. Asher lay back on the sand. Elizabeth leaned over him. She drew two intersecting lines over his heart with her right finger and then touched his lips.

"I know," he said. "I wondered when you would say it."

"When I would say what?" She laughed and drew closer. She moved her leg between his. "I didn't say anything."

"I know we can't be lovers," his voice cracked, and he swallowed. "The cross you made over my heart."

"Cross?" She laughed, genuine amusement. "A cross? I made an 'X marks the spot' on your heart, and I'm going to sleep next to you in your little tent if you will invite me in." She laughed more gently. "What do you mean? About a cross." She propped her left elbow in the sand. "What are you talking about? You look so sad all of a sudden."

"Well, I am a Jew, and you could never love me. The Jews killed your Jesus, and in the end you could not love me."

She stared at him, a wide smile. "Asher. Nonsense. Two thousand years ago. It's not a Jewish national crime against me." She laughed and crossed his heart again with her finger. "I am laughing because I once was married to a man named Dan. Another of the tribes of your Israel. Maybe that's why it didn't work out!"

"He was Jewish?"

"No. Dan was Danish." She laughed again. "But Asher, seriously, Jesus was a Jew, and he was part of Jewish history and taught in the synagogue and read from the prophets and pointed out the hypocrisy of the Jewish leaders. He was a troublemaker in their book, no?" She rolled on top of Asher and straddled him, her knees in the sand. He laughed.

"It is nice that you know the names of two of the sons of Israel. What is 'X marks the spot,' then?"

"Right, Asher, and remember Lev too. That makes three of the twelve. And the X is your heart. And I think the spot is also in your tent. Let's go into your little tent, if that's OK with you. I can't sleep in my hut tonight. I had a girl. My daughter. Rita. She's gone, and I'm remembering her too much in the nighttime, alone."

Asher reached up and cradled her face, drawing her close. They held each other, rocking gently. After a few minutes, they helped each other to their feet and made their way to the tent. They crawled through the screen flap and lay on their backs on Asher's open sleeping bag, side by side. Asher turned onto his left side and brushed Elizabeth's hair away from her face. Elizabeth pulled her shirt loose from her shorts. She took his hand in hers and placed it on her stomach, unfolding his fingers and holding his hand against her skin. His hand was warm.

"I wanted just to see if your hand was warm. It was sort of a test, and to see if you were gentle and would let me just hold you, or guide you, without you taking over. You know, trying something."

"No, Elizabeth. Never," he said, pulling his hand away, but she tightened her grip and then brought his hand to her mouth, easily, and gave his palm a light kiss, a whisper, then placing his hand back on her stomach. She turned toward him.

"Tell me a story about something really nice, Asher. A story with a happy ending, and with a little girl like me in the story. A little girl." She hoped he couldn't see her tears for Rita. Elizabeth waited. "Tell me a story," she said again, barely a whisper.

"I knew a girl," he said. "Once upon a time, I knew a girl." He hesitated and gently moved his hand from hers, and swept his fingers lightly over Elizabeth's stomach, as if cleaning crumbs off a tablecloth, and began to draw a map of his story. "This is a story about a girl I knew in my hometown, at the kibbutz. She taught me how to love and how to want someone. But she did not teach me what to do with my love. To sing to her or write poems, or hold her close as we walked. I wish she had told me what she wanted, so I would not have to try to figure it out, and be shamed if I thought too much or just didn't know what to do. And I think she got tired of me not knowing how." He paused.

"One night we were walking back to the kibbutz. We stopped along the way, and we were standing so still, and holding close, and I think she was waiting, and all at once she said, 'Never mind,' and pushed me into the bushes. She walked away, and I quick tried to follow her, but that was it. I never could get up the nerve to just do what other guys talked about all the time, just having girls. I thought I was afraid, but she said all men are afraid. At least the good ones. We did try one thing and another, and it never was easy. It was nice, but not easy. I miss her very much. She went to live with her mother, to take care of her mother, and we stopped writing, and the time just passed. Too bad, huh?"

"Not really," she said. "It's how things work out. The way things work out," and she caught her breath, thinking of Rita again. "Asher, I'm thinking about the girl, maybe my little girl, who would ask me one day how to get her boyfriend, Asher, to love her with all his heart and soul, at least for a few minutes. And I would tell her maybe Asher is shy, and you could just show him how. Not wait. And not tell him."

Elizabeth rolled onto her right side, pulling herself closer to Asher, and as his arm circled her waist, she planted her elbow and slid her body over his. Her knees and elbows pressed into the sand beneath the tent's floor. She whispered to him, close to his face, "And then all of a sudden you have him, and he is yours, and he knows, and is glad because he doesn't have to do anything."

She sat up on his stomach and straddled him, her knees pressing harder in the soft canvas. The sand still held the afternoon heat. She leaned forward and kissed Asher's lips lightly, just once, while she held his head, combing his curly black hair with her fingers. "And if he tries to do anything, you just tell him, 'No, you just wait, Asher,' and you just do what seems the easiest thing, because there's no right and wrong just now, especially if he doesn't think he has to do this or do that. You got that?" Asher tried to answer, but Elizabeth stopped him. "Not you, Asher. I was talking to my little girl. Be still, please?"

He laughed. "OK, sure," he said, "I guess. It's really easy, Elizabeth. Really nice."

"Yes, Asher. It is really nice. And if we said good night right now, you would never forget this lost moment. It would be the one moment in time forever and in the entire universe that maybe if we had only tried a little harder. If only."

"Yes. I think you are right."

Elizabeth pulled her shirt up over her head, a breeze and shadow in the waves' night shimmer, white softness and a line of sunburn at the neck. A silver chain and tiny cross glinting between her breasts.

"Just hold me close, Asher, and don't let go. You don't have to do anything." Safe harbor, low waves, rolling toward shore. Waves on the sand, ebb and flow. Blue-green glow. Tiny creatures in the endless universe, energy on the wave's edge. Blue and green lights.

Chapter 15

BILLY KATHRYN'S MANY STORIES (2016)

Bodil poured boiling water into the glass and chrome coffee press. She brought a pint carton of cream and three ceramic mugs to the table, next to a squeeze bottle of honey and a bowl of what looked like raw sugar. Brown and glistening crystals.

"Søren is in his workshop, maybe making plans for his day. He will write it all down very carefully."

"His story of the day," Billy added, smiling. "Does he write what happened? After?" He laughed.

"No. It's just his schedule. He is very particular. Meticulous, I think one says." She pressed down on the plunger in the glass coffee maker, brought it to the table, and poured into two of the cups. "Speaking of writing things on paper, how did you get started in all this? The book. Were you a taxi chauffeur and writer and college student all of your life?"

"No. Six or seven years ago, I was in a jam, and a very kind lady gave me a chance. One of Elizabeth's friends from way back. At their high school. The lady, Elizabeth's friend, was on the school board where I went to high school. I was turning out bad and didn't have a clue. I got in trouble, and she gave me a chance and then followed me around for the next few years, making sure I wasn't slipping again. I never did. A couple of my friends jumped onboard too, when they saw what was happening with me."

"Jumped onboard?" Bodil asked. "A ship?"

"No. It's like when a train is pulling out of the station, and you run along the platform and hop onto the train before it leaves the station. Just in time." Billy stirred a spoonful of sugar into his cup and poured in some rich cream. "Wow. That's thick cream. Is it something special here?"

"No. It is cream you use for whipping cream. The real thing." She looked at Billy as he stirred the fat into the coffee. "Maybe that's what this lady was for you. Like sugar and thick cream, making the black coffee rich and full of flavor."

"No. It was more than coffee. It was my life. She demanded I write my story. It was all about stories."

"Tell me what she did. Then we will call to your Rita's house and see if it is OK to come driving over."

"You want to hear this? It's in the book too. It's about a dumb high-school kid. And a tough lady. Her name is Kathryn."

"Quit avoiding the truth. It's your story. Tell me."

Billy shook his head. "OK. But Bodil. It's simply one of her many stories. Each has a name. But the story is hers. Miss Kathryn's story. I was there when she told Elizabeth the story. Last year, when we were writing Elizabeth's book."

Chapter 16

KATHRYN ECHOES IN A DUSKY HALL (2010)

Kathryn pulled open one of the double gray metal doors and went into the dim hallway. An old elementary school converted to school board office. It was quiet, smelled of floor polish and dust. And old book jackets. Her steps echoed off tile walls. A late-afternoon disciplinary committee hearing, another hopeless case. Hopeless. Kathryn halted her thoughts midstream and reflected how her spirit had just fleeted away again, like a bird barely escaping a hawk's shadow. Kathryn was weary of her two terms on the Carmer District School Board. She was glad she had not sought another four-year term. The end was in sight, and it was a chore to make it to the finish line.

When Kathryn had retired from teaching, her thought had been to keep active and work within the school system on the board. At first her role had seemed helpful and full of energy. However, the last two years were all tied up in arguments about discipline and budget cuts and depressing test scores. Politics. And fear. She was tired of the work, but the hopeless part of the job was meeting with children who had really gotten off track, when the school administration said they had tried everything they could and the final option seemed to be expulsion. In those cases it was the school board disciplinary committee's responsibility to hear the cases and decide, usually incidents involving weapons and drugs. That was the law. The board had to vote on those cases, and the collective attitude was simply to get rid of the offenders. *Maybe that's why the day holds no cheer,* she thought. No cheer. The expulsion hearing today was for a very young high schooler. Billy something. She couldn't remember the name or what this one was about, selling drugs maybe. Billy something. Billy Johnson.

Kathryn approached a woman and a boy sitting on a bench in the dusky hallway. Her own echoed footsteps sounded as if someone were walking with her. She wondered if this was Billy. He looked too young. Too small. Harmless. The woman was thin and dressed in plain best clothes, a small butterfly pin glinting on her collar. The boy had on basketball shoes. The shoes seemed too big. *He will be tall one day,* she thought. He wore chinos and a blue dress shirt. Mother and son looked up.

Kathryn nodded. "Hello," she said. "Are you here for a meeting with the disciplinary committee?"

"Yes, ma'am," said the lady, a cautious apology and tight smile.

"Are you Billy Johnson?" Kathryn asked, wondering how in God's dear name this child could be in this dark hallway. He nodded yes, looking away.

"Speak up, child," snapped the lady, swatting at the boy's leg. "Speak up!"

"Yes, ma'am. I'm Billy Johnson." He looked down, and his mother swatted him again. His eyes came up, and he met Kathryn's gaze. He wiped at his eyes with the back of his hand and swallowed hard. Kathryn shook the woman's hand and then Billy's.

"I am glad to meet you both. They will be calling you in shortly, I'm sure." She turned and walked to the meeting room door and went in.

Billy had nothing left to claim. Except his name. Billy. Billy Johnson. He and his mom sat. And waited. They had gotten there early. "To show respect," his mother had said. An expulsion hearing, they called it. He had no good explanation or excuses, and there was no one else he could blame. He was guilty, and they said he was a danger at the school, only his first year in high school. He had done wrong, but he wasn't big, not any physical threat. He was certainly on a wrong path, and they said he was bringing others down with him.

Here he was, a dusky afternoon, fading light in an empty hallway. Waiting. A school board hearing to deal with his case. He was beaten. He felt dull and stupid. Suspended was one thing, and his mom hadn't even noticed, really, but now they were saying expulsion. The thought gave him a dead feeling. Nothing to do but sit, for a month or more, or a year. His mom kept saying no television or video games.

Billy had hoped to attend the homecoming game this weekend with Gina, maybe the dance, and now he was forbidden not only at the game and dance but on all school property, anywhere in town, not even on the playgrounds or the outdoor basketball courts at the elementary school, where they always met after school and weekends. Or used to meet, he thought. With Gina too. They would sit on the benches and watch, and they even held hands a couple of times. *Who would she sit with now?*

He wondered how long it would be before the meeting would begin. And how long it would take. Billy and his mom, in the accusing silence. The hallway outside the meeting room filtered a dim light from the heavy push-bar doors at the end of the corridor. There were muffled voices in offices down the hall. Someone laughed. Maybe it was a joke. Or maybe they were talking about him, sharing the foolishness of his mistake. His mistakes. He had brought some weed to school to share with Milo. A lot of weed, in a ziplock bag. But the bigger mistake was letting himself get caught by Mr. Wilson. Right in the hallway, at his locker, as if someone had told the assistant principal he had brought the marijuana in. And the pills.

Mr. Wilson had simply appeared and told Billy to come along, and Statton, the black school-squad officer, was with him, and they had just said, "Come on, no trouble." He had never been in any really bad trouble, and at first he tried to wonder what they meant, tried to angle and twist off the hook in his mind, knowing he was caught. He knew, because Mr. Wilson walked ahead of him, and Statton behind. Statton had his left hand on Billy's shoulder, lightly, just enough pressure to know he wouldn't be able to slip free if he tried to run. He prayed it was nothing. Other kids watched silently as they passed. A girl giggled.

Maybe someone else is in trouble. Maybe they want to ask me what I know. They had asked him before if he knew who had started a fight or messed with a teacher's car, but he had never let anything slip out. Why would they think he knew anything? He never knew that much. And here he was now, on a bench in a dark hallway, after a long two weeks just sitting at home, suspended for bringing grass to school. They said he brought the drugs to sell, because there was more than just for having in your pocket or something like that. Too much just to have in your pocket. For distribution, they said. And the five pills he had taken from his mom's medicine cabinet. The pain pills, they were in the bag too. He had figured she wouldn't notice, and the pills would impress Milo. Billy had no answers for the principal, so the meetings and phone calls and letters home flowed quickly toward this final hearing with the school board's disciplinary committee.

At home Billy had asked his mom when he would be able to go back to school and sit with his friends again.

"Just you be quiet," she'd said. "Don't you know they are not suspending you? You're getting expelled. Depending on what they say, it can be a month or a full year, three hundred sixty-five days, Billy. And if that's it, you can't go to any other school, not nowhere in the state. And I can tell you this, Billy, we can't afford no Catholic school or no private school or—what in the world were you thinking of anyway? What in God's name were you thinking, boy? Marijuana? And my pain pills? Dear Jesus, God in heaven!"

She had walked away, and his heart flinched. She had never hit him, never even spanked him, not that he could remember. Just those quick slap swats to his leg or his rear end. He sat on the sofa, and the clock was the only sound, then a honk from the street or maybe it was a drawer slammed somewhere in the house. Mom had said no television, just do whatever homework he could find, so when they went for the meeting he could say he'd been keeping up, and that he wanted to make a fresh start.

Fresh start, he thought. He knew what they had done with Elgin, threw him out for a year. But Elgin was really bad, a tough guy and in a lot of trouble all the time anyway.

Maybe they'll give me a second chance, he thought. His heart was empty. *Maybe*, he thought, but he couldn't think of what it would be, what the *maybe* could be. He heard the voice in his head, ringing.

Something. Dear Lord, something!

There were footsteps in the meeting room, and his mom grasped at his hand. The door inched open while last words were shared inside the room. Billy could see a hand and shirt cuff on the inside doorknob, and someone said "OK." Someone in the room laughed and said, "If you say so." They were motioned in.

Billy followed his mother into the room. Mr. Wilson was there, and he pointed Billy's mom to the two chairs behind a small table, across from the five school board members on the committee, four men and one woman. The woman they had met in the hallway. Each had a microphone in front of his or her papers, and there was one in front of an older man with glasses, shuffling through papers on the table. His title was on a triangular wedge. "Superintendent," it said.

They spoke, and Billy could tell the microphones were off, but he could taste the danger and disappointment in the air. There was no way he could weave an explanation or an excuse. *No way out*, he thought, even though he really hadn't done anything that bad, just trying to be cool and fun and easy, like freedom, and here we are. Here we are. He clenched his fists hard, fighting an urge to run, breathed out and put his head down, almost touching the table with his forehead. His mother slapped his leg with the back of her hand under the table, and he sat up.

The expulsion hearing played like a scratchy recording from a neighborhood window, pieces and sketches and quips of fact. He heard them tell his misdeeds and the possible consequences, tried to sell marijuana, pain pills in school, a year's expulsion. Billy shook his head to most questions, having difficulty answering anything, mostly, "I don't know." They asked him why, and what were you thinking, and what will you do now? Billy swallowed, trying to moisten his tongue and mouth, and there was a whistling ringing behind his left ear. He felt something break inside, just let loose in his chest. A dry twig underfoot, on concrete.

Billy's mom offered no excuse either. She showed bewilderment and regret, and then the hearing was over. He had prayed for no more. *Please, no more*. Billy and his mother shuffled to get up to leave, shamed, both dreading the silent evening together. The superintendent stopped them with a politeness Billy didn't recognize and then asked if any of the school board committee members had any final question or wanted to make a final comment. Billy's heart faltered. The superintendent asked again, as if scripted, as if someone had told him to ask. The four men on the board seemed uninterested, gathering papers, having completed their duty. But Billy saw their faces behind the silent microphones, their eyes and the edges of their mouths hardened, shoulders tensed. One or two deep and impatient sighs, boredom. Anger.

"I would like to add a word. Or two." It was the woman. She seemed to be the oldest board member at the table. The lady from the hallway. She had soft eyes and had spoken gently during the hearing. Through the maze of details and shame, he remembered her kind eyes. She looked at Billy.

"You're just fourteen years old. Just starting out, right?" Clearly an accusation, but as a question.

"Yes," he said, barely a word, looking down.

"Yes, ma'am!" his mother hissed close to his ear, with a quick swat at his leg.

"No, Mrs. Johnson, this question is for Billy," and the lady went on before he or his mother could respond. "It really feels bad today, doesn't it?"

Billy nodded lightly, head falling farther, his neck deflating.

"You know," the lady said, "I'll bet it feels almost like your life is over, like you don't know what will happen next, if anything, if ever. Like it's over, right?"

Billy sank down deeper, and it appeared as though he might be crying softly. He nodded, just once.

The kind-eyed lady continued. "You know, it feels as though this here today is the last chapter in a lousy book, a book with a bad ending. Chapter ten in a really lousy ten-chapter book. Don't you sort of get that feeling, a bad ending in a bad book?"

The board members shifted in their seats, looking at the superintendent. Billy's mother stared at the lady, mouth open. Billy cried silently.

"But let me tell you something, Billy," the lady said, and stopped, waiting. He looked up, and his mother tried to wipe at his eyes with a tissue. He grabbed the tissue and held it. The school board lady went on.

"I happen to know it's not quite like that. In fact it's not like that at all. You want to know why?"

Billy didn't know if he was supposed to answer, so he looked at his mother. She was crying. His chair scraped the floor as he pushed back to run, but the lady continued, loud enough to freeze his steps.

"It's true, Billy. It's true it's a ten-chapter book. But your tough chapter here today, it's a tough chapter in a wonderful book." She stared at him, silent room, a clock ticking somewhere behind him. Ticking. She went on.

"Billy, today's chapter is only chapter two in that book, or maybe chapter three. And Billy, you know who's writing the book? You know who the author is, and who makes it turn out to have the best ending, the happiest ending you could imagine?"

Billy could barely hear. The lady's question came out almost as a whisper. "Do you know who?"

He held his breath and shook his head, looking quickly at his mother.

"No, it's not your mom," the lady said, "though your mom tries to help. The only author of this book, and it's a great book with a wonderful ending, lots of surprises and adventures along the way, lots of wonderful things. That author is you. It's a ten-chapter book, and you are in chapter two, maybe three, and you are the author of the book, Billy. It's you who has to write the pages of each chapter. And as you finish chapter two, you will begin to see how it leads to chapter three and how it will go on from there." She paused and waited. He didn't know if he was supposed to answer something. One school board member was tapping a pencil on the table, looking toward the superintendent, anger in his eyes and fingers. Billy wondered why the man was so angry. The lady waved her hand at the pencil. The man stopped tapping.

She went on. "Only you can write it, Billy. And it will begin to feel as though it's all connected together in really nice ways, opening doors and settling troubles, and making it the best book ever. It's called the Billy Book. You know that, Billy? It's called the Billy Book, and it's the best book ever written, and it's ten chapters long, and the chapters get better and better as you get better and better at writing it. You begin to pick out the right words and ideas and places and companions, and whatever it takes. The Billy Book. It's the best book in the world. You want to try that?"

He looked at the lady, eyes fixed.

"Come on, you want to try that, Billy? The Billy Book?"

His brain was clicking on one idea and then another, and nothing made any sense. He had no idea how to answer, and if he could have run he would have.

His mother was pressing her hand down on his leg hard, pinning him to the chair.

"You going to try that, Billy? Write that book? The Billy Book?"

He wasn't sure if she had said it again. It was an echo. He wanted to go home.

After Billy and his mother were dismissed to wait in the hall, the school board debated the facts and the consequences. They joked lightly about Kathryn's closing comments, which they had heard many times. Like a stuck record, they said. Scoffing. Chapters in the Billy Book. Three of the men made brief comments: Billy needed a harder chapter this time, he needed a lesson to realize his life was going to hell.

"Let's write a real-world chapter for him, the real world," said one.

"It's no fairy-tale ending, that's for sure," said another. They shook their heads, smiling, agreeing on the amusing thoughts.

"Listen, this kid is a loser, and he doesn't get it. He doesn't realize he's heading for real trouble. Selling drugs. Stealing mom's pills. And who knows about her? That boy will be in prison before you know it, the way that mom stroked his tears."

"I wonder where Dad is," said the district five member, from the tough, hardworking blue collar part of the county, chosen for his strict ideas on discipline: schoolchildren needed rules and consequences, zero tolerance for trouble. He had made it clear that Kathryn's "book chapters" speech was a waste of breath; he had heard it at least five or six times since joining the board. He told anyone who would listen that he didn't like Kathryn's soft approach.

Kathryn's term was up in January. She was satisfied to leave it behind, but she knew the children were fighting more battles on the streets and in their homes than they could weather on their own. Certainly not as children. The board was right, the children were on tough paths, but she could see a glimmer of hope in each, and this boy, Billy, had really been beaten down. In the hallway he had looked worn out, and she was sure she had caught something in his shamed glance, some last-chance plea. Something she couldn't put her finger on. Salvation, maybe, or redemption. But she would have told the Billy Book story no matter what. It wasn't just a show. She knew it was the truth of the matter.

A year on the streets would truly be the end of the line for most, if not all, of the students who came before the board committee that heard the expulsion cases. In one or two instances, Kathryn had been able to steer the decision toward a second chance, placement in an alternative school, bleak hopes that usually didn't turn out well. Maybe that was why she had pushed so hard with Billy, her final chance to steer the committee toward some compassion.

Three of the four men on the board expressed satisfaction with the state's limit for sale or attempted sale of drugs in school, 365 days' expulsion. The fourth seemed undecided. He too felt expulsion was justified but didn't want kids on the street, where they'd just get into more trouble. They all knew that the working mother, and no evidence of a dad, couldn't afford a private school for the boy. Nor would he be likely to find even a menial job—too young. Too hopeless. They knew that Billy was done for, but he had earned it. Even a three vote majority would put Billy out for a full year's time, and since it was now mid-November, Billy would have two entire school years compromised beyond repair.

Kathryn also knew it was all over for Billy and thought she might even beg for his case, since there was nothing to lose, likely her final expulsion hearing. Her decision not to seek a third term had been simple. It was time to quit. Her sight and her energy were slipping away, and she struggled for words from time to time, not just forgetful. It was something else. She searched for a thought. Anything. But it was her last chance. And Billy's too.

"Listen. This is my last hearing. At least I hope it is. I have an idea for that boy, and you'll never hear my Book Chapters tale again. You remember where I got it, right? My best friend in high school? Elizabeth. We got it from a really good teacher. He told us. Writing our chapters, great novels, even with the bad turns here and there, great endings. We had every advantage, good homes, lots of support, but my friend Elizabeth needed something to guide her steps. Her mom had died, or something had happened to her, and Elizabeth was worried all the time. And unlike our Billy here, she had a wonderful dad, a father's love. Billy, he's beat up, and his mom doesn't seem to know what to do."

Kathryn caught a glimpse of one of the three board members who had said expulsion was clearly the right thing to do. He kept looking away, looking down, biting at his lower lip, some battle going on in his head. A couple of blinks of his eye. She wondered. Maybe something about a mom or a dad, or some trouble he had gotten into. Some private disaster. He was looking out the window as she talked.

"Listen. Let me prove the Billy Book thing to you once and for all. I have an idea. Just humor me this one last time, and I'm gone in a few weeks anyway. Heck, you've all written your books, haven't you? One chapter at a time, right? And as hard as it may have been for some of us, it was easy compared to our Billy. Right?" The board member brushed at his eye with the back of his thumbnail. He looked away, and she went on.

"Give me one chance to work with this child. I believe I can get to him, and maybe one or two other kids in the Alternative Center. Get them back on track. I have an idea. For Billy and a couple other of our lost kids at the center. What do you say?"

The district five member tapped his pencil on the table, anger welling up. "OK, Kathryn, we have to hold the line here. We've been tough, and we've cleaned up the high school pretty good. It's no time to let up. You can vote your soft dreams, but we've got four who want to do the right thing. I say no more talk. When we get to open session, I'll move for expulsion, and the committee's vote is four to one. Come on. Let's go."

The superintendent nodded and prepared to dismiss the hearing. "OK, we'll have the matter before us," he said.

"Wait a minute!" It was the undecided board member. "It's my vote, and nobody is going to count it for me, not yet. Not until I vote."

And then another voice and a hand slapped hard on the table. It was the board member who had looked away. He had stared out the window most of the time Kathryn spoke, as the discussion heated. He looked surprised that he had slapped the table.

"Hang on," he said, and smiled. "Let's not get bent out of shape. You know, it's sort of true, the way things turn out, lots of the time we have to plan and figure, a lot like writing a story. Like writing chapters as we go. And sometimes it does seem like we're right at the end, a bad ending and a bad story. Something hopeless." He swallowed hard and went on. "I'm sure it's been easier for us than

Billy has had it. There certainly are some awful chapters here and there, even for those of us who seem to have had it so easy. I would like to see what you're talking about, Kathryn." He turned to the superintendent. "If we vote to keep Billy off the streets, can we put him in the Alternative Center, day or evening? If so, I'll vote no on this expulsion."

"We could. But it depends on the vote," the superintendent said. "That would still be three to two for expulsion."

"Or two to three," said the undecided member, no question in his voice now. "We still have to vote."

Billy sat in the dimly lit hall and waited for his mom to come out. The janitor nodded each time he passed with his broom or a trash can or empty boxes. Billy did not understand what the school-board lady had meant, but it sounded like a strange ticket to something, maybe something better than all this confusion. The school board lady had come out of the office where Billy's mom was signing papers and getting information on a new school. She sat on the bench next to him and asked questions and talked about her own life as a teenager, and some girl named Elizabeth.

Billy couldn't quite focus on what the lady was saying, because it looked like he had not been expelled, and he would go to an alternative school, and this lady was going to go there and work with him and one or two of his friends. Maybe he could get Eddie or Hollister to go along with him. The lady lived in a little house on the edge of town, and she had a garden and a cat, and she had even invited him to come for tea one day. For tea? The lady's name was Kathryn.

"Miss Kathryn will do," she had said. "Just call me Miss Kathryn." He had no idea what was happening, but maybe. Just maybe. The janitor was sweeping in the shadows. Billy's mom emerged from the office, and Miss Kathryn stood up.

"It's all set," his mom said. "You can start next Monday. Billy, it's lucky you didn't get expelled. You better not mess up again, 'cause they said another drug situation and you will be gone. Gone! You understand? You better thank this lady here."

"No. Billy will have a plan. We've been talking about it," Kathryn said.

"Billy will behave. I promise, ma'am." Billy could hear his mother's fear.

"Call me Miss Kathryn. That will do for now. And Billy can do the rest. I'll come down to the Alternative Center on Monday, make sure everything is set to go. Some of the program will take place there, and some he can do at home."

"At home? All he does is watch TV. And play video games."

"No, he'll have some things to work on there, writing, maybe some reading. Making plans. We will talk. You OK with this, Billy?" Miss Kathryn was friendly, but there was something hard underneath. More than just stern. He didn't know what it was.

"Yes, ma'am. It's good, I think. I think I know what you mean. And I think I have an idea about Eddie. Maybe Hollister too."

"Hollister?" Billy's mom shouted. "I thought he dropped out. He's no good, Billy."

"Yeah, I know. He was going to drop out, but he's too young, and they made him stay after he got out of detention. But I think he might catch on to some things Miss Kathryn said. Make a plan, maybe. We could be like a gang. That goes straight. You think, Miss Kathryn?"

"Billy. I think one step at a time. Day by day. You know, and then all of a sudden, you're sixty years old. Or more, like me. Right, Mrs. Johnson? Though you're not that old."

"Yes, it goes by pretty fast. I hope I make it to forty even. Thanks, Miss Kathryn. Thanks for everything. I hope Billy understands what he has to do."

"Don't worry. It'll be clear. And I think he'll do just fine. Right, Billy?"

"Yes, Miss Kathryn. Yes. And. And thank you." He looked down, and then up again. "Thank you. I can't wait to see your garden. And your cat." His mother stared at him.

"See you Monday, Billy. And it was nice meeting you, Mrs. Johnson." Kathryn turned and walked toward the late-afternoon glare from the doorway at the end of the hallway. Sunlight through a break in clouds, she thought. She traced her fingertips along the wall to keep herself from stumbling in the dim light. She heard Billy's anxious voice.

"See you, Miss Kathryn." Billy's voice trailed off the walls, a child's hope call. Billy's hope. Billy. Kathryn stopped. She turned and made her way carefully back down the hallway, as if she were lost, or blind, her left arm outstretched, her hand following the tiled wall back to where Billy and his mother waited, frozen in place, waiting. Kathryn stood over Billy, her gaze fixed on his stunned eyes. She pointed her finger at his mom.

"Mrs. Johnson? Can I ask you a question?"

"Yes, ma'am. What do you...?

"What's this young man's name? I mean, on his birth certificate?" She stared at Billy. "What is this young man's name? His full given name?"

"William, ma'am. His name is William. William Starr Johnson. Starr, that's with two *R*'s, my grandma's family's name. William Starr Johnson."

"See you Monday, then, William." Kathryn turned and walked toward the door, her footsteps echoing the promise. "See you Monday, William," she said again, testing the sound as she walked, an echo in the dusky hall. "William Starr Johnson. Sounds like an actor. Or a chef. Mr. William Starr Johnson." Her steps on cold terrazzo. "Or an author." The push bar clattered as the door slammed shut, locking out the sunshine-bright breeze.

Chapter 17

———◇◇◇◇———

HOLLISTER. IN THE LINE OF DUTY (2010)

The following Monday morning, Kathryn drove to the alternative education center. The program was located in an old elementary school building on the edge of town. It was easier to find than she had figured, and traffic had been light. She was early, more than a half hour before the school day would start. She parked in an empty spot in the school parking lot. Chain-link fence. A knot of teens sat on a low brick wall next to steps up to the school's back doors. Several taller kids shot a basketball at a metal backboard. The rim had no net. The worn ball landed with a heavy thud on the pavement. It didn't bounce. Or roll away.

The air was cool, blowing in from the coast. It might even rain, she thought. She had driven with the window open, enjoying the fresh air. When she rolled the window up and shut off the ignition, she realized how tired she was. Not sleepy, just tired. There was a heaviness weighing on her heart. Something crowding out her spirit. She wondered if the troubles of this world were simply the normal state of affairs. When would it all let up, the worry and strife and conflict, over things that should be so full of joy, so easy?

Kathryn thought about meeting Billy's mother the previous week, how worn and scattered the boy's mom had seemed. Or afraid. Kathryn closed her eyes, breathed in deeply. A recurring dream floated close by, street sounds mingled with cottony fear. Billy's mom was dabbing at Billy's face and tears. The mother's tears, and then the child's, the tissue floating on a warm breeze.

A quick backhand slap on Billy's leg. Another slap, then two more taps. Kathryn was jolted awake by tapping on the car window. Tapping.

"Hey! Ma'am! Hey! You OK, ma'am?" It was a young boy, a teen. Orange T-shirt and worn black chinos. His hair was swirled into a shocked look, standing straight up, gel or some spray, Kathryn thought. A scarecrow for her garden. She turned the key in the ignition and stabbed at the button to roll the window down.

"No. No, I'm fine," she answered. "Just resting my eyes for a moment. Thanks for waking me, might have slept all day. That would look bad." She composed herself. "Do you know if Mr. Racey is here yet? Do you know?"

"No, ma'am. I don't know, just getting here myself. Running late. Hey, you sure you're OK?"

"No," she said. "I'm not sure. I mean, I'm not really OK, but it's just worry. No need for alarm. I'll be OK."

"Hey, I'll walk in with you, if you want. Hey, I'm not leaving you here, all worried."

"Just a minute," Kathryn said. "I'll take you up on the offer. I think I need a hand, and you just answered a small prayer. Something I was thinking about."

"Hey. OK, lady. Whenever you're ready." He held out his hand. It was softer than she expected for a teen, a boy.

"Thanks. What's your name, by the way?"

"Hollister," he said.

"You have a first name, Mr. Hollister?"

"Hollister is good enough. Don't really like my first name."

"Hollister will do, then. Let's go. I want to talk to Mr. Racey and meet with a new boy here, maybe he's one of your friends."

"OK, and you take my arm, ma'am. Just to be sure your worry don't trip you up." He laughed, his grin a diagonal slash across his face, and Kathryn laughed too. "Plus, all these bad boys and girls in here. Hey, you might need protection." He laughed again.

"How bad are they?" Kathryn asked, wondering what he meant. They were all ages, middle school through high school, but she knew none were in the Alternative Center for any violent crimes. Weapons or assault. Things like that.

"No," Hollister said, "I was just kidding. People think we're bad, being sent here. It's just we get off track, and no one has any good idea what to do with us. Runaways, drugs, skipping school, fighting, talking back. Most of us are just bored. Or lonely. Hey, or afraid."

"You weren't afraid to tap on an old lady's car window, thought something might be wrong. What about that?"

"Hey, you can't rightly walk past something where someone might need a hand. That's why I'm here anyway, stood up for a kid who was being bullied, and after a couple of times too many, it was a fight, and I guess it was actually me what started it all. At least that's what they said."

"OK, yes, I think I remember your name now. You tell it a little different than I remember it, but I remember. It was about a new kid, a Hmong child, Vietnamese, right? Kids were picking on him?"

"Yeah. Hey, how do you know about that?" Hollister asked.

"I just hear things. And now I remember about your father. Police force, right?" Hollister looked down and then keenly at Kathryn.

"Yeah. That was my dad."

"But he was sort of doing the same thing you seemed to do, protecting the people who were down and out. Or bullied, right?" Hollister kept his gaze on Kathryn.

"Yeah. Line of duty."

"That's been a number of years. It was a shame to lose him that way. He was one of a kind. Defending the weak ones. I remember how proud you were of your father. Let's go. We're late anyway. And thanks, Mr. Hollister. I owe you one."

"Maybe, ma'am. Maybe." She grinned. An idea. A moment.

"Hey, Mr. Hollister. What's your full name? Like, on your birth certificate?"

— ⌘ —

Billy seemed to choke, stumble on the words. He closed the book and then opened it again, tried to find his place. "Sorry, Bodil. Miss Kathryn knew how to capture us. Stop us in our tracks. I'll go on now."

Bodil interrupted Billy. "And this, then, is another of Miss Kathryn's stories?"

"Yes," Billy said. "Hollister is one of my best friends. And he's also part of Elizabeth's Story. Part of a very sad chapter. And then a pretty funny one. In fact, Hollister may have saved Elizabeth's life." He closed the book.

They heard Søren's footsteps in the workshop and then the furnace room entryway. Bodil quickly rose from the table and took her coffee cup to the sink. She busied herself swabbing it with a wooden brush and straightening utensils and dishes in the drying rack on the counter.

"What's the story of the day, children?" Søren asked, broad smile. The kitchen was silent. Bodil did not turn toward him but raised her hand, a finger asking for a moment. Søren looked at Billy, an unspoken question, and Billy answered with a silent shrug and a wry smile. Søren stepped to Bodil's side and put his right arm around her waist. He leaned his head to her hair, and then her shoulder. They stood in a loose embrace, swaying, as if the house were the silent ferryboat bringing them home. To Jutland. After a moment Bodil shut off the sink faucet, turned and gave her man a quick kiss. She wiped her hands and then her eyes and went to the living room. She called back to her man.

"Søren, you cut some bread and put the butter and cheese on the table. And the yogurt. I will call to Terndrup and see what William's Rita says."

Søren took a large piece of cheese in plastic wrap from the refrigerator, foil-wrapped butter, a jar of marmalade, and a loaf of crusty French bread. The cheese was light yellow, a hint of tan. Rind on one end. Søren shaved several thick slivers, pulling a small plane across the surface of the cheese. He placed silverware and small plates on the table.

"*Værsgo,*" he said, putting the cheese slices on a porcelain dish. He sliced the bread. "Go on and take the butter and cheese, and I will get bowls and granola, if you are liking some yogurt too." He placed the things on the table and reached for his food.

Billy buttered a piece of bread and put a slice of cheese on it. "You were working this morning? In your shop?"

"Yes. I will show you a little bit before you go. Or before we go. I do not know what Bodil wants to do about going to Rita's place." He reached for a bowl and the yogurt. "You can also drive there by yourself. The way would be very easy to find."

Bodil finished talking on the phone and returned to the kitchen. She smiled broadly, and then seemed to catch herself, an apology on her face. Hiding a smile. "Yes. Rita will be at home. But first tomorrow. She is in Århus today to visit the doctor and will not be back until late this evening." Bodil could not contain her smile. She reached for the bread and the butter, beaming. "So we are stuck with Mr. William Starr with two *R*'s Johnson for another day and night." She laughed. "Too bad for us, huh, my big Danish man?"

Søren grinned. "OK, then. William may stay for another day." He paused. "If he will tell us a story here at the table. This morning, right now." He beamed at Bodil, and then his face clouded, serious, deep concern. "And then he may stay another night, but only on one condition. Listen carefully, William." He paused, pointing at William. Billy wondered what had gone wrong.

Søren continued. "You may stay only if you will also read to us another bedtime story tonight. So we are sleeping good again." They all exchanged glances, turning into smiles. "And maybe if you will let me show you my workshop today, and maybe help me clean it up a little while my excellent woman, Bodil, is making a nice supper for us. What do you say?"

Billy rose from the table and retrieved the book in the living room. "I'll read you a short chapter, which comes a while after the one I read last night. Elizabeth is in Thailand. I had dreams about this last night. And about writing the book with Elizabeth. We worked very closely. So, she has visited Koh Samed and will go to Koh Samui, a very popular spot for European tourists. She also meets some Thai students on the taxi boat from Koh Samed, and in the next chapter after Koh Samui she tries to visit them, in another part of Thailand. It is a chapter that doesn't turn out well. Also Koh Samui. It's actually very sad. But not so sad either. You will have to decide." He opened the book and paged to near the middle. "You will have to decide."

Chapter 18

ELIZABETH MOONLIT SHARDS.
NIGHT'S DUST (1986)

Sailing from Koh Samet was bittersweet. Mr. Visith and Mr. Tu waved good-bye from the shade of the bar, Mr. Visith bowing only a hint of his pleasure, having hosted Elizabeth for the two weeks. He did not show any disappointment that Elizabeth had declined his offer for her to stay for a month or two, no charge for the thatched hut, just help out around the grounds, cook and translate for the few foreigners who arrived from time to time. For a moment she had caught her breath at the thought of an island home for even such a short time, or maybe longer.

Elizabeth did not see Asher in the morning. His tent was gone, and there were no signs of their midnight on the beach, except for ridges of sand flattened where the canvas floor of the tent had cradled their conversation. Elizabeth wanted to walk the mile to the bayside pier, but a pickup truck with young Thai students stopped and insisted she ride with them. They too were leaving Koh Samet, returning to their school on the mainland. It had been a final-year trip, celebrating their graduation. She had talked to some of the students on the beach, and they laughed at their own stumbling English, jabbing at each other, asking outrageous questions of the friendly yet shy and sad girl from Denmark. Or was she from America? She told them she did not know yet, and they laughed.

"What wonderful gift, can choose," one girl said. She had showed photographs of herself in bright fancy gowns, serving trays of exotic food and tea and flowers. "Serving my husband, maybe," she said. "When I married. I hope."

"Maybe you will travel first, or find a good job," Elizabeth countered.

The girl darkened and looked away. "Yes, maybe. Maybe job," she added, drifting words, sand and wind. "Maybe."

"But you are graduating. Have a diploma?" Elizabeth asked.

"Yes. Diploma. Nice paper. But no job, no husband. Not yet." She cheered on the final note. "Maybe you come visit us? Beautiful school. No ocean, but very nice and green, near mountains."

"Well, I don't know. In Rayong? Nice and green? I guess not Bangkok."

"No." The girl laughed. "Work in Bangkok soon enough, nice and green in Buri Ram, next two months."

"Buri Ram?" Elizabeth asked.

"Not too far by bus from here, but take too long, bad roads. Easy by train, from Bangkok."

"Well, maybe. I'm going to Bangkok to get tickets. Maybe. I could write and let you know." Elizabeth imagined the trip. "Is there a train?"

"Coming to Buri Ram?" Faces shining excitement and promise. "Elizabeth coming to Buri Ram?"

"Maybe," she said, knowing how the word usually meant "probably not," and statistically it meant "no."

"You come, and we talk about jobs and school, and travel and marry nice man. You come to Buri Ram? Sure?"

"Yes. I will come," and Elizabeth knew she would. "I will go to Bangkok and get my tickets ordered, and then I have one other place I would like to see. Then I will send you a letter about when I'll come. Can I stay with you in Buri Ram?"

"Yes, stay. In school or with family. No hotel Buri Ram for you."

The small truck stopped near the fishing pier on the bay side of the island. Ban Phe shimmered in damp heat above the ocean, a mile and a lifetime away. Elizabeth held her hand to her waistline, wondering if Asher was still on the island or had moved on.

"Let me tell you a story, little girl." She felt warmth, and knew it would just be gentle hands, her fingers, tracing a map.

The bus ride to Bangkok was uneventful, except for the thoughts running in Elizabeth's mind. The beautiful land, the sky and sea, but a new undercurrent of uncertainty and fear, the young people clinging to her on the fishing boat taxi to the mainland, trying to ensure she would visit them at their school in Buri Ram. They made it clear they wanted her somehow to share in their future. Or help protect theirs. One young man asked her if she would invest in his graduation idea, setting up an import and export business in Bangkok.

"Only five thousand dollars, for sure," he said. Elizabeth asked what the business might be, and he said he had not decided yet, but it would be a big success. "Make lots of money. Import and export."

The girls echoed even more insecurity about their futures, maybe jobs as secretaries in a big company in Bangkok. One or two said simply they would marry, if things worked out. But they pressed Elizabeth again and again about visiting them in Buri Ram.

"You will come and visit, sure?"

"Yes, I will come. I will write a letter, let you know when I come," and she gently reminded herself not to mirror their tentative English, and to respect their efforts with honest words. She showed the girls she had their names and school address in her pocket notebook. "Yes, I will let you know when I am coming. In a letter. I will visit in maybe two weeks, three at the most."

"Very good, Miss Elizabeth. Very good. Nice train from Bangkok to Buri Ram."

In Bangkok Elizabeth checked in to a large and modern hotel near to the bus station, regathering her strength and patience, hiding from the hectic diesel fumes and blaring horns of the city. She paid more for one night in the cool room than for all the days and nights on Koh Samed, two weeks in paradise. But the island had been draining in a very basic way, keeping clean and rested, and ever aware of the language strain. And the young Thai girls' uneasy sense of their futures nagged at Elizabeth's heart. What was their fear? She asked the hotel desk clerk for an air-conditioned room with hot water and bath, lights in the evening hours, and if someone could wake her in the morning, nine o'clock, please.

"Certainly, miss, nine o'clock." The desk clerk smiled. "And plenty lights. All the rooms nice."

Elizabeth shared the elevator with a young couple, certain they were speaking German. She was relieved it was not Danish. Her room was on the fourth floor. It was small but clean and cool. She bathed and stretched out on the bed, thinking about her plan for the next day, wondering whether it was a good idea. *Only in Thailand once*, she thought, closing her eyes, and everyone talked about Koh Samui.

She woke hours later, chilled by the air-conditioned draft from under the windows and the constant waterfall of sound. She realized it was not the cooling fans but the street and traffic reflecting onto her room's ceiling and walls. Elizabeth hugged two pillows to her ears, drowning out the noise. Maybe she would go down to the street before turning in for good, maybe walk up the avenue toward smaller and busy side streets, flood her senses with the stalls and markets. Maybe a restaurant was still open. Maybe. She slept.

Elizabeth woke to glaring sunlight and a knock on the door. A distant muffled soprano. "Nine o'clock, miss?"

She padded to the bathroom and showered, settling her mind. She would take the bus south to Koh Samui, visit the island everyone talked about, at least the European tourists, even though many of them wore ragged shorts and had long, matted hair. She asked at the desk about the bus to Koh Samui.

"Sure, miss. Everyone visit Koh Samui. Buses leave all time, two or three buses together." Elizabeth walked the short distance to the southern bus terminal. The agent, a young Thai girl, asked if she had a bag or backpack to check, and Elizabeth raised the khaki shoulder bag and smiled.

The agent nodded, a slight compliment. "That good. Very little worry about."

Elizabeth remained unsure about this side trip and felt her decision to visit the island was being swept along by the combined recommendation of touring young people, mostly from Europe and Australia. She didn't feel young or free, just heading home to see her father, perhaps delaying the visit, or avoiding it. She didn't know what her father's questions would be, about Rita or Dan or her future, and she didn't know herself. Nothing had changed, but she was suddenly captured in an awkward moment of indecision, yet a settled mind.

"No more," she said, shaking her head.

"Excuse, miss?" The agent's voice a musical counterpoint to her doubt.

"Oh. Sorry. It's nothing, just thinking."

"Yes, very good. Thinking. I think all the time, what to do, why, get married, university, get rich, travel. Very exciting. Maybe America. One day."

"Yes, America," Elizabeth answered. "I am going there."

"You are English?" the girl asked.

"I don't know, really. I lived in Denmark. Seven years. My father lives in the States. I think I have to make up my mind."

"Ah, very lucky, miss."

"I don't feel lucky, just confused. Some problems I don't know how to settle. I have to decide."

"Oh no. You very lucky, decide one wonderful opportunity, decide another wonderful opportunity. Freedom. Travel. One small bag." She smiled at Elizabeth. "One small bag, free. Like beautiful bird. Choose this one, gold. Or can't decide, choose that one, silver. Can't decide, gold or silver. You very lucky, miss."

"Maybe you're right."

"Oh, I right. Believe. I right." Her anxious smile.

The bus left at eight in the evening and would arrive after dawn, almost twelve hours. Elizabeth felt helpless as she stepped in line to board, seeing there were three buses loading and preparing for the trip. She remembered the tales of bus convoys, Burmese rebels, stopping the buses, robbing passengers. And to make matters worse, as she was gathering her thoughts and her bag, preparing to board, she spotted a bulletin board for the Thai railways.

She looked for the schedule for the eastern rail, which would take her to Buri Ram, and saw as well that there was a southern rail line to Surrat Thani, the port serving Koh Samui. That would certainly have been quicker and safer and more comfortable than the bus, she thought. Too late. She checked the one daily express train to Buri Ram and made a quick decision to visit earlier than she had told the girls.

Deciding gold or silver, she thought and smiled. *I will see this southern paradise, come back and go visit my new friends, and then home, see Dad. Go home. Decide. Silver? Or gold?*

Elizabeth took out her notebook and made a hurried calculation, wrote a brief message to one of the girls from Buri Ram. She would be there in a week, ten o'clock in the evening. She would not get swept up in the south Thailand tourist haven. Elizabeth made her way back to the ticket clerk and asked if she had an envelope and if she could mail a letter for her.

"Certainly, can do." The girl rummaged in the shelves below the desk, producing an envelope.

"I am going to visit friends in Buri Ram and have decided to visit them earlier than we planned. I will come in one week. Earlier than our plan." Elizabeth seemed to be talking in the same halting language, straining for clarity. "Letter get there in time?"

"Yes, and I will mail for you, right away. You catch bus."

"I have decided." Elizabeth stammered. "Decided, I go home. But visit friends first. I promised them I would come."

"OK. Home America? Or home Europe? Gold or silver?" the girl asked, hesitant, straining for Elizabeth's decision. Suspense, a lifetime hanging in the moment's balance.

"I don't know," Elizabeth replied. "One decision enough for today. Home America first. You can mail the letter?" She placed several paper baht on the counter. "Stamps, and thanks for envelope. And the advice. You've been very kind to me."

The girl looked away, drew in a sad breath and exhaled. She reached under the counter and produced a small placard, "Be Right Back" in several languages. The Sanskrit Thai script danced in comparison. Notes and pauses.

Elizabeth stepped into the bus. It was cool, and its low diesel hummed already. Within a few minutes they were in the city traffic, heading toward a southern highway. She took out her notebook and wrote herself a reminder, thinking at the same time. *If only I had asked about the train. Damn! Just asked.* But she had the round-trip bus ticket in hand, and within an hour they were riding on the floating concrete carpet, low music in the air, the bus intercom, stringed instruments and distant high-pitched voices, Thai angels and children. Innocent choirs. Elizabeth wondered if the school in Buri Ram had such an orchestra or choir. Decisions and choices played across her mind, frets and fingers plucking harmony and discord. Gold and silver decisions. Choices. Children's voices. The Buri Ram school girls. *There had to be jobs and professions and families and futures, like anywhere. Certainly.*

On the fisherman's taxi boat to the mainland from Koh Samed, one of the students had taken photos of Elizabeth with one girl and then another, sitting on the crates or gunwale. The girl with the camera showed Elizabeth several worn photographs of herself, proud testimony, a gold and silver and yellow sequined dress, floor length, tight fitting, feathers, cascade of curls, broad smile, golden shoes. Girl and serving tray, holding gifts of food for the party or for the family. Or for the man of the household. Gracious service, a promise, satisfaction. Its chord was off-key in Elizabeth's memory, and the girl's smile had been tense, maybe a plea.

Please, the girl's smile begged. *Please. Me.*

They passed the first burned-out bus three hours into the trip. She would have missed the scene in the silver moonscape, but excited voices in front of her alerted her senses. The bus was a skeleton only, front windshield missing. *Smashed with rocks or branches*, she wondered. *Or guns.* The side of the bus was blackened, tires flat. Elizabeth could hear the conversation; the bus had driven alone, rebels from just over the mountains, Burma, plunder, disappeared into the woods. The convoys of three or four buses would likely have armed guards aboard, automatic weapons, safety in numbers, and they would seldom be stopped. She could feel the diesel engine behind her, steady high pitch inter-cooler, smooth power pushing her toward an island of hopes. She calculated they were speeding well beyond the limit. If there was one. She shook her head.

Ten hours. Elizabeth slept most of the night and didn't know if they had stopped for refreshment. The toilet in the rear of the bus was surprisingly clean and fresh, and the bus unloaded the passengers at the island ferry terminal in Surrat Thani. Elizabeth paid for the ticket and sat on a bench in the boat's crowded inner gallery, a two-hour sail to the island. The boat was over-loaded with people, and any thought of refreshment was ruined by the long lines of travelers, waiting, and her growing hunger. But paradise was in sight. She would find a beach cabin and a mattress and a quiet meal.

Once on the island, Elizabeth found there were huts available, despite the many tourists. The choices were not expensive, but twice or three times the cost of Mr. Visith's huts. The visitors to this island clearly had resources and foreign currency. Elizabeth suddenly wished for the simplicity of Koh Samed, Mr. Visith's and Mr. Tu's polite kindness, attentive to her singular wish for quiet and peace and escape. Elizabeth promised Rita in gentle secret whispers that the new warmth beneath her worn and faded shorts was the promise given her by Asher. A child. She was certain, and had prayed in the night that it was for certain.

Elizabeth was hungry and decided on food before lodging. The snack bar cafeteria closest to the hut rentals had scrawled messages, pictures of food on plates, prices and special handwritten offers. Omelet, ten baht. Omelet with mushroom, fifty baht. She wondered at the substantial difference, perhaps the cost of shipping vegetables to the island. Maybe the eggs came from a few chickens on the island, cheap enough, but garden vegetables trucked to Surrat Thani, then hours by boat. She asked the young girl serving up small platters to a loud group of German tourists.

"Ah, with mushroom. Special with mushroom. You know."

Elizabeth didn't understand but wanted more than an egg or two. "OK. Mushroom omelet, maybe some onion too? Bread? I will go and pay for a cabin, OK?"

"OK, sure, mushroom and onion OK. Rice. No bread." The girl looked pleased.

Elizabeth went out and chose a cabin rental kiosk. Every sort of tourist mingled in the dusty yard, middle-aged couples and bearded hippies with backpacks and hollow looks, no children. Elizabeth settled on a tented hutch with mattress and night-light. And a secure door, they promised. Elizabeth longed for one of Mr. Visith's six wooden-floored single-room thatched bungalows on Koh Samed. But she could still sleep within twenty or thirty yards of the water, and the small waves provided a constant and soothing audible backdrop. Comfort and refreshment. Elizabeth wondered if the waves would glow green-blue in the moonlight here. She felt a stirring in her stomach. Maybe Asher was somewhere nearby. Or Rita.

She returned to the café and waited for the omelet. It came on a paper plate, beaten egg with crisp edges, fragrance of olive oil, bed of rice, fresh cilantro sprig, and the usual utensil, a single large soup spoon. Elizabeth cut into the omelet with the spoon's edge. The fragrance of oil and onion and mushroom enveloped her tiredness, fatigue, and wonder about the future. The taste and rich warmth coated her mouth, hopeful and secure. She didn't realize how hungry she was.

The serving girl returned to the table. "Is OK?"

"Yes. Perfect for today, for now," Elizabeth responded, wondering at the words, which flowed so easily. "I am fine. Warm and satisfied and everything is fine." The food and the moment cradled her worries and wonders.

"OK. Good. When you go to cabin, I will go with you, make sure you OK."

"I'll be just fine. And what's your name? I need to say thank you for being so kind today. For caring."

"Call me Kim. Is good enough, Kim."

"OK, Kim." Elizabeth finished the last bit of her food and drank from the bottled water. "I'm ready to go. I think I can take a nap, maybe until supper."

"Or until tomorrow," Kim said. "If you are tired. Is long trip from Bangkok. Come on. I will walk with you. What is your name?"

"Elizabeth."

"OK, Liz. I will watch out for you. I just call you Liz."

Elizabeth pulled the khaki bag's strap over her head and stepped toward the sunlit doorway of the café. She suddenly wondered if there was a door to open, and then wondered at the very thought. *Maybe it's the sunlight.* Kim opened the screen door, and they walked arm in arm toward the line of hutches along the sandy ridge above the beach. The waves made gentle slow motion invitations to sleep. Or to swim to the horizon. The sun was high in the sky. Nighttime and sleep were distant thoughts, part of a faint plan. Kim brushed aside the screen into Elizabeth's hut.

"Here your quiet place, Liz. Take rest, and tie screen shut when I leave. Not come out after dark. There be guards keep you safe. Not come out."

"Thank you, Kim," Elizabeth said, but Kim was gone, and the words floated on the wall, a thought only. A wish. *Thank you, Kim.* She tied the thong latch on the screen, and fingers of afternoon sun filtered onto the fabric wall behind the low platform and thin mattress. Elizabeth loosened the net canopy and curled on the bed, gathering filmy covers and pillows and dreams. She was tired. The earth turned beneath her dreams. Cilantro and olive oil and mushrooms. The spoon.

A shout and hard padding footsteps startled Elizabeth to wakefulness. Someone was chasing after another, then more footsteps, and more shouts. Angry. Or in fear. The hut's walls were dark, faint moon shadows where the warmth leaked to the open night air. She wondered what time it was. She had no watch, and there was no clock or sound other than the island's shore line. She loosened the screen. The shouts were far down the beach. Receding toward the jungle's edge. Maybe.

Guards, she remembered, *to keep me safe*. *Safe*. She sat on the sandy floor of her cabin, and it swung in a wide arc, toward the moonlight, and then the shore. She was a teacup on a server's tray, miraculous journey from the kitchen, through a crowded bar, to the table. Tivoli dreams amid guards' shouts, pounding feet and sharks at the water's dark edge. A swim in cool water would clear her mind. She waved the screen aside and crawled toward the black mirror and silvery edges of waves. Blue-green-silver lights.

"The mushroom." She heard her voice. "Mushroom. Fifty baht, not ten. I can just slip under the edge of the water, and it's just the mushroom. Pulling the covers over my head. No shout, no guard. Safe."

Elizabeth crawled on cool sand, her knees sinking into warmth beneath the surface. She remembered Asher's tent, but this was loose sand instead of canvas and the closeness of angled tent walls. The sky a billion electric flecks, stretching down to the horizon, white infinite points joining the blue-green knives' edges of the waves, slicing onions and mushrooms, preparing the evening's garnish. *Mise en place*. Everything ready for the chef's orders.

She slid her fingers and then arms and face into the water, surprised how warm it was, gathering her body in a clean, inviting embrace. Tiny creatures, lights and energy, everywhere as the water rolled and lifted and dropped her to the sandy ocean floor, then rising. Falling again, blue and green. Clean and fresh, bringing her home. Rita and Asher called, and she knew she would invite her baby girl into her, to join what Asher had planted, new life.

Maybe. Honey. Baby. She sat on the shallow ocean floor, rising and falling with the low waves. Drifting away from the beach.

"Liz." A voice, calling for someone Elizabeth knew. "Liz." Again.

"Yes. Maybe."

"OK. It's Kim. I will bring you home." Steady wash of waves and legs approaching.

"OK, Kim. I'm ready."

"Yeah. You ready." Elizabeth felt Kim's strong arms, steady and sure. She was gathered up and guided, coached, counting steps to the beach, water heavy at her waist, slow steps, but surely planted toward the shore. She did not recognize the line of hutches and tents, dark splotches, trees and moonlight.

"You long way from your place, Liz. Come. Let's go." They made their way to the sandy beach and walked arm in arm, close bodies, warm, Kim's arm around her waist, relief. They stopped, and Elizabeth embraced Kim, clutching her close. Warmth and softness. Safety. Kim turned Elizabeth toward her hut.

"OK, girl, you safe now. I put you in bed, and this time you sleep, stay in home."

"Yeah, I'm safe. My own place. Safe place. Friend Kim."

They reached Elizabeth's hutch. Kim spread the screen wide, and they went in. Kim retrieved a towel from the wicker chest at the door and dried Elizabeth's back and shoulders.

"Take off wet clothes; I dry you and put you in bed," Kim said.

"OK, Kim. My girl Kim. Thank you for bringing me home safe. I was OK, but now I am safe too."

Kim dried Elizabeth's legs and stomach and breasts and back, and finished by covering Elizabeth's head and hair with the towel, tousling the hair and laughing.

"OK, in the bed. I hold you quiet a minute or two, be sure you don't get up and go swim again. I think you done tripping in waves."

"Yes. Maybe. You stay with me?"

"No. You got to sleep, and I got to work tomorrow. I just knew you be alone and you do something foolish. I knew you not know about mushroom. No more, OK?"

Elizabeth exhaled into the bed covers and pulled Kim and the thin blanket to her. Their arms entwined and held each other close, a long moment. Elizabeth's bare body was a shadow on the mattress, Kim's rich, darker reflection. Moonlit shards of moisture and the night's dust in the air. Kim straddled Elizabeth and held Elizabeth's face, thumbs stroking her cheekbones gently, fingers in her hair. Kim leaned forward and kissed Elizabeth's forehead. A whisper.

"You pretty girl, and sad. Real nice girl. And sad. I stay a minute or two. Make sure you not swim. Not come look for me. I right here, little girl. You sleep, I hold you." The words echoed. A dark tunnel. "You sleep, I hold you."

Elizabeth remembered a party. Going away. Bethlehem. A dark room. The going-away party. A lifetime.

"I will just hold you," he had said. A lifetime. His hands had stroked her gently and slowly, loving fingers caressed her wonder, tracing the warmth of her stomach. "Just hold you," he repeated. "Going away."

Kim breathed a soft promise, close to Elizabeth's ear.

"I right here, little girl." Kim kissed her neck.

Warmth rising in Elizabeth's stomach, excitement and fear. Rolling waves. Pause, top of the world. The inevitable and safe fall.

"Yes. Me too. I'm here."

Elizabeth woke late and went to the ferryboat landing to check on the next boat and a connecting bus to Bangkok. She was tired. And wondered if it was shame. Not since college had she felt shamed for an adventure or a chance, or even an indiscretion, and she couldn't recall which one the night before might have been. She remembered the kids on the dorm hall in high school, her senior year, rooming with Kathryn. She knew the mean girls whispered ugly rumors, snickering glances, and some displayed open disregard. She wondered if anyone on the island knew or cared. A cascading moment or two, or a lifetime. A memory. Or just a dream. It replayed in her mind, and she wondered if she could retrace the steps to what had actually happened.

The mushrooms? Maybe it had all been an orchestrated encounter, a rehearsed island trick. But she didn't carry much loose currency, and all her things were in their place, the khaki bag in plain view. Even so, Kim was not there in the morning, and Elizabeth decided it was time to go. Back to Bangkok, rethink visiting Buri Ram, get tickets to the States. Just go. Or was maybe the Buri Ram visit also some plan, some attempt on her goodwill? She recalled the boy's proposal for a five thousand dollar investment. Import and export.

She would think it over, Buri Ram, even though she had promised. Foolish girl, she was. And the night. The waves and the emotion, and the wonder. She shook her head and looked back at the ferry and bus timetables posted behind glass on the ticket kiosk. The reflection in the glass surprised her. A smiling and then surprised young woman. Beautiful and tanned. The smile broadened as she continued to shake her head.

Billy closed the book. Silence. They sat for a minute. Then another. Søren released Bodil's hand and pushed his chair back from the table. Billy wondered at the chair's soundless glide on the bare wood floor. *Soap?* he thought.

Søren cleared his throat. "Maybe you can read that again. Tonight?"

"Well. Sure. I can do that."

"OK. It will be a good day, but maybe go too slowly."

Bodil smiled and looked away. "Søren. You two go out now. You and William can clean up in your workshop. Søren! OK?"

Chapter 19

$$\cdots\!\!\!\Longleftrightarrow\!\!\!\cdots$$

ELIZABETH — TURNING POINTS (2015)

Arthur Newcomb and Elizabeth sat in silence. The train's wheels strained between westward urgency and a thousand tons of steel. The weight of passengers' impatience. They were finally well on their way. More than halfway through the western leg of the trip. Flat land. The cab ride in Chicago had been brief, but the wait for the train to leave had taken hours. Delays and confusion. Equipment failure. The only explanation.

Elizabeth had politely declined Arthur Newcomb's repeated offers of a compartment, though the anxious wish for stretching out and for sleep gnawed at her pride as the train rolled westward. He had arranged for a coach seat next to Elizabeth.

"There is much security between the sleeper cars and the coaches," he said. "But I want to hear more. My company's connections allowed me some free passage." The train finally felt as though it was rolling forward more easily. Downhill. Toward home. Elizabeth was aware how many hours had passed in welcome conversation, about writing and Newcomb's work and Elizabeth's travels.

"It's quite a story. I can tell you have written from the heart. Your emotion." Newcomb paused and shook his head. "That was very hard, about your daughter. Rita."

"Yes. What happened with her was something I have never really settled."

"Was that the turning point? And when you came back from Denmark?"

Elizabeth considered the question. "There were other turning points too. Certainly on the trip back, and through Thailand, and then in the States. There were many turning points." She glanced at Newcomb. He was thumbing through her notes, straightening the papers. She felt a rush of pride, his genuine interest.

"Arthur, our turning point is not always that farthest last place going away from where we should be. You know, where we come to our senses and then begin to make our way back? Like a rubber band being stretched and then released? But Elizabeth's turning point in Thailand was her last stop. Buri Ram."

"Buri Ram?" he asked. "Where is that? How did you get there?"

"It was *Elizabeth*, Arthur. She took the train this time. Buri Ram is in the northeast part of Thailand. Near the Cambodian border." Elizabeth took the notes from Newcomb and shuffled between yellow and white sheets of legal pad paper. "Do you want to hear about it?"

"A turning point, right?" He nodded. "Yes, read it. Or tell me about it from your notes."

"OK. I have the notes to go by." She paused and thought about his question. "And about the turning points. This is the main turning point in Thailand, on her trip home to the States. But there are other turning points too. When she was younger, a teen. And later, when she moved to Virginia. And when she was married."

"That's a lot of turning points, don't you think?"

"Every day, Arthur. Every day." She smiled. "Every moment. But here you go. I'll try to tell it like a story." Elizabeth heard soft clapping behind her, tiny waves lapping at the edge of a swimming pool. Encouragement. Somewhere behind her in the car. She felt a silent smile. Smooth rails and wheels. She surveyed the notes. And began.

Chapter 20

ELIZABETH THAI COOKIE. MIDNIGHT TRAIN (1986)

Elizabeth stood at the edge of the train station's platform, where the concrete met a curtain of darkness. Stranded in Buri Ram for the night. She had imagined a bustling square, certainly a restaurant or coffee shop, or a bar, maybe even running into some of the students she had planned to visit, surprised by her arrival, an unexpected celebration. She surveyed the dusky scene and breathed in a wave of fearful green foliage and dust. She heard a faint singsong strain of a violin somewhere in the dark, beyond the gravel path and trees.

"This must be the edge of town," she said aloud, surprising herself with the sound of her voice in the stillness. Nothing confirmed which direction might take her into the city, if there was one. She was also beginning to wonder if this was the only train station in Buri Ram. Maybe she had gotten off too early, and there was a station in a town center. She was sure the city was larger and busier than this silent outpost. Even the school would require more than this. She thought of the train station at her high school, a quiet hiding place for her and Kathryn, where they had talked of their future, and books, and Hemingway. This station was smaller.

Or maybe this was their old school station, dreams playing a mean trick. She clutched her bag, suddenly afraid she might have left it on the train. A manuscript, papers. Hadley Hemingway. A lifetime ago. Tracks disappearing into the forest, the end of the line in one direction, and the other toward the Neshaminy Creek trestle and thirty miles on, to Philadelphia and life. Holding Kathryn's hands. No, Kathryn holding hers. A dream, but this was Buri Ram. Elizabeth was sure now she would leave as quickly as she could, fear rising quickly to panic. She turned and walked back toward the small concrete building, a light over a barred ticket window. She would make the station master listen. Somehow.

Elizabeth had awakened when the train jolted to a stop, and she asked passengers in the compartment if it was Buri Ram. Several nodding smiles.

"OK, Buri Ram. Buri Ram here," and she gathered her canvas bag and quickly stepped off the train. She had not expected that anyone would be there to greet her, but the silence enfolded her in the doubts and questions that had wrestled in her mind during the six-hour trip from Bangkok. Another foolish adventure. She had gone directly to the ticket window and asked about a train returning to Bangkok, trying to make her words as demanding as her heart.

"I need a ticket to Bangkok. Next train." She would end her trip, end the flight. She would go home. To the States and her father. To her daddy.

The station master spoke with certainty. "Tomorrow, train." He blinked and nodded.

She studied the printed schedule on the wall. Three languages, French and English and the exotic Thai script puzzle of sweeps and dots, clearly a train for Bangkok just after midnight, in only a few hours.

"Here, train, twelve thirty. Train to Bangkok," she said.

"No, miss. English train tomorrow. You looking Thai worker night train. Women worker cars, too. English train tomorrow." He was polite and firm. "No train. English train tomorrow," he repeated, stepping from behind the small caged window onto the dim platform. He pointed to the morning train on the schedule. "You English train. Nice train. Air-condition." Then he pointed to the night train, where Elizabeth's finger was planted. "This Thai train. Workers. Women. Thai train." He bowed slightly.

"I am women," she answered. "I am women. Thai train is fine. For me too." She was exhausted. It had been such a mistake to come here. Buri Ram. The middle of nowhere, or somewhere. They had said Cambodia was just through the dark trees and fields, closer than Bangkok's familiar noise and diesel clamor. She wanted to go home. Anywhere. No, home. No. Rita.

Elizabeth had begun to realize her fatigue and hopeless wonder during the train ride to Buri Ram. A mistake to venture into truly foreign territory, just to visit the vacationing students she had met on Koh Samed, as if it were an afternoon appointment in the neighborhood. She had spent only twenty minutes on a fisherman's taxi boat with them. She wrestled with the thought of their excitement. That she might visit them at their school. Her letter must not have arrived in time, and she hadn't even said exactly when she was coming, so of course they weren't here to meet her. But on the train she began to feel certain she did not want to spend even one more moment or ounce of energy to find them. Simply to be polite. Simply to follow through on their hopeful invitation. Hopeful and polite, but more than hopeful. Nervous, maybe. Or frantic. Frightened for their futures. Particularly the girls. The young women, their uncertain future.

The string music in the trees stopped, then began again. Elizabeth returned to the station master's window cage. He was sweeping the floor inside the small room. He looked up and opened his mouth, breathing in to speak.

"No!" she said. "You must sell me a ticket. I will go to Bangkok tonight. No place to stay here. Not sit on platform all night. Is dark, and I will be afraid. I sit on women worker train, or I sit here in dark until nice train tomorrow? No," she said. "Not good. Not good!"

"Not same people, miss," he began, but she cut him off.

"Yes, same people, but no matter! I sit here in dark night not good. Not good for me, not good for you!" He stared at her, blinking, and she repeated, "Yes, same people. Please. I sit on Thai women worker train or I sit here in dark! Please, I go home now. To my father." He stared at her. She did not move. The station master leaned the broom against the wall. The broom handle slid along the wall to the floor, a flat cracking noise.

"OK. You wait. Five minute. Come in. Sit office. Safe." He ushered Elizabeth into his tiny space and turned the wooden chair at the desk for her to sit.

"Five minute. Not go out. Too dark." He handed her a colorful travel brochure and left the office, closing the door as he left. She heard his steps, running on the gravel road. Perhaps toward the string music. A violin in the trees. She leaned back in the chair and closed her eyes, welcome music, distant. A sing-song voice. Loneliness and hope. A girl's small voice, a solo in a children's choir. Rita. The violin. She breathed in a prayer, drifting words.

"Hello," and soft tapping. Elizabeth sat up, shaking loose from her sleep. The voice called again.

"Hello. Coming in, please." A woman's voice, at the door.

"Yes, come in," Elizabeth answered, and the door opened tentatively. A small woman's face appeared, almond skin and eyes. Elizabeth saw the station master directly behind, expectant and hopeful. An apology written on his face. Elizabeth also saw his relief in the protection of this woman. Elizabeth blinked, unable to place the woman. Probably his wife. Or his daughter. Elizabeth smiled at a thought. It could also be his mother. The woman's hair was gathered in curls on top of her tiny frame. She carried a brightly colored fabric bag in two hands and put it carefully on the desk. Then she turned and took a small tray from the man, with several quick, direct words. He stepped back into the office shadows. The woman turned to Elizabeth, holding the tray. She beamed joy, a sudden small statue, gracious hostess in a golden satin tunic and close-fitting skirt, long, almost to her shoes, proud pose. Motionless. A photographic portrait.

"Bring tea and cookie. Thai cookie. For you. Very nice. Welcome Buri Ram train." She put the tray on the desk and uncovered the tea pot and four small cups. Porcelain gloss and Thai script, no handles.

"One cup guest. You." She smiled broadly, pointing to the cup nearest to Elizabeth. "One cup man. One cup hostess," and she poured tea into three of the four cups.

"And this cup?" Elizabeth pointed to the fourth tiny bowl.

"For guest not here. Never know. Guest always welcome. Always prepare for guest." The woman beamed. She picked up the tray and held it out for Elizabeth, bowing, eyes down. "Thai cookie. Lemon. And spice from garden. Make self."

Elizabeth took a cookie and nervously bowed in return, unsure how to reciprocate.

The woman giggled. "Not often entertain in train station office," she said. "Not often entertain. Man have train station job. Good job. Government. Not much entertain."

"You are beautiful. Your hair. Your beautiful dress," Elizabeth said. "And the cookie is wonderful. Where did you learn to bake? Your mother?"

"Oh no." She laughed. "Learn at school. Learn at school in Buri Ram. Since many years. Learn English there." And she laughed again. "Man go to school Buri Ram too, not learn much English. He forget English, not use too much at train station. Not many English come here."

"I'm not English. I'm from America, and I lived in Europe. Denmark. The past seven years," Elizabeth explained. "I was going to visit some students from Buri Ram school, but I want to go back to America, quick. See my father. He is old. I am sorry for trouble. I have to go."

The woman turned to her husband in the shadow and spoke quickly, tones and a rhythm Elizabeth could not translate. But she heard the interplay of power and purpose. The man responded in short assents. His wife turned back to Elizabeth.

"Boy in Buri Ram school learn business. Money and counting. Girl learn cook and sew and serve, polite and friendly. Man not understand woman. Maybe Buri Ram student boy ask money. Start business? If Buri Ram schoolgirl, show nice picture? For good wife? Cook and serve?" She turned to her husband, and words flowed faster. He backed farther into the shadows. Giving orders, Elizabeth guessed.

The woman returned to Elizabeth, a gentle smile again. "Man correct, night train not for tourist, but OK, most Thai friendly. You go tonight, OK. Or welcome stay, drink tea, sleep our very small house, and nice air-condition train in morning."

Elizabeth wondered at the efficient resolution. She could sense the welcome was as genuine as the tea and cookies. But she knew also that either option was generous, the midnight train ticket as much of an accommodation as a night in the station master's house.

"Thank you so much for your offer, and for the Thai tea and cookie, but I will go tonight, if I may please have the ticket." Elizabeth sensed a relaxation on the woman's face. Relief. "You both have been wonderful to me. I will never forget the generosity of Thai. And the beautiful hostess. Tell Buri Ram school they educate you well." The woman beamed and bowed.

Elizabeth boarded the train at twelve thirty, on time. There were several freight cars attached at the front of the train, behind the engine. The passenger cars were older than the one she had arrived in, with compartments of several rows of facing bench seats, and a middle aisle. No air-conditioning, but open windows allowed a breeze and relief. The night air was cool. Fifteen or twenty passengers boarded with Elizabeth at Buri Ram, women and girls, and one man. Elizabeth's car was nearly full, but not crowded, and the man who boarded at Buri Ram sat in Elizabeth's compartment. He looked at Elizabeth closely, not pleased, she thought. She wondered if this was the station master's concern. But the train seemed to be full of friendly women, talking and joking. One held a very young child in her lap.

The train moved suddenly, slowly pulling away from the station, car couplings clanging and jerking sharply. Elizabeth could not see the station master on the platform and thought he perhaps might not wave anyway. He had counted her money and stamped the ticket politely, without comment, but he also handed her a Thai magazine. His wife stayed at his side until the transaction was complete. She wrapped several cookies in a small sheet of waxed paper.

"For trip. You have good trip," she said.

Elizabeth was glad for the visit with the woman, and for the tea and cookies. But even more so, she was relieved to have had the use of the remarkably clean toilet in the station. She wondered if the station master kept it that way, or if perhaps it was his wife's job. Elizabeth had stared in the spotless mirror. A moment. A tired and gaunt woman in the crystal clear glass. A life.

As the train gathered speed, Elizabeth thought of the station manager and the broom. And his golden hostess. A man and a woman. A life. Two Buri Ram students finding each other, a pretty good team, perhaps a business arrangement too. A man and a woman. Elizabeth had not thought of Dan since leaving Denmark. She opened the magazine, looked at the pictures and the flowing secrets of script. She turned the pages and was soon asleep.

First light was streaming through the windows when Elizabeth awoke. The compartment seemed familiar, but her dreams had been complex and confused. Her father spoke to her sternly in one dream, scolding her. She could not remember what about, maybe about Dan. Why had she not told him? She had never been disrespectful or careless as a child or teen. She would have time to explain it all.

The windows in the compartment were open at the top only, an inch or two, and the morning breeze was still cool. Lights were on, and there was a bustle of activity as passengers seemed to be preparing themselves for food that was being delivered at the far end of the car. Young girls carried plates, stacked in hanging racks, one on each arm, five or six plates on each rack. The girls were efficient, and each plate had the same food, rice piled high, a fried egg on top. There was some sauce in a tiny plastic cup, and a large stainless steel soup spoon on each plate, the spoon's rattle indicating the plates were restaurant china.

Elizabeth asked the woman seated next to her, loud enough so someone else could answer if her seatmate didn't speak English.

"How much breakfast food cost?" she asked. Several women eyed each other and bowed their heads, looking toward the man across the aisle, next to the far window. Elizabeth noticed one young girl staring at her, sudden wide eyes, the girl's mouth opened in surprise. The girl silently mouthed the words "Koh Samed. Ko-Sa-med!"

A woman near Elizabeth's elbow answered her question very quietly. "Worker food on train. No cost worker."

"Can person buy a plate food?" Elizabeth asked. The woman looked down and toward the man. Elizabeth saw he was watching closely. The girl sitting next to him spoke quickly to him, close to his ear, too quiet to hear. Elizabeth wondered if the girl was translating for him. The man's eyes were dark, squinting, and his mouth tightly set. Angry. He said two or three very soft words, like air hissing from a cracked pipe, and a final command, clearly "no!" in Thai. He rose from his seat and walked to Elizabeth's seat. He shouted several words at the women as he stood over Elizabeth. She did not understand what he was saying, but the message was clear, that she was not one of them, and he was warning them away. Suddenly Elizabeth was alone in the train.

A serving girl entered the silent car with twelve more plates of food and began to pass them to the very quiet passengers. She realized something was wrong and joked, clearly asking what was going on, in a happy tone. The man turned on the girl and shouted another command. She became silent and hurried to unload the last several dishes. The man growled tight, angry words, this time directly at Elizabeth, pointing his finger at her, and went back to his seat. The child in the woman's lap next to Elizabeth began to cry. Elizabeth started to apologize for the trouble and was cut off by an older woman who sat across from her. The girl across from Elizabeth was still staring at her.

The older woman spoke. "No. Man correct. Worker train food for worker."

Elizabeth saw the girl translate for the man again. He smiled grimly. The old woman continued, and Elizabeth caught the eye of the girl opposite. One of the students on the boat. Koh Samed. One of the girls and boys she had come to visit. Graduated? On the worker train? One of the lucky ones, with a job. Or was this her fortune, the man her manager? Or guard?

The old woman continued, the man listening to the girl translating at his side, and Elizabeth could see that every woman in the car, including the old woman speaking, was looking away, away from Elizabeth and away from the man. This was no challenge to the man, but neither a defense of what he had said. They were simply considering the words directed to no one, to the ceiling.

The old woman spoke, silent support from her friends and coworkers. "No. Man correct. On worker train, worker train food for Thai worker only."

The man smiled more broadly, his argument honored. A serving girl pushed through the car's far doors with two more racks of plates. The silence stopped her, and she waited. The child cried. Elizabeth counted the serving plates. These were the last. The old woman talked on, looking away, talking to the air. Maybe talking to her father, or to the Buddha.

"Thai food good. Worker train food very good. We lucky, have job and food. Thank man." The old woman waited, certain the translation was complete, and then continued. "Thai woman make good food. Serve good food. Thai woman always grace, and Thai woman not eat until man and family eat. Children eat. But Thai grace, very important. Before any have food, guest have food."

The woman's eyes glanced past Elizabeth, and then back to the ceiling, perhaps praying, Elizabeth thought. The child on the woman's lap next to Elizabeth still cried. Elizabeth unwrapped the Thai lemon cookies the station master's wife had given her and passed them to the mother, who gave one to the child, The child stopped crying immediately. Someone clapped.

The old woman smiled and continued. "Yes, children eat sweet cookie that our guest give child. But most important, before anyone eat, Thai woman make sure guest eat." The serving girl, not knowing any of the drama in the car, handed a plate to Elizabeth. Everyone had a plate. Elizabeth noticed the man was eating too, and the girl translating was also eating. Plain white rice, fried egg, Thai hot sauce, plate and clink of soup spoons on porcelain. Elizabeth was hungry, yet worried the old woman would lose her job, the man's target in the evening or the next day.

As if she had spoken her worries aloud, the woman with the child whispered, "No trouble. Man always angry something. He know we stronger than him. Too many us." She giggled and then straightened her face to serious again. Her child laughed and reached for Elizabeth's dusty blond hair. Elizabeth noticed the women across from her were laughing with their eyes, tight lips bursting with pleasure. The women were hurrying to finish their food, as they prepared to leave the train, a stop on the outskirts of Bangkok. Near factories or hotels, Elizabeth wondered. The girl from the Koh Samed boat was gathering her things, looking back to Elizabeth again and again.

Elizabeth nodded and smiled. "I remember you," she whispered. "Koh Samed. Very nice students. I came to Buri Ram for visit, but I must go home to my father. I met the station master wife. Very nice lady. She was student at Buri Ram school. Maybe long time ago. Made cookies, serve tea. Very nice."

The girl's eyes filled with tears. "I think it was you. I wish you visit and we talk in Buri Ram." The girl was searching in her bag for something. The train had slowed to a stop, final screeching brakes, and then a deep breath, shuddering wheels, and rest.

"Something for you," the girl said. "Photo from school, when I graduate. My very nice tea party." She looked to see if the man was watching, but he had exited with two young workers. The girl placed the photograph in Elizabeth's hand. "For you. You give, maybe your brother or your friend or your uncle. Young uncle."

Elizabeth stood up, and the girl hugged her quickly and rushed toward the door, as a whistle shrilled. Elizabeth sat down, tumbling thoughts. The next stop would be the city center. She would go to the ticket agent and see if he could get a ticket. She would take the first flight that could get her to New York or Newark. Home. To her father. She would visit Kathryn on another trip. She needed her father, to tell him everything, search for an answer.

Elizabeth held up the photograph. It was the girl. She wore a yellow and gold and orange satin tunic. Overlapped sequins, like fish scales. Her skirt fitted tightly and covered her legs. She stood, a small statue, much as the station master's wife had presented herself. The girl's hair was curled and piled on top of her head, shiny black ringlets. She held a silver tray. Treats and sweets, Elizabeth guessed. The girl's eyes showed pride. Elizabeth looked closely. The eyes were proud, yet uncertain, and edges of the girl's mouth showed fear. Elizabeth slid the photograph into her canvas bag. As she tucked the glossy paper in, she noticed there were words written on the back, handwritten, ink, and a name, signed. She held the photo up, to read.

"So sorry I miss you Buri Ram. Please come back soon. We be friend. Please tell brother in America I make wonderful wife. Please. Have safe trip to America." Elizabeth drew a long breath, closed her eyes and exhaled, "America."

Chapter 21

ELIZABETH FEARS IN
THE DARKNESS (1986)

Elizabeth rode upstream without effort, the Lackawanna taking her toward greener parts of Northern New Jersey. At this early hour, the heaviest current of humanity flowed eastward, toward Newark and New York. She watched travelers on the opposite station platforms, Hoboken, Newark, then East Orange, waiting to push onboard the crowded commuter trains to the city. She skimmed against the flow, her westbound train cradling passengers on their way home from a night shift in Newark or the city, or traveling to small jobs in the western suburbs, where she was bound. Home.

A couple more stops. Maplewood. She had the seat to herself. Passengers in the car were quiet and tired. She remembered her amazement the last time she had traveled to visit with her dad from her cozy and quiet life in Denmark, during Tivoli's off-season. The sheer flood of human hope and fatigue cascading toward Manhattan in the morning, lines and crowds and traffic, and noise. And then home again each afternoon, an echo and a reflection, motion and tense hurry. She marveled at so many people. Each face a story, a history and a future. A wish or a dream. A life. Told in a stranger's brief glance. She was cruising easily against the awful flow this morning. On her way home as most were just beginning another day.

Her plane had landed late, well past midnight, but her schedule was her own, and of course there was no welcome party or family at the airport to greet her. She had no way of knowing if her father had even received her letter from Thailand. She had called from Denmark before she'd left, but the conversation was lost in her incoherence and tears and rage. Her Rita. The memory of Rita still surprised her several times each day, odd moments of panic, deflating to guilt and regret. The calendar's grid calculated the days since Rita had been wheeled away from Elizabeth's outstretched hand. A month and a week and two days. Or three now, in the morning light. She wondered if crossing the international date line made any difference in the count. Would it be one day more or one day less? Would it matter?

"If I could turn back time," she wondered. Rita's bluish lips and fingernails. Elizabeth's father had never held his granddaughter. He had promised to visit Denmark to see the baby, and again later, as she grew, but his plans always remained fuzzy and tentative, and nothing had come of it. Too late now. Elizabeth focused beyond the train's streaked windows. East Orange. Then Brick Church, the name colonial, or British maybe. Elizabeth had never learned where the name came from, maybe a long-dead Preacher Brick, or perhaps just for its red façade, the bricks. Brick Church. It didn't matter. Dust to dust either way.

She met a man's gaze across the aisle. He was staring at her, head cocked to one side, his eyes trying to understand the tired and disheveled and pretty young woman. Elizabeth smiled at him, weary at the thought of explaining herself to anyone, as had been required the night before at Kennedy airport. She surprised the man with a quick summary, as if he had dared to ask.

"I explained it all to the customs agents in the airport. JFK. Last night. And they let me come in," she said, smiling.

The man leaned back, startled, and then laughed aloud. "Yes. I was wondering too. I am glad for you," a thick accent, but American. He smiled and looked away. He continued to glance at her, still curious.

The customs agents at the airport had asked familiar questions, trying to gauge her intent, alone and without any luggage other than her small canvas shoulder bag. She had begun to realize her tattered shorts and wrinkled blouse were out of place, not to mention the chilly March morning ahead. Cold. It had been hard to freshen up in the plane's lavatory, even harder in the bustling air terminal. She had started to accelerate her pace there, wanting to be home, a sudden child's fear that her father might have died or moved. Or left her. Simply forgotten about her. Her hair felt stringy, almost sticky. The customs clerk had repeated his questions, perhaps trying to unearth some inconsistency.

"You've been out of the country for the past year? Where are you headed?"

"I've been living in Europe for seven years. Married there. Denmark. I'm coming home to visit my dad. New Jersey. Same as last year. Yes sir. Maplewood. Yes." Easy questions surrounding a hazy picture, she imagined. He asked several other quick questions as he thumbed through her passport.

"No sir. Nothing to declare. No sir. Nothing of value. No sir, not going back. I'm going to stay with my father. For now. No. I don't know how long." Elizabeth was thankful she had not renewed her passport during the years she had been abroad. It would have been harder to explain her married name, foreign. And hyphenated, at Dan's insistence. That would have complicated her explanation. That son of a bitch Dan.

The passengers from her plane had crowded at the luggage claim, and once through customs, Elizabeth gained her freedom, striding toward the waiting area, parents and lovers and friends and children anxious for reconnecting, eager eyes focused on the swinging double doors, Elizabeth a sudden and lonely being, a leaf on the human stream's surface, breaking the crowd's expectant reverie. Tumbling over rocks, light and agile, as she flowed through the waiting area and terminal and away from the knots of people. Fellow travelers, become strangers again.

The shuttle bus to New York had taken a long time to load and finally pull away from the curb, straining diesel whine, the driver in a careless conversation with a female ticket and baggage helper on the seat directly behind him. He spoke with her over his shoulder, glancing back at the roadway ahead from time to time. The lights of the city ten miles distant were beginning to melt, a glow of morning at their backs. Full sunrise within an hour or so, she guessed.

The bus stopped briefly at Grand Central, unloaded some more passengers at the Port Authority bus terminal on the West Side, and a final stop ten blocks farther downtown, at Penn Station, where Elizabeth could catch the Lackawanna under the Hudson River to New Jersey and to her dad. The railway's name had changed so many times. There were signs for Conrail, but it was still the Lackawanna for any regulars from the area, regardless of who ran it. It would take her through the tunnel, to Hoboken and Newark and the Oranges, where the tracks turn south toward Highland Avenue and Maplewood. What a long way it had been just to return home, three quarters of the way around the world. The final short steps seemed to be taking the longest time. She thought of her books, so many stories about journeys. Circling home.

"To my father. I will go to my father." She mouthed the words. They sounded so familiar, but she couldn't place them. The previous month felt like an eternity. Rita and Dan and Amman and Thailand. Mr. Visith and Asher and Kim. Buri Ram, the station master's wife. The night train and a young girl begging. The girl had begged for rescue. A safe place. A refuge.

"I will go to my father," Elizabeth intoned, a whisper. She had written him from Bangkok, before leaving for Koh Samed, well before Koh Samui and Buri Ram. She had explained she was coming home, needed some time, maybe stop in California on the way, visit with Kathryn, her high-school friend. She wondered if a letter from Bangkok could take longer than three weeks. The fear welled up in her again, that he might not be there. He had talked about moving for some time, but wouldn't he have told her? She was uncertain.

"Miss? Are you sure you are all right?" The man who had stared was leaning toward her, across the aisle, kind eyes blinking.

"Yes, I'm OK. Just thinking. Wondering about my father. Whether he'll be at home."

"You're sure you're OK? You looked scared all of a sudden."

"Yes. Well, I'm sure he'll be waiting. Somehow." The man leaned back in his seat. "And thanks for your concern," Elizabeth said. "Here's my stop. And thank you."

Elizabeth stepped onto the cement platform. Solid. Maplewood. She walked down the steps and through the station, a dusty smell, faint odor of urine. It was dark and shabby. She remembered the spotless restroom in Buri Ram. She still had a few dollars in loose bills from Amman. The bus on the main street might come within two blocks of her father's house. She looked down the street and began walking the ten or twelve familiar blocks toward her childhood home.

She walked quickly, and then began to jog, almost a run. She hoped her father would be at home, not off at some job or out driving around. Or wherever he might be. He needed to be at home this morning. He had to be there. She ran the final block to the corner of his street.

Elizabeth turned off the main street into her childhood neighborhood. East Park. She stopped and stood for a moment, catching her breath. The street and sidewalks were much narrower and closer than she remembered. Trees shaded the pavement where she had played as a young child, roller skates and hopscotch and bikes and laughter. And the gray frame house, waiting. Black shingle roof. She walked briskly, breathing in the memories. Everything was smaller, the neighborhood, tight lawns between the homes, little more than pathways to tiny backyards.

She slowed. Home. Her eyes focused on a figure on the porch, interrupting her wonder about the neighborhood and the house. Her father. He stood with his hand on the rail, dark tree branches brushing at the porch roof. His face was turned toward her, his gaze expressionless, then reflecting a worry, as if trying to unravel a puzzle, beginning to recognize the slight form turning in at his front walk. His girl. His only child. Elizabeth. His face broadened in pain and then surprise, and relief. He began to uncoil and move toward the edge of the porch.

"Elizabeth! Honey. It's you!" He grasped at the railing guarding the four steps down to the sidewalk. Careful steps, one at a time, eyes looking down, hand over hand on the railing. She realized he was hurrying, moving as fast as he could, holding on, fears he might fall. Her father. Suddenly an old man.

"Elizabeth. It's you. I couldn't see who it was. I was waiting. You're home. You've come home!"

"Daddy," she cried. Her voice echoed. An echo in a dark tunnel. A twelve-year-old's cry, junior high school. She heard her own relief, her father at the principal's office. And the fear in his eyes. Her entire life's cry, an echo.

"Daddy!" And then the news that her mother was gone. Daddy anchoring her hope and her worst fear. The principal's office and the final bad news. His voice was suddenly much closer.

"Elizabeth, you're home. Thank God. I was starting to worry. I was waiting." They clasped each other close and rocked, a child in a parent's arms. "My

Elizabeth, I'm so sorry about your baby. Your little girl. About Rita. And I thought you wouldn't get here in time."

"In time? What do you mean, Daddy? Are you all right?" They stood at arm's length.

"Oh heavens, yes. I'm getting old, but I'm fine." He turned her toward the steps, holding to her arm tight. Frail.

"Come on in. Let's make us a pot of coffee. My Elizabeth is home. I have so much to tell you." He seemed relieved as Elizabeth slipped her arm under his elbow. They made their way up the steps and across the porch.

"Your room is right where it's always been. I haven't packed any of your old things. Go on and get cleaned up if you want, and then I can tell you what's going on. There's a guy coming to look at the camper. I was waiting for him. He should have been here by now. Go on up."

When Elizabeth came down to the kitchen, her father had cups on the table, next to her mother's hummingbird sugar bowl and a carton of coffee creamer. Her father didn't wait for her to sit down and began as she poured the coffee.

"The house is sold, and I'm moving next week. Earlier if I can tie up the last few things. Like your room. I'm glad you're here. You can decide what you need to keep. And we can put stuff in storage too. Or pack it up and send it over to you." He stopped and coughed.

"Daddy, I need to tell you," but he continued, focusing on stirring the coffee and creamer.

"You know I'm not getting any younger, and some things are setting in, getting worse, like my memory and my eyesight. And that cough. I had it last winter, last time you were here, and it keeps getting worse. Doc Ward says he wants to check me out for that, and for my driving. I had a couple of small fender benders last month. Two in a row, and it makes me extra nervous. Doc Ward says he's more nervous than I am." Elizabeth's father paused.

"It's time, Elizabeth." He looked down. "All I have are the memories, and way too much time on my hands. But even when I have to do something, it's like one thing after another is getting too hard to do, or too hard to figure. And I'm not shoveling snow for another winter. Or bills and balancing my checkbook. It's getting tricky."

Elizabeth interrupted him. "Daddy, I can help. I can take care of some of those things."

"No. You have your own life. I'm not going to tie you down. And anyway, as soon as you go back to Denmark, then what?"

Elizabeth was relieved that her father's news had crowded out any sharing of what had happened in Denmark. And about Rita. Elizabeth did not even want to start on Dan. She let her father go on.

"Well, I quit smoking because of my cough, and I don't really drive anywhere, so I bought a share in a little duplex house. A retirement community. In Virginia. I can live in the house as long as I can manage, and then I move into the retirement home when I get old." He laughed out loud, enjoying the thought. "When I get old." His laugh turned into a cough, wheezing enjoyment at his thought. He pulled his handkerchief out of his back pocket and swiped at his mouth. She noticed dark stains on the awful wrinkled cloth.

"Fresh air and mild winters. Friendly people. I'm the only smiling face on this block, it seems. No joy living here anymore. Everyone's scared. Things changing too fast. No joy. Not since I retired, or since you left. How long has that been? Four years? Five?"

"More than seven years, Daddy."

"It won't be so lonely, either," he continued as he stirred in his coffee. He put the spoon on the tabletop. A small brown puddle. He took Elizabeth's hand and went on. "Maybe you can help me with the last few things. I've sold all the extra furniture, and a lot of stuff in the basement and garage the people who bought the house will keep. I was so afraid you wouldn't get here in time. I didn't know how to get in touch with you. But I knew you were coming. I got your letter. Praise the Lord, you're here. Maybe you can stay long enough to drive down with me. Next couple of weeks. Before you go back home. Usually you stayed a couple weeks," he added, a hopeful look.

"Daddy. I'm not going back. I'm not going back. I hope you won't be mad, or disappointed in me. For not sticking it out. You know, not sticking it out when it gets rough."

"What?" His surprised eyes, a smile that broadened in hope, wondering. "You're not going back? What about Dan?"

"No. Never. If I went back, it wouldn't be to him. Dan's a jackass. He wasn't even there when it mattered, with Rita. He was with some woman. He was running around. Well, really that's not what they do there. They don't run around. It's not like it's cheating and hiding. They just go with each other. Hello and good-bye. I hated the way he flirted all the time, and it was dead serious flirting, always. So that's it. I loved the place, so clean and safe and smart. Maybe too smart. But it was all just too much, Rita and Dan. I'm home, and the noise and the traffic and the speed, I'll just have to get used to it again."

"So you could drive down with me? Help with a couple of things? Maybe you would like it in Virginia. It's nice. And you'd be near your old dad."

"We'll see, Dad. For now I'm just worn out and need to get a shower and get some rest, maybe take a nap. An hour or two."

"OK, honey. I'll get you a towel, and your room is just like you left it last year when you visited. All I have to do today is talk with the guy who's coming to look at the camper. It's the last thing I have to find a home for, really. In fact he may be here already. It's about time. I was waiting for him. On the porch. He and his little boy are coming." He smiled.

"Imagine, you still have that camper. I remember. It was your hideout."

"Yes, it was my secret place where I could laugh or cry and nobody to worry me about it. Back when this home was a real home, with your mom. And later, with you here during college, and when you started teaching. The camper was my clubhouse, my little chapel. My foxhole. I hope this guy takes it. He seemed nice enough on the phone. Give my camper a good home."

"OK, Daddy. Let me get cleaned up." Elizabeth went up the stairs and down the dark hallway to her bedroom. The room was clean and neat, the bed and dresser still in place. She drew back the curtain and saw her father walk across the back lawn to the small camping trailer. A man was inspecting the hitch while a young boy stood back, looking at the trailer. He might have been four or five years old, probably the man's son. His hands were clasped on top of his head. He twisted his upper body, treetops in the wind.

Elizabeth watched at the curtain. The man returned to the boy and took his arm. The boy pulled away, and his father walked him back to the camper, awkward steps leading the boy from behind, holding both his hands. The man lifted the boy and opened the camper's screen door. The boy twisted loose from his father's arms and jumped down to the grass, shaking his head, then pulling his father back, away from the camper. Elizabeth couldn't hear the boy's voice, but the drama of fury and fear was clear. The man picked the boy up again, and held him close, stroking his head and rocking him back and forth. The man laughed while he talked with Elizabeth's father, holding the boy at his shoulder. They talked for a few minutes, shook hands awkwardly, and walked back toward the house and driveway. The man and his son headed for the street.

Elizabeth looked at the camper. It was smaller than she remembered. White aluminum, several windows and vents, an air-conditioning unit on the roof, leaves and dark stains scattered across the top, comfortable and quiet. A small place. Streaked with rain spatters and dust. It looked cozy in the backyard.

"It would be cozier than this room," she thought out loud. She turned and went to the bathroom to shower, and a thought repeated itself, a breeze crossing her mind. Something. Elizabeth caught sight of herself in the bathroom mirror and looked closer. Her hair was longer than she remembered, having not tended to mirrors and brushes and trimming. It wasn't clean, either, too many hours since her last shampoo and rinse and dry in the hotel in Bangkok. The trip had just accelerated, trying to get home. She could have stopped over in San Francisco and tried to see Kathryn. Maybe later, in the summer or fall. Not going back.

She looked in the mirror, closer. Her eyes were tired, and tiny lines pulled toward her temples. No sparkle or gladness. But no fear or anger either. It was time. For something. She needed time, enough time to make a plan. A new chapter in her book. She felt like she had lost a manuscript. Left it on a train, forgotten her beloved companion somewhere along the way, the one for whom she was responsible. Trust. Special friend, where are you? She remembered the words, from so long ago.

Unique in all the world, she remembered. *In all the world*. Elizabeth unbuttoned her shirt, a tear at the back of one sleeve. Her shorts were frayed and stained with coffee and something sticky from the train. The Lackawanna. There were old clothes in her dresser, and she could buy a couple of things in the morning. She turned on the shower and surveyed her body in the mirror. It was still athletic and smooth.

"Most places, at least," she said to the mirror. She reminded herself she would buy tennis shoes and a tank top, maybe a gym membership wherever her dad might end up in Virginia. She stepped into the shower and closed her eyes. A flickering light, expending energy on the edge of dreams and wonder. Waves. Something. She was so, so tired. Elizabeth showered quickly and toweled off the water and dried her hair. She padded down the hallway to her bedroom. She closed the door, pulled back the covers on the bed and slid between the sheets. *Between pages in her book*, she thought.

It was late afternoon when Elizabeth came downstairs. Her father was sitting at the kitchen table, looking in the phone book.

"What's up, Daddy? Can I help with anything?"

"No, just calling Camper World out by Parsippany, about the trailer. They might be able to put it on the lot, sell it on commission. Or maybe buy it outright. Hey, you want anything to eat? I have some pizza we could heat up. Or we could go out."

"No, I'm still worn out. I'll eat a slice of pizza maybe. I need a full night's sleep, or more. The trip. So the guy didn't want the camper?"

"No, he really liked it, but his little boy was scared stiff to go in. The kid saw a spider. He couldn't get over it. And you know, the spider was dead. Dried up, like teensy twigs and a fleck of dirt. Once the kid saw it, he cried and cried, and finally his dad took him home, said he would call. But I know he won't."

"Well, maybe," she said.

"No, his dad was buying it for the two of them, himself and his boy, for camping out. I bet they'll go to the beach instead." And he laughed. "You were a bit like that yourself. If you got upset or scared, that was it."

Elizabeth went to the kitchen door and looked out at the trailer. One room and a couple of windows, a door and breezes in the night, sounds in the forest, or just the backyard. A water hookup and electric, a gas stove, porta-pot, and tiny shower.

A little piece of heaven, she thought. Her father's hideout.

"Daddy, I don't have much money to pay my way or anything, a little bit left on my credit card and a few dollars is all. I mean, maybe could we take the

camper to Virginia and park it in your backyard for a week or two? I could figure a way to buy it from you, find a place to park it, maybe a year-round campground, a cheap long-term rate. I could have my own place for the summer at
least, while I make some new plans. Maybe even work at the campground to pay
the rent. What do you think?"

Her father looked at Elizabeth in disbelief. A smile spread across his face.
"No, you can't buy the camper. How about you help me pack up the last things
and hitch the camper to the car, and you drive me down to Virginia? And you
can have it! What do you say? Deal?"

"OK, Daddy. Deal!" She hugged his neck and rocked, thinking of the
camper and then the boy and the spider, and the boy's comforting father, smiling confidence and care and forgiveness. Her childhood welled up inside and
rocked her back and forth, holding on to her dad. The kitchen table. Her childhood home. She was so tired, and the tears began to fill her eyes and her heart,
and the years gathered on top of other years, and she cried for her father slipping
away and for leaving her Rita and her mother gone so many years, and she cried
for Kathryn. *How many years, Kathryn?* Her father patted her hand on his arm.
He wiped at his eyes.

"OK, Daddy. Thank you, thank you for the camper, my own hideout. Just
what I need. Now I can sleep for real. I'm going upstairs. I'm still worn out. Is
that OK?"

"Yes, honey. You're home. Safe. Sleep. We'll hitch the camper to the car in
the morning. We'll check it out."

"Night, Dad. Even though it's not late." She went upstairs and to her room.

Elizabeth pulled the covers up to her eyes and rolled to face the window,
wondering if there would be raindrops on the porch roof or the windowsill.
She lifted the sash several inches and surveyed the backyard. It had always been
a comforting spot, especially as a child and then as a teen, when it rained and
drops spattered on the window screen, fresh cool air breezing across her face.
When she had returned home from high school for college, her bedside dreams
were an apartment in the city, New York or Boston or Paris, raindrops on a
metal fire escape, like Hemingway in Paris. A candle and a bottle of wine. A
lover maybe. And here she was, home again, preparing to take to the road with

her father. Taking her own tiny home along. She closed her eyes, praying the fresh promises would outweigh the old fears.

The window and breeze transported her to her childhood in the house, and she floated in a waking memory. Mommy sat at her bedside as Elizabeth wrestled with the fears hidden in the darkness. She could feel tender fingers brushing her hair back from her face, a gentle voice in the evening shadow asking if she was afraid.

"No, Mommy, it's nothing. Just wondering what will happen. My life and where I'll go and what will happen." She always left out the fear, the gnawing chasm of death and the universe splitting open and the earth stopping turning and everyone spinning off into the blackness. Forever and ever. Specks of dust. Lost in darkness. She asked her mother questions to steer away from the frightful shadows.

"Will the sun ever go out? I mean, will it stay warm forever? What would happen if it would go out?" She pulled her little black stuffed dog closer. She knew the obliteration of being, deep in her soul. The nothingness. Where could a person run, to hide from death? How far would a person have to run? She covered her eyes with the worn plush dog. Who would hold her and make her safe?

Her father remained in the kitchen until midnight, reworking a list of things to do. He needed fatigue to be able to sleep. He sat at the kitchen table, his usual midnight cup of coffee, still no sleep possible. He heard his daughter cry out in her room upstairs. Once, and then again. He held his breath a long time, and silence settled on the house. The beloved space, full of love and struggle and hope, but finally the emptiness. He considered the beloved hummingbird sugar bowl, a Christmas present from a ten-year-old girl. To her mother.

"Thank you, dear Lord, for bringing my baby home to me," he whispered, putting his list aside. "Let me be a happy chapter in her story, dear Lord. When all's said and done. A happy chapter." He prayed she would not have the nightmares, just for returning home.

He had tried to be a good father, raising his only child since she was eleven. Even so, he had always been cautious about the slight and tense girl. He could never truly say he knew what made her tick, especially during her teen years, a fear around the edges of her frame. The way she held her hands, more tightly than necessary when holding nothing. Her ninth-grade year he sent her to a boarding school in Pennsylvania. He knew he would prefer the awful loneliness to his helpless wonder at Elizabeth's private intensity, her interest in books and geography and maps. Stories, and tense wondering about far-off places. Elizabeth called him Daddy, but never with the same intensity she bestowed upon her mommy. He knew that Elizabeth confided her deepest wishes and fears in her mother, and he was just part of the backdrop of the house.

Elizabeth's father had visited her at the boarding school once or twice during her four years there, when his business travels took him from Northern New Jersey to Pennsylvania or Ohio. He also came to her graduation. Elizabeth had seemed engaged in activities at the school but never talked about any specific friends until her senior year, a new roommate, a girl from California whose mother was ill, or hospitalized, Elizabeth didn't say why. They seemed to be good friends, close in a special way. Very much like Elizabeth's relationship with her mother. Confidantes and best friends. Roommates, yet so much more. He took a sip of coffee. It was cold. He put the cup down very carefully, to make no sound. He listened, a faint creak upstairs.

Elizabeth swung her feet over the side of the bed and padded to the dark corner of her childhood room, next to the hallway door, faint shadows from a distant streetlight. Or the moon. She turned the doorknob slowly, no sound that might expose her secret hiding place. She pulled the door open slowly.

She had heard her father's chair at the kitchen table, legs scraping on linoleum, and held her breath. A midnight cup of coffee. The house sold, another piece of her life gone. Gone. She thought of Rita, her child's outstretched hand, opening and clenching, reaching. Her last echo, forever.

"Mommy."

I could have reached her. Or I could have stayed, Elizabeth thought. She stepped back against the bare interior wall, brushing her fingertips against the dusky wallpaper, retreating into the corner of the room. She carefully opened the hallway door all the way, as she had done as a child, quiet and cautious, so her parents would not hear, pulling the door toward her, blocking the window and bed from her sight. The corner walls and the open bedroom door shielded her in a triangular hiding space. The doorknob tapped the interior wall, brass on wallboard, and Elizabeth slid slowly to the floor, fingertips sliding on wallpaper. She huddled, knees touching her chin, holding her breath. The perfect hiding place. For a little girl.

"Mommy," she whispered. "How long is forever?"

Rita's fading echo, "Mommy," tiny blue fingers just out of reach.

"We'll get our little camper and make a cozy little home, just you and me, honey. Just you and me. And Mommy." Her heart filled with regret and loss. *Why did the world stop turning? Why did you leave me here? Everything is flying off into space.*

Mommy. She heard raindrops on the porch roof. Relief on the windowsill. The night would be soft and soothing.

In the kitchen, her father heard the bedroom door open upstairs, so cautiously, and then the familiar single soft beat of the doorknob on the wall. And now the rain was tapping on the kitchen door and window. He looked at the clock on the wall.

Good. The rain. Five minutes, he thought, and let his mind wander through the day's events, Elizabeth home, gathering a few of his beloved things and preparing to retreat to a safe place. And the camper. He thought of the final tasks necessary for the coming days and hoped he hadn't forgotten anything important. He looked back at the clock and watched the second hand move through an extra minute, then two.

Time. Gone forever, he thought. He set his coffee cup on the table, a clear ceramic note, and scraped his chair back from the table. His little girl needed a gentle warning. She would close her bedroom door ever so cautiously and tiptoe back into bed. She would be able to sleep now. She had told him so often how she loved the sound of rain at her window.

He moved coffee cups and a bowl from the dish drain to a cabinet, smiling at the familiar kitchen sounds. He heard the bedroom door latch shut upstairs, the faintest click. She would be fast asleep in minutes, worn out from her long flight, and maybe be able to stay asleep this time. He thought about the coming week. He would hitch the camper to the car in the morning. He turned off the light. He knew he would now be able to sleep.

Newcomb put his hand on Elizabeth's arm.

"So. Your father knew about your struggles, then? Did he ever tell you that? Did you ever talk about it with him?"

Elizabeth folded her notes gently, no crease, just a safe packet, words closed from view. The scene was fresh in her memory. An evening's recollection of the afternoon. She still wondered about her father's complicity in the nightly scare. The tiny triangular bomb shelter. The despairing walled womb. The house's secrets.

Newcomb interrupted her thoughts again. "And then they drove to Virginia? Did anything happen on the way?"

Elizabeth heard someone's low hiss. The seat in front of them. A woman's soft voice. "Shut up." Then even more quietly, "Go on, honey."

She unfolded her notes and shuffled white papers on top. The train rolled westward, splitting the silence of the northern plains.

"OK, Arthur. They drive to Virginia. One stop on the way. An important stop. Special. One of the turning points, I think. At her old school. Train tracks."

Chapter 22

ELIZABETH   CHAIN LINK FENCE (1986)

Elizabeth backed her father's old Buick carefully toward the small camper. The grass and gravel were wet from a nighttime shower that lingered through the early-morning hours. Her father directed the operation. After several tries she had the ball hitch nearly under the trailer's tongue, and he cranked the jack down. With an extra last shove, the car and trailer were ready to go. His car and her camper, the clock turned back almost two decades. Father and daughter, thrown together against the odds. He attached the safety chains and brake light connectors and told Elizabeth they were ready. The house sold, a few pieces of furniture and personal belongings already shipped, his move to a Virginia retirement community and a fresh start. They were ready.

Elizabeth sensed her father was relieved she was going to drive. She hadn't told him much about leaving Dan, and she wondered if he might ask her to stay with him for a while, even throw in her lot with him again. She had lived at home while attending Montclair State and during her first five years teaching. Then a gnawing yearning to travel, and the study grant that opened the door to her European travel dreams.

"Dreams." She laughed the word aloud in the front seat of the car. "Or nightmares. Homecoming." Elizabeth adjusted the driver's seat. Her father called out from the back door that everything was set, that he would be right out.

Elizabeth's last night in the house had been fearful, at least until the rain started to tap on the porch roof outside her window. The breeze and misty drops through the screen transported her once again, Mommy sitting on the bedside, tightening the covers as she leaned over Elizabeth, her only child, who wrestled with the fearful darkness. In the night Elizabeth startled awake, certain she felt tender fingers brushing her hair back from her face, a gentle voice asking if she was afraid. She pressed dark plush softness to her face, the faint and familiar odor of tears on her little childhood stuffed dog. Where could a person run, to escape the darkness? The night bathed the house in the awful quiet she remembered. Desperate loneliness. Her mother. Elizabeth prayed nothing would delay their departure in the morning. Her camper, and the good fortune that her dad had been unable to sell it. Strangely, his gift of the camper had not surprised her.

She sat in the car, suddenly aware of her knuckles, clenched white on the steering wheel. Her hands and shoulders and jaw ached. She shook her head, sure the hollow loneliness of the house had been the same for her father, the years without Mommy, especially the past five years, since his retirement. She wondered what he had done with each day. He joked about how his mind was playing tricks on him, or maybe it was his body, dropping things, forgetting. Small accidents around the house. He said he was glad he was moving into a retirement village where he might have regular contact with neighbors.

"Older folks in the same boat," he said. "Maybe I'll get better, or maybe even meet some nice lady who would pamper me with some attention. Maybe, huh?"

Elizabeth wondered why she had never thought about her father having a lady friend. Or more than a friend. Her father returned to the car. They had agreed on an early start.

"You ready?" he asked. "I left the kitchen door open in case you needed anything. The new folks are coming this afternoon. They're going to clean out the last stuff, or keep it. The house is all theirs now."

"OK, Daddy. I'm ready, but let me run to the bathroom before we drive." Elizabeth jogged to the rear door, the lawn spongy and cold. She went in and then climbed the steep back stairs from the kitchen, a favorite childhood escape route, and went to her bedroom. The closet door was open, and she reached to the upper shelf, under old pillows. She pulled out the small stuffed dog, worn black plush fabric. Floppy ears, a handmade present from an aunt to a three-year-old who cried at night, the familiar smell, and safety. Elizabeth clutched the dog to her chest and turned to leave the room. Her bedroom door stood halfway open, and she noticed the wallboard's old doorknob scar.

Elizabeth went back to the window. Her father was getting into the passenger side of the car. He pulled the heavy car door shut. He wouldn't hear. Elizabeth went to the hallway and turned back. She gave the open bedroom door a sudden solid kick with her right foot. The door slammed against the wall inside the room and bounced back toward her. She kicked it again, even harder, and then again, and as the door hit the wall the third time, the doorknobs on both sides broke loose and fell to the floor, one of them spinning on its shaft and the other rolling under her bed. She turned to go.

"Good-bye," she whispered, and skittered down the back stairs, one step ahead of a shadow.

In the car, her father rummaged in the glove box. "You ready, baby?"

"Ready as ever, Daddy."

He seemed satisfied and fresh. She slid the soft plush nighttime companion into her khaki bag on top of her father's belongings in the backseat, giving the bag a gentle pat.

"Let's go down Route 1, like the old days, just not turn toward the shore," her dad suggested, laughing.

Elizabeth stared at him. "Daddy. Route 1 is clogged with traffic and lights and the worst part of any town we drive through. This old car would never make it. Not with the camper. Either the brakes or the transmission will give out for sure."

They haggled about the map and memories of trips, but when they finally pulled out of the backyard drive, she told him they would simply head west and south, looking for ways to get on Route 22 West or one of the interstates. She began to fear she really didn't know the way.

He father sulked, still looking at alternate routes on the tattered and faded map he had retrieved from the glove box. He unfolded it and then refolded it into a more convenient square. His fingers drummed on the brittle paper. She could tell he had his heart set on old Route 1.

Something from his childhood, maybe, she thought, *or when he was on the road, selling painting contracts to factories and schools.* She also remembered Route 1 in Pennsylvania, where it met the winding country road to the boarding school she had attended instead of high school in Maplewood. Her thoughts drifted to Kathryn, rooming together their senior year. Hope and comfort. And their plan. She tensed and felt a wave of guilt, the months or years between letters to Kathryn. And most of her letters simply about travels. Nothing about plans or futures. Or stories.

Elizabeth never reminisced much about the school except for her senior year, when Kathryn arrived. Their quiet conversations, the books she loved, walks down to the train station. And how they would stay in touch. Sharing and building the chapters of their lives. Otherwise, the four years passed in a cloud of nervous activity. Tasks and deadlines, homework and clubs, and the yearbook. As well, she carried nagging fear and guilt during those years, knowing her father was alone at home. He always assured her it was only an hour away. She remembered the train from Trenton, occasional quiet weekends and holidays at home the first year. But she also remembered the silence and memories that haunted the house, and her father's quiet grief for her mother, which made it harder and harder to visit. As she grew, she also began to understand that her own fears were beyond her father's ability to fathom or sooth.

"OK, Daddy, we can head west on 22 to Mountainside and Plainfield and get on 206 at Somerville. Then down to Princeton and Lawrenceville and meet up with your beloved Route 1 just above Trenton. Then we cross the river and drive down to Langhorne." She hesitated. "You know, from Langhorne it's less than five minutes to the school. You always said it was only sixty miles home, and you joked at sixty in a car it would only take us an hour. It sure seemed farther."

She thought about the distance and the loneliness. And then the warm and comforting moments of her senior year. She closed her eyes momentarily as she let her foot off the gas. Then she glanced over at her father. He was looking out the side window. His left hand scribbled wandering notes on the open road map, two fingertips connected to memories and faded paper. A thought stirred her.

"You know, Daddy. Once we're safe on Route 1, we could take a quick side trip to the school. It might be neat to drive through and see the old train station. A quick stop. What do you think?"

Her father sat up in the seat, looking out the front window, as if they were going to make a turn onto Route 1.

"Well. That sounds like fun. Your graduation, I remember we all walked down to the station. Yes. We prayed together, about your future, and your roommate, what was her name? Kathy? She was there. We held hands and prayed. Do you ever hear from her?"

Elizabeth did not know how to answer. "I was going to write her. Regular, you know." She maneuvered the car and camper around a slow-moving truck, which honked an all clear. She concentrated on the road and weighed the question. The two wide trailer mirrors attached to the hood reflected more clearly than her memory of the years that had passed.

"I think I once told you. We were going to help each other write our chapters, our stories. Particularly the big decisions." She braked carefully at a busy intersection, reminding herself it might be difficult to explain her Danish driver's license if they were pulled over for any carelessness. She and Dan had never owned a car, and he joked about her busy insistence at exchanging her New Jersey driver's license for a Danish license as soon as she had moved to Denmark. There had been no difficulty or cost, but he said it was needless, that cars and all the related taxes were a huge and unnecessary expense.

"Just in case," she had said. "We might need a car, when we have kids." He had laughed at the thought. The buses and trains were very adequate, she knew, but it always seemed they were waiting at a station or bus stop. Late at night. In drizzly and cold weather. Or had he laughed about having kids? she wondered.

"Elizabeth," her father said, "the light. You can go. You dreaming? Or thinking about writing to Kathryn?"

She pushed on the accelerator. "No." She hesitated. "No, I wrote, but maybe only when I had already decided something. When it was too late for a smarter head to prevail." She took her hand from the steering wheel and bit at a cuticle she had been picking at with her thumbnail. The fingertip was wet and raw. She focused on the road.

"I didn't write often, except when I was traveling or in a new and exciting place. Like I was reporting home. I loved the travel. Especially the trains. You could see everything as you were riding, and you could walk around and stretch your legs. And usually get some coffee to drink. Or something to eat." She looked in the mirror and pulled out to pass another slow-moving truck.

"The food. I think I wrote Kathryn more about the food and wine and coffee than I did about anything else, like people or history or family. It was like I was at a huge banquet, and I wanted to eat it all, one thing at a time, and I never got full, and I never got fat. I must have burned it off wondering about it all. Or worrying along the way. But it was like a book. Fascinating scenes and people and stories. More than enough. I stayed hungry. For more."

Her father glanced sideways, at her. "So why didn't it work out, honey?" Caution in his voice. "Or did it? I've never been sure if you were happy."

She wondered at the question and didn't answer. The road was a treadmill unwinding under their tires, the remains of her dad's belongings in the car and trailer, and Elizabeth's green khaki bag. Traveling light.

"Baggage," she said.

Her father studied her face and smiled. "Well, we certainly have left a lot of things along the way. But you have a little home now, hitched behind us. I hope the camper is comfortable, until you figure what you're going to do. It's clean, and small enough to be sort of like a nest for you. Or a cocoon." His voice trailed off as he watched the road signs.

"Right, a cocoon," she said blankly, shaking her head to scatter the echo of her night's thoughts and dreams. "Or a coffin," she wondered out loud.

"What did you say?" her father asked, distracted. "Hey! Here's the sign for Route 1. Be sure we get on the southbound lanes." Elizabeth steered the car smoothly onto the busy highway, auto dealerships and malls and billboards, but fewer traffic lights than she remembered, the road more sheltered from stops, skirting the towns, it seemed. There were signs for Pennsylvania.

They made a brief rest stop, bought gas and paper cups of coffee, deciding to wait to eat until after they had visited the school and were on their way toward Virginia again. Elizabeth remembered the few yearly taxi rides from the school to the train station in Trenton, crossing the Delaware River. The bridge. There had been a big sign on the bridge. About Trenton. They always laughed and made up rhymes about it. Part of her seldom weekend trips home to the quiet house in Maplewood. It wouldn't be long to the turnoff toward the school. She imagined Kathryn in the backseat, listening. What would she say today? Elizabeth perked up at the thought.

"I wish Kathryn was with us, to see the station and the tracks and the trestle, the river. Or creek. Daddy, I remember the time we were down at the station, talking and reading in a book. Hemingway. Hadley had lost his manuscripts. His fiction, originals and carbon copies. We were talking about it and getting ready to go back up to the school for supper. All of a sudden, out of the blue, or out of the woods actually, a train came thundering down the tracks, not moving real fast or anything, but it was right there before we could even think what the sound was. Booming and creaking and clacking. And then it was gone. Just like that. An engine, or maybe two, and a couple of empty cars." She tried to picture the scene. "We never saw any passengers in the cars and didn't even see the engineer. I wondered if he would blow the horn. I waited for that, like I was scared." She looked over to her father. His head was slumped on his chest, and he breathed easily, shifting in his seat for comfort.

She smiled. "You glad we're finally driving on Route 1, Daddy?" she whispered. Her thoughts returned to the train booming out of the woods, and she spoke the words softly, to her sleeping father. Or to Kathryn, in the backseat. "I always thought it was maybe a ghost train, Daddy. No engineer. Gathering up people's dreams. Booming along. No engineer. No passengers. Just the train and the noise. Exciting us and scaring us to death. Our future, what we were going to do or be. Our dreams." She could see it. "Ghost train," she whispered again. She looked in the mirror to see if Kathryn was there.

The turnoff toward the school came sooner than she had expected, and everything seemed smaller, more crowded, dark trees and bushes. The highway was narrower than she remembered. She had driven from school to Langhorne and back many times. She remembered the driver's training her junior year, usually in evenings. Two or three miles from the school and then up a steep grade toward Route 1 and Langhorne, through an ancient tunnel under the main line railroad tracks between Trenton and Philadelphia. In Langhorne they would turn around and drive back to the school. An old Nash Rambler. The driver's ed teacher would encourage her, shouting, as they came from the school and neared the tunnel. "Give it the gas. Let's go. Don't slow down going up the hill."

She would step on the clutch pedal and push the shift on the steering column up to second gear, let out the clutch and press on the gas. The man would laugh as the car accelerated. She couldn't remember any other real instruction. She could see that the car did not have any special brakes or controls for the instructor.

Brave man, she thought. *Or a fool. Or something else in between. Something practical?* Elizabeth reached over and patted her father's arm.

She slowed the car and camper as they neared the school, looking for the entrance and a place where the trailer would not be in the way or a distraction. She wondered if anyone would mind their visit. Then again, she had attended the school. Graduated. An invisible alumna. She slowed to a stop in a small gravel parking area under towering oak trees. There were only a few other cars in the lot, middle of the day.

Perhaps a holiday. Or Easter vacation, she thought. *We'll be here for only a short time. And on our way again. We're just a footnote on the page.* She realized she didn't even know what day of the week it was.

"Come on, Daddy. We're here." She ruffled his arm and folded the map as he sat up and stretched.

He opened his door and swung his feet carefully to the gravel. "Are we there? Are we in Virginia already?" he asked, leaning forward and rocking, trying to gain enough momentum to stand, pulling on the sides of the open door.

Elizabeth went around the front of the car and helped him to his feet. "You OK, Daddy? You got a nice nap, and it will be lunchtime soon. No. It's not Virginia yet. We're at the school. Remember, we were going to visit the train station. That's all. We'll be on the road in just a little bit." She hooked her arm under his, and they walked along the service road behind the school's main building, toward the path that led to the station. The trees were silent, and the air was cold and still.

"This is where we used to walk, Daddy. Kathryn and me. Before supper, or on weekends. Kathryn seemed to know how to steer my thoughts, when I was sad or nervous. She was strong. And smart. She's a teacher now."

"You were a teacher," her father offered. "I was proud of you. But I knew you wanted to travel. See the world. You've had an exciting life, and some ups and downs." He stopped her and turned her toward himself. He looked at her, and then down. Elizabeth feared he would want to talk about Rita. Or Dan. She looked away, and he continued.

"I know I didn't make it any easier. Without your mother, life was pretty sad. I know. I felt it too. Lonely and too quiet. I didn't know how to fill in, and I knew you were unhappy. And afraid." He felt Elizabeth pull away and stopped. She was staring down the path, eyes wide open, her mouth straining to breathe in. He followed her gaze.

"The station. It's gone," she whispered, then louder, "it's gone. Our station and our bench. And our pond. It's all gone," as she shook her head. They walked, faster, toward a flat expanse of gravel. Rusty tracks, clearly visible in the weeds and underbrush. A few young saplings between dark railroad ties. "It's gone. Our pond. They drained it. Look at the pipes. The mud." Frank put his arm around his daughter's shoulder.

"Baby, it looks like the rail line has been out of service a long time. Years. Rust and weeds," he said. "How long has it been? You've been gone for more than twenty years, right? Trees beginning to grow between the rails." Elizabeth stood silently, looking down the rails, first in one direction, then the other, and back to the gravel and railroad ties. Weeds. Rust.

"Our station. Our special place." Whispers more than words. "This is where we made our plan. From here we could go anywhere. I was going to just take the train. Follow where the tracks might lead. Like Hemingway. Or poor Hadley." She stepped into the rail bed, between the two rusty steel threads. Adventure in weeds and decay. She gently pulled free from her father's arm.

"I'm going to walk down toward the creek, Daddy. Take a look at the trestle. If it's still there, and the creek." She began to walk away.

"I'll come with you, Elizabeth," he said, and started toward her.

Elizabeth called over her shoulder, and tripped on one of the heavy wooden ties. She caught herself, regained balance. "No. I'll be OK. I need to look. By myself. I'll only be a minute or two. It's only a couple hundred feet. I have to go look. Alone."

He began to protest, but she stopped him. "You wait here, Daddy. It's too rocky and rough. You'll fall. I'll be fine."

She walked on, not looking back, stepping carefully from one tie to the next, an awkward gait, each step too long or too short for the distance between the ties. She kept her eyes on the ground, focusing on her feet and the ties. The shock of the demolished station began to fade as she counted her steps toward the trestle, toward her teenage freedom and adventure. Toward Hemingway. And Hadley. Her pace became a quicker skipping jog, toward a new and exciting place down the tracks, just out of sight, the arch of young birch trees and undergrowth, an invitation to the unknown, the next chapter in her story. She stepped more quickly as she found the match between steps and ties, counting, years and miles, turning pages in the story. Fresh hope.

Eyes down and with no warning, Elizabeth careened headlong into gray chain-link fencing stretched across the tracks, a dim steel curtain, the trestle ahead and the black surface of the creek fifty feet below. Elizabeth's fingers cut into the wires, and she cried out in shock as her head and knees and chest hit the fence. She fell to the ground, an instant surprise that a train must have hit her. She lay on the tracks, the shock fading slowly, only the echo of her cry drifting in the archway of trees.

She heard her father's voice; he was coming to help. Elizabeth rolled onto her side and sat up slowly. She called to her father. "I'm OK, Daddy! I'm OK! Wait there! You'll fall. Wait there!"

She shook her head and looked around. A chain-link fence. Ten or twelve feet high. Wrapped around the trestle's concrete foundation and steel frame rising among tree branches. "Of course, stupid. Ran right into it." Her fingers stung from the collision, but it seemed as though she hadn't broken any bones, and she didn't see any deep cuts on her hands, just torn skin. The shock dissipated, and she looked through the steel wire weave, across the trestle, a matching barrier on the other side. For the curious. Or kids. The creek below, glistening dark water, liquid steel.

Stupid me! she thought. *All the years and stupid dreams. Rails disappearing around a bend in the woods. The dreams.* She laughed out loud. *Hemingway and Hadley. Lies.* She laughed again, through tears. *Or fiction? The lost manuscripts? Hemingway's memoir? Or just plain lies!* She laughed again and heard her father's call.

"Elizabeth! Are you OK? I'm coming to get you!"

"No, Daddy! I'm coming now! I promise! Stay there!" And she laughed again. "Damn railroads and mystery and adventure." She swallowed salty blood. "I promise. No more." She rolled to her knees and stood up, one shaky leg and then the other, pushing herself up with her hands. She took two steps and stopped, calling to her father.

"I'm coming, Daddy. I'm coming." She sat down again among weeds and gravel. She clasped her knees and pressed her head forward. An ache growing in the hollow of her being. A reminder of fertility. "No more." Silent canopy of trees, carpet of weeds. "No more." After several minutes she heard her father's hesitant footsteps in the gravel. He helped Elizabeth to her feet and then to the car. He tended to her hands and forehead with paper towels and first aid kit supplies from the camper. He offered to drive, but they agreed Elizabeth would still be safer to drive, even if she had broken an arm or a leg. They laughed about that all the way back to Route 1.

"Even both arms," he tried to joke. She pressed the accelerator to the floor under the hillside tunnel. That brought nostalgic and sad warmth to her heart, an echo, "Give it the gas." The remainder of the trip to Virginia was silent except for directions and turns and a stop for gas and coffee. And tampons. They drove south to Route 30 and turned west to Downingtown, then south on Route 11, through the Maryland and West Virginia panhandles and into Virginia. They arrived at the retirement settlement just before sunset. New one-story brick duplexes. A quiet cul-de-sac. Freshly planted trees, mulch and wire supports.

"Where will we park the camper, Daddy?" Elizabeth asked. "Maybe the street would be OK for a day or two."

"There's a grassy space behind my half of the duplex, he said. "The back of this unit faces a town street. When I came down to look, that's one thing I liked about this unit, on the edge of the village. Let's drive around to the back, see if there's a curb. I think it's just grass. No sidewalk."

"Are you sure? I don't see any trailers or campers parked anywhere. They might have a rule against that, Daddy. In a place like this."

"Drive around the other side, honey," her father insisted. They drove through a labyrinth of dead ends and circles and finally emerged onto the quiet town street that bordered his edge of the retirement village.

"Here it is," he said, pointing to the back of the darkened unit. "There's no curb. Just back it up toward the house. The left-hand side. That's mine."

"OK, Dad, but I bet you'll hear about it tomorrow."

"Right. That's tomorrow," he said. "Tonight we'll go out and get something to eat. You must be tired and hungry."

"No, not really. My head hurts a little bit, though."

"It looks like it might hurt. Nice bruise over your eye. A cut too. Like you've been in a fight."

She smiled. She was tired, and maneuvered the car, backing and angling the trailer onto the grass and toward the house. The car labored, and then one of the rear tires spun quickly, and she let off the gas. She got out and walked to the trailer. The small camper wheels had dug into the soft grass. She could see squares of sod, one or two pieces disturbed by the trailer's wheels. She got back into the car.

"Looks like the trailer might be stuck, Dad. It's fresh sod, new lawn. I'll give it one try, to pull it out, but if it doesn't move, we'll have to unhitch it where it is. At least it's off the street, but they won't like those ruts on the grass." She put the car in gear, and it inched forward, and then one of the car's rear wheels slipped again. She shifted gears and rocked the car and trailer once, and quit. "You'll have to unhitch it, Dad. We don't want to get the car stuck. Might already be."

Her father walked to the back of the car and unhooked the chains and electric cables, put a small piece of plywood from the camper under the jack and cranked the trailer off the car's ball hitch.

"OK, Elizabeth. Ease it out. Easy."

She started the car and put it in reverse first, rocked it slightly, shifted into drive and let it roll forward, then with some gas. The big tires rolled smoothly on the grass, and the car pulled away from the trailer, out onto the street.

Elizabeth parked the car and shut off the engine. She got out and went to where her father was inspecting the grass and the ruts.

"It'll be OK, but we'll probably catch hell for the grass," he said. "We'll need some help to move the trailer, though. It's not dark yet. Maybe we can see if there's a gas station, or someone with a truck. We'll be OK."

"Yes, Daddy. It'll be OK." Elizabeth wasn't sure how much bother it was going to be. Her head hurt, and her left knee too. She went back to the car and slumped in the front seat. She was running low on energy and patience. And hope.

"Running head down on train tracks. Stupid." She closed her eyes.

"Hello." A voice from across the street. A man passed the open car door, glancing in at Elizabeth, and then approached her father. "Got yourself stuck? I saw you all backing in, and I knew they had just laid sod the other day. And it rained yesterday. Didn't get my shoes on in time to come over and stop you."

"Well, probably not a smart move, not to walk on it first," her father said.

"If you want, I'll bring my four-wheel drive over and ease it out. This little trailer, I could even do it with my four-wheeler, bigger tires and not so heavy, less damage to the sod. I'll bring that over, if you like." He walked to the trailer hitch and then looked at the tires." If you don't have any place to park the camper, we can put it over on my gravel pad, right over there under the shade trees. Till you decide what you're gonna do. Can't leave it on the street, for sure. The town don't allow it."

Her father nodded in agreement. Elizabeth felt a gentle wave of relief flood through her legs and stomach and arms. The stranger had brushed aside every care from the evening. She and her dad could drive out, or walk even, get a sandwich and a cup of coffee. Or a beer, maybe. The man left her father to get his four-wheeler and then returned to the car. He looked in at Elizabeth.

"Hey. How are you doing? Got the trailer stuck, but you sure knew how to get the car out OK. I saw that. No spinning wheels and mud." The man grinned. "That would have been something."

"Yes. I guess we got out easy. Thanks for offering to help. You've been very kind. I was about worn out."

"Well, you look like you've been beat up too. What happened to you? A fight?" And he smiled. He was younger than Elizabeth, maybe his mid-twenties. Jeans and T-shirt.

"An accident. I ran into a fence," she said. "Stupid me."

"No. It's just the way things happens. You moving in over there? You seem a little young for the village. I think you have to be fifty-five or sixty to move in there."

"I'm just riding with my dad, getting him settled. He gave me the camper, and I'm going to stick around until I know he's OK. Sleep on his sofa if I have to. Or I was going to find a campground nearby, be close while he gets settled. My dad is getting pretty forgetful."

"Well, I'll pull the camper off the lawn and put it over there, under the trees. It's a gravel pad for a fishing boat I used to have." He turned to go, and then came back. "My name's Donner. Glad to meet you. You'll feel better when you get your dad settled." His smile was serious. "Hey. While you're making up your mind what you're gonna do with the camper, I'll attach the electric and the drinking water hose. No septic, but it'll be all right over there for now. And you'll be close, either way, on your dad's sofa or over there. No one to bother you, just my three-year-old. Michelle." He beamed. "She's my sidekick."

Elizabeth drew a deep breath, a wave of relief and sudden weariness, as he walked away. She called out, "Donner. I'm Elizabeth. Thanks."

He was gone.

Chapter 23

ELIZABETH STRUGGLE TO LOOSEN THE KNOT (2015)

The conductor entered the car, reminding passengers that Sacramento was the next stop. Elizabeth and Newcomb sat in silence. Elizabeth had reached the end of her manuscript pages and notes.

"So we've come full circle," Newcomb said. "You were friends with Kathryn fifty years ago. You made plans to share and write your stories. You lived in Europe, lost your child, and then traveled around the world to come back and spend twenty-five years in Virginia." He paused. "And then you leave home and family to visit with Kathryn in California. Because something is missing or wrong in Virginia. You will replace Virginia knots with California knots. And you are writing about lots of things along the way." He sat in silence. "And the turning point in your story is running into a fence on abandoned railway tracks in Pennsylvania."

The simple summary shocked Elizabeth. She laughed and caught herself. "Well, I guess it felt like more than that. At least while I was writing it." She thought about her response. "And when I was living it too. Each day was pretty complex. And so many of the days along the way were turning points. Or could have been. And could have sent me off in any direction. A life."

"Yes," Newcomb said. "You will be searching for the main conflict. The knot your life has struggled to loosen." He smiled at Elizabeth. "The stories are very good. Some pieces are funny, and some of your ideas for writing about Denmark and the trip to Thailand will make for an excellent memoir."

"Well, maybe." Elizabeth started to shuffle her pages into a neater pile. "I think I could write a truthful memoir. But I'm not sure it would sound like anything more than a list. Days and places turning into years. And so often when I was writing, I felt like trailing off in a different direction. Fiction or fancy. Or fantasy. And I think I did, here and there. I don't know. I've sort of lost track, but I don't think it really matters. I'll have some time to figure that out. I hope. Maybe that was why I decided to see Kathryn." She shivered. "Oh boy. Kathryn."

"You look worried about that," Newcomb said.

"Yes. Well, I'm going to go to the ladies room real quick." She laughed. "We're on time, six o'clock, but only off by twelve hours. Late. The sun will be coming up soon. I'm actually glad we're arriving early morning rather than in the dark. I'm not sure where I'm going or how I'm going to get there." Newcomb stepped into the aisle and let Elizabeth out.

"I'll be right back," she said, and walked forward, toward the lavatory. Newcomb watched her go. He lifted his attaché to his lap, opened it, and took out a trade magazine. And two more.

Chapter 24

BILLY HEART'S DESIRE. TURNING POINT. HADLEY'S GHOST (2015)

"So what you going to do next year? Your mom back at work?" Hollister asked, unwrapping a piece of gum. He offered a piece to Billy, who shook his head and nodded to Hollister to drop the wrapper in the small litter bag hanging from the taxi's dashboard. Hollister knew if their paths crossed on night shifts, it would be at the Sacramento train station cabstand. Billy had learned it was the quietest place in town at night. Usually no trains, plenty of time to study for classes, few interruptions. Hollister's question.

"No. Mom's still off work. Her back is still hurting. She'll be out a while longer." Billy put his textbook on the seat and fished for his calculator in the door's side pocket. "Not sure about next year. This spring I have only two classes left to take, but I can get a head start, a course or two that will transfer. Cheaper that way, in the long run. What about you?"

His friend was shaking his head. Hollister's loud gum chewing irritated Billy. Hollister answered between chewing and swallowing.

"I don't know yet. I'll keep driving cab. It's an easy way to get along. A little money and time to study. We've knocked 'em dead, haven't we? Another couple years and we're college grads. I'm going to City in the fall, I think. Social work or administration of justice. Or both. I can drive a cab, either here or over there, take day classes or online." Hollister looked toward the train station. "Almost time to start real life."

"Hollister, this is real life. Study and work, straight and narrow," Billy said. "Hey, some people coming out of the station. Must have been a really late one. You better get up in your cab. You're first out."

"See you, man." Hollister opened the door and walked briskly between the two taxis, waving back at Billy. He got in his car and started the engine as a man and woman came through the glass doors onto the sidewalk. The man carried a slim attaché and a suitcase. Billy could see he was a businessman of some sort, expensive dark overcoat. The woman was much more informal and looked younger than the man.

The man opened the door to Hollister's cab, spoke briefly to Hollister, and then put his bags in the backseat, motioning to Hollister to wait. Hollister must have said something. Billy could see the man laughing in response. The man held a finger up for Hollister to wait, and turned to the woman.

The couple spoke briefly, holding both hands, and then hugged. Billy could see the embrace lasted longer than the woman wanted. She patted the man's arms and stepped back. He reached into his pocket and handed her a card, which she took and put in her jeans pocket. She nodded and smiled. Polite. Billy smiled, easy to see she didn't really want the man's business card.

Friends, but not friends. Met on the train, maybe? Billy thought. The man got into Hollister's cab and pulled the door shut. Billy opened his door, got out and spoke to the woman over the hood of the cab.

"Ma'am? You need a cab?"

The woman turned toward Billy's voice, distracted, as Hollister's cab pulled away from the curb. She clutched a worn green khaki shoulder tote, a crumpled airline tag twisting on a strap. The bag was the first thing that had caught his attention, in contrast to the man's coat and suitcase and attaché. The khaki bag didn't match her style, or her jeans and light-tan rugby sweatshirt. The woman was athletic, or at least she kept herself in shape, for her age. Her silver-blond hair was pulled back in a ponytail.

Pretty, for an older lady, he thought. As he looked more closely, he also saw worry, her mouth tense. Tired eyes. Or maybe she had been asleep on the train when it pulled in late. He always liked a puzzle. The train's late arrival was unexpected, another major Amtrak delay. This one was almost twelve hours late, if it was the regular evening arrival from the day before. The woman had to be a stranger, maybe a little down on her luck, with just the one small khaki bag. And jeans. No, she was trim, and carried herself with grace. And pride.

"Lady! Need a cab? You OK?"

She ignored him, looking away quickly, up and down the early-morning street. He wondered if he had frightened her, and called out more gently. "Ma'am. You need any help? Or directions?"

The woman approached the taxi, still looking about. "No. Well, I don't know. Maybe yes. How far would it be to take me to Carmer? I think it's north from here."

"Oh," he said. Relieved. He was off the hook. "That's quite a ways, ma'am. More than forty miles. Almost fifty, depending on where in the county you're going. It's spread out. Mostly farming. I can't go that far, and I'll be off my shift at six. Sorry, ma'am."

"How about a bus? I'm going to Carmer Hill. Is there a bus?" she asked.

The mention of Carmer Hill took Billy by surprise. "Only city buses here. They'll start running regular, but later on. Maybe Trailways, other side of town. I could give you a lift, but I don't know if any Trailways would be going to Carmer. Probably not too many people heading that way. For sure, no bus to Carmer Hill."

"All right. And thanks," she said, turning back to the station door.

"OK. You be careful. Stick around the station until you decide what you're going to do," he warned. He watched her pull the door open and go into the station, uncertain steps. She was probably older than he had thought at first.

Still a pretty lady, though, and polite, he wondered. Someone off a train, a small green canvas bag. Lost. Going to Carmer Hill, of all places. He took a deep breath and straightened up the papers on the seat next to him. Yes, he knew Carmer County. And Carmer County High School too. He had lived in the county for years, from a young kid almost through high school. He remembered how glad he had been when his mom told him they were moving, when she got a job in Sacramento. Carmer County was truck farms and unfriendly irrigation ditching crews, crop spraying, seasonal work. Migrants and some drifters. A couple hardware and grocery and liquor stores. And the dry wind and hot summers. Cold in the winter. Even so, Billy never forgot that Carmer County had also saved his life. In the end. Gave him his chance. No, the chances were always there. And it wasn't Carmer County, really. It was Carmer Hill, the garden. The lady with the soft eyes.

My wake-up call. And now I'm getting close. He looked at the papers and books on the front passenger seat. Final semester coming up at the community college. *Last two classes.* He smiled. *I'm still just at chapter two, maybe three, in my book.* He repeated it. *Chapter two. Maybe three.* The lady's magic words reminded him often, just like she had said them. His book. Her stern demand, and his promise. She had been right.

Billy liked the train station cabstand. It was the quietest place in town at night, no trains scheduled to arrive or leave during his shift. Unless they were running real late. If he got a radio call, he answered quickly. He was near enough to some of the projects and bars, but otherwise he had the night to himself, unless Hollister was on the same shift. *Great place to study too.* He nodded. *Getting paid to get ahead.*

And the end in sight, he thought. Then maybe to Berkeley, or City College across the bay, San Francisco. He knew it wouldn't matter where he went. For his plan, anywhere would do, for the next chapter in his book. *Chapter three. Maybe four*, and he laughed aloud.

The Billy Book. He answered the kind lady with the soft eyes often, in the silence of his cab, or in his room at night. Her demanding question, and the only answer she would ever accept. Their words echoed often.

Will you do it, Billy? What do you say? You want to try it?

Yes, Miss Kathryn. Yes. I will. She had been right. It had always been his choice, so easy, once started. He had written the pages. Day by day, even when people hadn't believed he could follow through. It was hard, back when he was still scared, intimidated by his more fortunate or brutal classmates in school. But as he showed determination, and as he began to catch on to the simple tasks, they began to step out of his way. He quickly found that work and study were easy, that he was moving faster than the other students in school. It was the same now too, in community college, or at the small jobs he took to make ends meet. Students and lazy coworkers were all just shuffling along and lounging around, thinking their good fortune was automatic. And permanent.

Weak, and stupid, he thought, surveying their confidence. Billy now saw the weakness in his mom too. A different sort of weakness. Always begging and politely giving in. Her apologies, especially when she was wronged or ignored or underpaid or laid off. He knew his own good fortune was his own responsibility. Even more, he knew his mother's survival depended on his success. He wouldn't let her down. His mom had tried but just didn't know how to move ahead.

He had finished his reading. The book was propped on the steering wheel, open to the chapter questions. He skipped through the paragraphs, knowing how to skim for main points or answers, how to arrive at a correct conclusion for each case study or statistical problem. Anticipation of likelihood. Trends. For him it was all good. The scales were tipping in his favor, for the least amount of extra effort. It wasn't even work, really. Extra hours, extra pay, extra notice, just for being on time and up to date and clued in. He would even be his own boss one day. Or maybe a teacher. Or write. But he knew none of it had to do with luck. It was assured, as long as he stayed on the easy smart track. On time, on target, in harmony with the storyline. The Billy Book. Didn't take much to tip the scales toward success. Every day. His promise.

Yes, Miss Kathryn. I will. You got that right! He savored the thought of the gift he would bring her one day. His diploma. Or maybe a real book, his book. He had come to love stories, especially about accomplishment, overcoming the odds. Sailors and explorers. Journalists. Writers.

"Ah, to tell her again! Yes. I did. I did it!" The moment he spoke out loud, he saw the lady with the khaki bag again, standing inside the station's glass doorways. Surveying her foreign territory, options slipping away. He knew the look. He had felt it. Years ago, but he had felt it.

That lady has no plan, the way she's looking up and down the street. No plan. Probably no cab fare either. She doesn't know which way to turn. Or what to do.

Billy looked back at his book and tried to cipher the child study group stats. The equation. The mean and median, averages and likelihood of where any one child would fall on a scale of possibility. Like himself in the third or fourth grade. He remembered. He could always do the arithmetic but couldn't read worth a damn. And back then no one ever spoke more than a single word or two to him, and if it was two, something like "hey, you!" or "sit down!"

He looked up, and the woman was gone. He went back to the book, but his mind was distracted by the woman's dilemma, and his eye caught a motion. She came through the doors again.

She probably went in to pee, he thought. *Or ask for directions.* The woman came all the way onto the sidewalk, looked each way, and turned toward the projects. Billy knew she was lost, the wrong direction for anyone to walk. Too many early-morning shadows, truly the wrong way. He lowered the passenger-side window and called out from the cab. "Lady, you need a lift to the bus station? Trailways?"

She stopped and turned, and walked to the cab. She looked in the window. "No, I just thought I would walk." Her mouth was tight. Frightened.

He stepped out of the car. "Hey, this is no place for a walk this time of day. And that's the wrong direction, for sure." He took a chance. "Ma'am, if you don't mind my asking, what takes you to Carmer County? If it's OK I ask. I used to live there."

She drew in a deep breath and stepped closer to the car. "I'm visiting a friend. It's been years. A dear friend. The one person who made all the difference in my life. A long time ago. I haven't kept in touch, and she made all the difference."

Billy stared at the woman. He was sure she was going to cry. And her words echoed in his mind. *All the difference.* No, she was repeating it. "Carmer Hill."

"She made all the difference, when I was struggling. She lives in Carmer Hill. She teaches English. Or used to."

"What?" He felt the hair on his arm stiffen, now an icy shadow of certainty. The woman hesitated and continued her explanation. No need now. Billy knew where it would lead.

"A friend. From high school. My best friend. She made all the difference. She was the only one who understood. She always knew what I needed to do. I need to see her."

Billy cut her off. "Miss Kathryn," he said.

The woman stared at him. "What?" she said, a whisper, tears glistening in her eyes.

Billy nodded. "Miss Kathryn. And I'm not surprised," he said.

"Kathryn? My Kathryn? How would you know her?"

"She made all the difference is how. It's all connected, lady. All the dots. The dots make the picture. The moments. Past, present, and future. And nothing's by chance." He paused and smiled. "OK, then, if you don't believe me. How about chapters in your book? You owe her for any chapters? Ever hear about them?" The lady stared. Disbelief. She began sobbing. Silent. Quick shallow breaths.

Like a baby, Billy thought as he stepped closer to the woman. He placed his arm around her shoulder and opened the cab's rear passenger-side door. She clutched her khaki bag and sat in the backseat. He closed the door and walked around to the front. He got behind the steering wheel and looked in the mirror. The lady held her bag with clenched fingers, the green khaki covering her face.

"I'll give you a lift to Carmer Hill. I'm Billy. Miss Kathryn called me by my real name. William. I was lost in a dead-end chapter, end of a terrible book. Ninth grade. Come on. I'll tell you about it on the way." He watched her in the mirror. The woman lowered her bag and sank back in the car's seat. She closed her eyes and shook her head, as if to erase thoughts.

"Dear God, this day has been so crazy," she said. "It's been so, I don't know what. Unexpected. I should have known. Kathryn."

"Well, the day has just started," Billy offered.

"No, the last few days have been an eternity. And the nights." The woman cradled herself, rocking, and added as an afterthought, "Elizabeth. My name is Elizabeth. Yes. My book has been a mess." She took in a breath. "At least, well, at least until I started writing it."

"Elizabeth. Let me call the dispatcher. And I better call my ma. Tell her I'll be late. She'll worry if I'm late. I don't have class til this evening." He stabbed numbers into his cell phone and started the car. "Let's go, Elizabeth. I haven't seen Miss Kathryn in ages."

Billy looked over his shoulder and made a U-turn onto the nearly deserted early-morning street. He left a message on his mother's phone and then spoke briefly with a dispatcher on the radio. He reported he had called home and his mother had not answered. He needed to go off-duty for an hour or two. He would call in if something critical had come up.

"Never lie, Miss Kathryn always told us, me and Hollister," Billy said to Elizabeth over his shoulder. "So. Tell me your story. In three good sentences." He laughed. "Your story, at least up to now. Three sentences."

Elizabeth surprised herself with a quick answer to the impossible question, about her love of train travel, living in Europe, her writing, and how the trip from Virginia had been a gift she had been waiting to give herself.

"To keep from dying." Surprising herself, she went on. "Here it is, in three pieces, sort of. Twenty-five years ago, 1986, I was driving through Virginia in an old Buick and a camper, and married a guy who was solid and handy. The rest of the story, well, I've been writing it, but the plot is still unclear. It's either a novel or a poem, or something." She hitched herself up in the seat. "How about you? You're lots younger than me, so what's your story? In one good sentence? Just one."

He laughed. "OK, let's see," he said, hesitating. "I was scared no one would love me, and a stern lady with gentle eyes showed me I had to start with myself."

Elizabeth tapped Billy on the shoulder and asked him if she could sit in the front, could he please stop by the side of the road. They were on a desolate stretch of fields and irrigation ditches and the dawning day. He looked in the mirror and scanned the roadside with a fleeting shadow of doubt and fear. He steered the cab onto loose gravel. Elizabeth climbed out of the backseat and opened the front passenger door. She moved Billy's textbooks carefully toward the center, placing them even more carefully on top of his notebook and papers, and slid into the front seat of the car.

"I wanted to be closer, instead of yelling from the backseat. Or maybe I'm getting hard of hearing," and she laughed. The sound of her laughter seemed to startle her, and it echoed in the car. "An uncommon sound," she said, as if to no one. "Unfamiliar."

Billy looked at her. "You haven't been laughing lately?"

"Not the last twenty-five years is all," and she laughed again. The echoes in the cab seemed to tear at her skin, the corners of her mouth and eyes. "Maybe thirty years in all, but no more than that." She paused. "Well, maybe," and Elizabeth laughed again.

Billy glanced to his right as the day's first sunlight laced the hood and windows, sudden splashes through a stand of walnut trees. She was gleaming, young and fresh and anxious, leaning forward, hitching herself up, then looking toward him.

"Thank you so much. All of a sudden I think I'm ready to meet Kathryn. I've been so afraid. It's been more than fifty years, and I have written her only a handful of times, mostly when I was in college and getting ready to teach. Then I went to Europe, and I wrote her a few times while I was there. I wrote her a few weeks ago. Told her I was coming. I've been terrified what she would say to me, but I had to come see her before, well, before it was too late."

"Are you ill or something?" he asked.

"No, not like that, maybe just that I felt life was slipping away, and I had to finish what I was writing. I mean, writing my story was one thing, like what Kathryn meant. But I started writing it. Like, for real. Or like something. I can't explain it. Words on paper."

Billy glanced at her. She was scanning the road, anxious. "Well, can I ask you a question, then? Sort of a writer's question? Or maybe about your life, Elizabeth. About your writing or your life, I guess. Either way."

She turned toward him. "Sure. What?"

"So then, where is the turning point in your story?" He hesitated, still thinking. "I mean, if we're trying to write stories, you and me, where is that perfect point that made all the difference, or where you changed course, or where things got easy, or on track?"

Elizabeth laughed again, and Billy went on. "For me, I used to think it was when I met Miss Kathryn, but now I'm sure there are more important moments. What was it for you? Or where? I mean, if you know."

She answered without hesitation. "Oh, I know, and as I look back on what I've written, there are more than one. But one of the big ones, when I was an adult, wasn't good. It was where I really gave up. Where all the air seemed to seep out of my soul, and suddenly I was empty, just wanted to lie down and die." She stopped.

Billy glanced away from the road for a moment. He could not tell if her face reflected sorrow or just the years. She was suddenly older, and tired.

"It was some railroad tracks. Abandoned railroad tracks, weeds and rust, and that was the first shock. It was a place where Kathryn and I had visited often, when we were high-school kids, teens. A boarding school in Pennsylvania. I loved the tracks and the little train station at the edge of the woods, and the creek, and a trestle high over the water. The train whistled through once each morning and again in the afternoon. A freight train every now and then, I guess." She waited for a moment, gathering her thoughts.

"So. Almost thirty years ago my dad and I stopped there, on our way from New Jersey to Virginia, when he was moving into an old folks' home. I wanted to visit our special place, mine and Kathryn's, and it wasn't too far out of our way, so Dad said it was fine with him. I think I had hoped the tracks might somehow spark me, my next adventure, you know, just out of sight, the old tracks curving around the bend in the woods, green light filtering through the trees. But the station had been torn down, so I started walking away from Dad, down the tracks. I was upset the station was gone, where we used to sit and talk and read. But even so, walking down the tracks was fun. No, it was actually pure joy. It was my adventure all over again. My future. Something good waiting, just out of sight.

"I was keeping my eyes on the railroad ties and the weeds, taking care not to trip and fall, you know, railroad ties are always too far apart, or too close, to just walk. And I was being so careful, counting the steps, head down, and getting more and more excited about seeing the trestle and the creek and my future, and all of a sudden, no warning, bang, I ran smack into a chain-link fence across the tracks. Twelve feet high, at least, and the trestle was there, and the creek down below, and my fingers cut into the wires, and I cried out, mostly shock, I think. My foot and my hands and my chest and my nose and forehead all hit the fence at the same time, and I wasn't hurt or anything, but I shouted out real loud. Not frightened, just the shock."

She paused and breathed in. Billy turned and saw her wide eyes, staring, alarm. Instinctively he pushed his foot on the brake, jarring them both forward in their seats. He looked quickly back at the road. Nothing. He shook his head, wondering what she had seen in her mind's eye.

"Sorry. Your face told me we were going to hit something, maybe a deer." He took in a breath of relief. "So. The tracks. You weren't hurt?"

She sighed and shook her head. "No. My dad called out, and I could hear him coming toward me, and I yelled back that I was OK, for him not to trip and fall. But, you know, I wasn't OK. So much had gone on, and my trip home from Europe had been confused and disappointing." She hesitated and swallowed. "I lived in Denmark for years. I lost my way and my child."

She was quiet for a moment, and then, "Well, there I was in the weeds and the rusty rails and the fence. And all at once, I was dead tired and disgusted with the mess I had made, leaving dreams behind, for nothing, for no reason, really." She closed her eyes. "Almost thirty years. Almost a lifetime. The end of adventures. The end of my story. My story."

Billy let the car coast and looked at Elizabeth. A question spoke clearly in his chest, silent words without conscious thought, the tires' muffled decelerating drone, hearts' desires for adventures and turning points. And love. He looked in the rearview mirror and then back to the highway ahead. Carmer Hill. The turnoff for Kathryn's. He flicked the turn-signal lever. His thoughts tumbled, an excited conversation in his heart. He glanced at Elizabeth.

She was staring at him, wide-eyed. "What did you just say?" Her incredulous whisper.

He stared at her, a glint of sunlight in her ponytail as she turned toward him. The unspoken words still echoed in his mind. "What? Nothing. I was thinking about what you said. Your turning point. The end of your story." He made a left turn onto a narrow stretch of country highway, peach trees and fencerows. "Here we are, only a minute or two."

Elizabeth placed two fingers on his arm. He turned quickly. "William. If you know where Kathryn's house is, can we stop and walk the last bit?"

"Yes. Let's do that," and he slowed, pulling to the side of the road, crackling gravel under the tires. They stopped and sat. "Two houses, on the left. The low porch and wooden fence. The garden," his words drifting toward a whisper and hush. Silence. He wondered how quietly Elizabeth wanted to proceed. It occurred to him she might well ask him to turn around and drive her away. The folds of silence were broken by a car passing on the road, slowing for a turn at a triangular intersection leading away from the hill. The sun rising. Clear blue sky promised a warm day. Elizabeth looked at Billy.

He smiled. "You want me to walk with you, Elizabeth? It's right here." He caught his breath. "Miss Kathryn is in the garden. See her?"

"Yes. There she is. An ordinary day in her garden. And here I am, wondering if I can do this fearful reunion." She shook her head, opened the passenger door, and swung her feet to the pavement. "Reminds me of my father, two feet flat on the ground, solid. He was always afraid of losing his balance. Falling." She stood and pulled her khaki bag to her shoulder. "Come on, William. Will you hold my hand? At least until we get up to the fence. Can you?"

He stepped around the front of the car, and she held out her hand to him. They walked to the concrete slab sidewalk. Weeds and stubble and cracks. Wildflowers pushing between gaps in the wooden fence, the paint, once white, blistered and comfortable. Her hand in his, suddenly a touch as light as a sparrow. A walk in the country, fresh air blowing from the north and west. Kathryn's house and garden, a small rise in the terrain.

"Carmer Hill," Billy said, following Elizabeth's eyes. The fence gate was propped open, a worn brick in the grass leaning against the slats. They stepped through the opening and hesitated at the edge of the garden. Kathryn was kneeling beside a large gray cat lying on its side in the dust, a row of tomato plants and stakes and props. Kathryn stroked the cat's stomach, and Billy could hear soft scolding words. Suddenly the cat's attention flashed toward Billy and Elizabeth, and the animal quickly rolled to a crouch. Kathryn's eyes followed the cat's alarm. A wondering moment, and then a smile spread across her tanned face. Her fingers reached up to her long, dark braid, strands of silver. She strained to straighten up, then walked toward them.

Billy felt Elizabeth's hand clench. He glanced at her. Her eyes were wide, looking toward Kathryn and then away, toward the western sky. She turned to face Billy, clutching his arm tightly. He thought she might turn and run.

"William. I was wrong. About the turning point. The main one wasn't when I hit the chain-link fence. At the old train station. You know, at the school. It was something else."

Kathryn interrupted Elizabeth, a tap on her shoulder. "Hey, you!" Kathryn grinned. "Elizabeth? And William? What in the world?" Kathryn spread her arms around Billy and Elizabeth, and gathered them in an embrace. "It took you fifty years to get here, Elizabeth, and then my own William Starr Johnson shows up at the same time?" She leaned back and surveyed them. She studied Elizabeth's face, and her grin widened. "And I should have known you would be worried about something, Elizabeth. I would recognize that look anywhere. It turns back the clock."

"No, not worried, really." Elizabeth hesitated. "We were just talking about stories and turning points. Something just hit me. Out of the blue."

"Like I said, it turns back the clock. Something you're reading?" Kathryn asked. "Come on in. My two favorite people in the world. Let's have a cup of tea, and you can tell me. Or do we want coffee?" Kathryn took Elizabeth by the arm and turned toward the house. "Come on in and tell me about turning points, Elizabeth! And William! Imagine my good fortune!"

Billy followed the two women, one low step up onto the wooden porch. Same squeaks in the boards he remembered. Summer evenings pulling weeds or hoeing in the garden. He looked back at the garden shed, pleased to see the tin chimney on the shed's roof was still there. His hideout and home away from home. "Worker's quarters," he whispered. "Saved my life. Wonder if the table and cot are still in there."

They went into the dark and low-ceilinged living room and through to the open kitchen at the back of the house. Kathryn motioned them to chairs at the round table that separated the kitchen area from the living room. She clattered cups onto the table and returned to the sink. She held a tea kettle under the sink's faucet, filled it, and placed it on the stove.

"We having tea or coffee, William? I bet you were working last night."

He laughed. "Not working, just studying in the taxi. Quietest place in town. Then this Elizabeth lady turned up and needed some questions answered, so I told her I knew someone who could answer any question. About anything. And here we are! Simple as that."

"What a coincidence," Elizabeth offered.

Kathryn pulled a tan and black foil bag from the shelf. The kettle began to creak and grumble on the stove. "Well, it's coffee, then." She spooned coarse ground coffee into a cloth filter ring and placed it on top of a blue-enameled tin coffee pot. Billy remembered the coffee-brewing ritual so well. Kathryn poured the boiling water into the filter. The coffee brewed and dripped into the pot as Elizabeth shared about the late train and how she and Billy discovered they both knew Kathryn. Billy told Kathryn his friend Hollister had been at the cabstand, and he too was finishing up at community college, making plans to transfer.

"Yeah, Hollister is maybe going to Berkeley. Criminal justice, like his poor old dad. Or social work. Or both. Hollister hasn't changed."

"What about you, William?" Kathryn asked as she poured the last of the boiling water into the coffee filter. "Are you still writing every day?"

"Yeah. Still poking words onto paper. We'll see. Or maybe I'll teach. I don't know."

"That's what we were talking about. On the way here," Elizabeth added. "About writing stories, well, or living them. And about the turning points, where everything changes, or begins to change."

Kathryn smiled. "And something occurred to you as you stood in my garden? Something about your story?" She beamed warmly and leaned forward.

"Well, yes, actually. Something really insignificant. Small. But I've never forgotten it, even though I've never thought about it being a turning point. Not until, well, standing in your garden. It was just a few insensitive words. About slow death." Elizabeth's eyes searched Billy's face, as if for help. "It was something my husband, Donner, said. At the dinner table. Ten, maybe fifteen years ago."

"Tell us," Kathryn said.

Elizabeth sighed. "Everything was set. Donner came in and sat down, surprised by the wine glasses. His daughter, Michelle, was excited. Her Pepsi was in a wine glass too. I told her that a teen in Paris would get to taste the wine, but we'd wait for that." Elizabeth smiled at the thought. "So I held up my glass and clinked Michelle's. And Donner's. The plates were beautiful. Steak, sautéed mushrooms, green beans. Salad. French bread, and Danish butter I found in town." She looked at Billy.

"Go on. What happened?"

"I passed Donner the sauce, extra Béarnaise for him. I had portioned the sauce onto each steak too. Proper presentation. Everything in place. I had thought and planned about it for a week. And cooked all afternoon. I lifted my glass and looked at them. Donner and Michelle. I was proud, and invited them to eat.

"Bon appétit?" Billy asked.

"My, my, William." She smiled. "Yes. I held up my glass and waited. But Donner was scraping at the sauce on his steak." She shrugged. "He looked up at me. Asked about the yellow sauce. The dark-green flecks."

"That's the turning point?" Billy asked.

"No, no." Elizabeth smiled. "That was just the sauce. I told him it was Béarnaise, like we served in Tivoli. So he tasted some on the tip of his fork and said it reminded him of something he had tasted before. Like licorice. And why licorice on steaks? And of course his Michelle went crazy about the yellow licorice sauce and that she didn't like it. And where were the mashed potatoes anyway? She just sat there, grumpy and disappointed."

Billy smiled at the thought.

"Yes. I should have known. But that's not it. Donner told her to scrape off the sauce and go get the ketchup. So she went to the kitchen. She came back with the ketchup bottle, and Donner had cut up her steak, but she could still see some of the yellow licorice sauce. So she took her plate out to the kitchen and scraped it all into the trash can. I'll never forget the clang of the lid. I looked at Donner and told him maybe I had expected too much. Just trying something new. For us all. For me."

"What happened?" Billy asked.

"Donner thanked me for the meal. I saw the ketchup on his plate, and I really didn't care. I said I would find other things to serve, things they would like. I said I had plenty of time to work on it. Plenty of time. I scooped my spoon through the Béarnaise on my plate, and tasted it. Slow, like a golden moment in time. A slow kiss. Or a touch that lasts and lasts. And lasts. Never forgotten. Then Donner said if I was bored, maybe I could get my aide job back. At the school. If I was bored. That night in my room I wrote down those words. But I wasn't bored. It was something else. And I began to write about it."

Elizabeth pushed her chair from the table and went to the open living room area. She retrieved her khaki bag from the sofa and returned to the table. "I brought what I've been working on. My notes, and the six or seven completed chapters." She stopped and looked at Kathryn and Billy.

He nodded. *Hesitant to share something*, he thought. *She's afraid. But not holding back.*

Elizabeth went on. "I wrote two sets of most of it. One is a little more factual than the other. Some different angles. Fact and fiction? But both are true." She stopped and thought. "Yes. They are both true. And it's my story. It's all here, almost done. Ten years of writing. Or more. But much easier than the seventy years living it." She laughed, and Billy stared at her. "I worked on it coming out here. On the train. I had three days alone. Well, sort of alone."

"Where's your suitcase? Your clothes and things?" Kathryn asked.

"This is it. I've got a couple of changes of clothes here." The coffee dripped in the pot as Elizabeth unbuckled the two olive canvas straps with shy fingers. She opened her bag and prodded the contents. She placed a small and worn black plush dog on the table and smiled. She lifted folds of cloth and withdrew a thick manila folder. Several industrial trade magazines slid from the folder onto the table.

Billy saw a puzzle darken Elizabeth's face. She took a paperback book from the bag, leaned back in her chair, and held the book on her lap, both hands. Tight grasp. Elizabeth looked up. Billy followed her glance toward the ceiling, then back to her face. She was counting to herself, nodding as the coffee dripped through the filter into the blue enamel pot. The drops slowed. And stopped. He wondered if she was adding silent numbers. Or trying to remember something. His heart paused for a moment as he shared her wonder. Her fear. Billy knew what she would say.

Oh my dear God, he prayed as Elizabeth whispered.

"It's gone." She swallowed and choked on the words. "All of it. It's gone."

Chapter 25

BILLY TRINITY FLOWER (2016)

Søren opened the door to the workshop, flipped on bright lights, and took several steps down from the house's entryway.

"This was the barn. The stalls are through that door behind the truck," he said. "The old Hanomag. It's old but runs good. If you are lucky, you will meet Ejs, the man who keeps our car and old truck running. Here is my woodworking bench and some tools. And there is our loom and this year's coat I have finished. If it is getting cold, I light the woodstove. This is where I spend my lonely weeks crying for my beautiful wife, who is always flying away."

Billy saw rows of small wooden objects on a shelf, and a striped gray and tan and cream wool jacket, its wooden hanger on a stout peg in a low beam along the wall.

"This year's coat?"

"Ya. I am raising the sheep, and gathering their wool, carding it and making the yarn, and coloring it and weaving the fabric. And then I sew the coat. By hand. I make two for a person who wants one, and they can choose between the two coats. The one he or she doesn't want, I sell in a shop in København. A shop where I sell my wooden pieces. Perhaps Bodil told you about them."

"No. And I am surprised. She told me you were a man of few words. It sounds as though you do OK with words."

Søren laughed. "Ya. She might say such a thing about me. We have known each other for a long time, and I am usually without words when I am with her." He laughed again. "Maybe one day she will not be flying away from me every second week. So, there is the coat our friend Krisser did not choose. Let me show you some other things, small figures and a little carving that is very popular with people at the shop, and I don't know why." He led Billy to the workbench. An assortment of knives and wood sculpting tools lined a low shelf at the back of the bench, gouges and files and small hand planes. A barrel beside the bench contained tree branches and roots and pieces of rough hardwood lumber.

"I am doing some carving of birds and chickens and animals like you see here on the shelf above the tools." He waved a hand at the small wooden figures. "But here is what I am making most of the time." He picked up a small piece of wood. Dark and bright shades mixed, smooth and flowing grain. "I am trying to find pieces of fallen trees in the woods, which make this figure possible. Three legs from where branches join, and then I carve leaves or flower or a bud on the other side. But the best part is finishing this. And then what happens to a few of them, part of their destiny."

"Sanding and varnish?" Billy asked. "Destiny?"

"Varnish? Oh my, no," Søren said. "Yes, some shaving, and almost no sanding. It is all in the final hand rubbing. And the special mix of things I work into the grain. I even rub in fine sawdust, which fills the grain and any small cracks. This is also adding streaks of color."

"And soap and salt?" Billy asked. Søren stared at him. "You rub these beautiful sculptures with soap and salt and sawdust?" Billy asked again.

"If I had told Bodil this," Søren replied, a broad smile, "I would think she had shared our secret." He went to a higher shelf and retrieved one of the wood sculptures, three legs holding a flower just beginning to bud, awkward inviting bits of bloom on a solid grained tripod.

"Morning glory?" Billy asked.

"No. But I have heard someone call it that before." He held it for Billy to inspect. "But I did not carve the bud." He turned it to show all angles. "No. I left it outside in a rainstorm. I put it down on the step to go back and close the barn doors and then some windows in the house before the rains came. Then the rains were coming down for two days. When I found it again, there was a bud spreading. My Bodil calls it the trinity flower. A bud sprouting. The three legs of faith and love and surprise held a special prayer to heaven, and the hopes are answered. Destiny. Maybe something like that."

"It's different. And beautiful," Billy said.

"Yes. One day it is Bodil and me too. Our hope. Our destiny. I keep it on the special shelf here." He replaced it carefully. "Come on, then. Let's wrap these pieces here in tissue and pack them gently in a box for Bodil to take to København when she goes to work next week. The coat too. And if you like, you can sweep while I make some shavings and then put away the tools and some wood I have on the pile. And we can open the bath and bring the carvings out and see if we have any special trinity flowers."

Søren unwrapped a large bar of olive oil soap and began to slide it across a kitchen grater over a clean piece of cheesecloth. He smiled at Billy. "I will mix my special rub here and work on one or two of the trinity figures, but I cannot let you do it, William. It gives a man's hands and clothes and breath a secret aroma, which my Bodil loves and which she thinks is just her Søren's natural smell." His smile broadened. "It is something I will not share with anyone." He whistled softly as the green olive flakes fell to the cloth on the workbench.

"William," he asked, "tell me, how is Elizabeth finding her papers in the end? Her book which was missing when she came to Kathryn? It sounds very serious. I will keep your secret if you will keep mine." He hesitated. "I am thinking. If I would lose such a large part of me, like my beautiful Bodil, I might just die."

Billy stopped sweeping. "Yes. Me too. And I was there. I was certain Elizabeth would have a nervous breakdown. Or a heart attack. I had only met her an hour or so before this all happened. But we had already shared so much. A ride in my cab. It was actually very easy to find where the manuscript was, since Elizabeth knew who it probably was, and we had all the information we needed. We had the man's business card and knew where he was staying, because my friend had driven the man there in his cab. My friend was the one who retrieved the papers and things.

Chapter 26

HOLLISTER. A DARKENED ROOM. ECHOES AND DREAMS (2015)

Hollister told the tale often, how he snaked the manuscripts and letters and the precious photograph from the train robber, Newcomb. Many people had heard the story numerous times and would notice small and not so small changes in each telling. And more suspense in each.

"It was in the hotel's dining room, pure serendipity." And then Hollister always clarified about serendipity, "It means luck. Or good fortune." Hollister had gone to the hotel desk and asked for Arthur Newcomb, Air-Ride Design & Engineering Corporation. Elkhart, Indiana.

"Giving a presentation. The convention." Hollister flashed his cabbie ID and put it quickly back into his pocket. The clerk pointed to the dining room.

"Mr. Newcomb checked in this morning. He just came down. Needed a quick breakfast before his speech. His train was late, I think. Important guy. Big wheel in the business."

Hollister always remarked that the real serendipity, or luck, was Newcomb's self-confidence and high opinion of himself.

"His weak point. His Achilles heel." Then Hollister would explain that key angle to the Battle of Troy. But just as important, there were two police officers in the lobby Hollister recognized. Two of his father's friends on the force, before his father was killed.

"Line of duty," he always added. He knew the two policemen would do anything for his father. Hollister asked them to wait in the doorway to the dining room. Backup. In case he needed them.

"Just stand there, looking very concerned and very dangerous," he said. He knew they were probably in the hotel looking for some free convention food anyway, and had time to spare. Hollister crossed his fingers and walked toward the man's table. He noticed Newcomb had his attaché case at his side, next to his seat. As Hollister approached, the man picked up the attaché and placed it on the table, opening the lid. Hollister introduced himself. "Mr. Arthur Newcomb? Air-Ride Design & Engineering? Elkhart, Indiana?"

The man hesitated and lowered the lid. Hollister put his hand on the lip of the open case, maintaining a gentle gap, the case's contents visible.

"Who are you? Get your hand off," Newcomb began, and Hollister interrupted, lowering his voice to a clear and strong whisper, like air brakes. Newcomb sat back as Hollister pulled back a chair at the table and sat down, his other hand still in the briefcase. Hollister leaned toward Newcomb and nodded toward the lobby.

"Mr. Newcomb. My two colleagues in the doorway to the lobby are aware you have items in your case here, or in your room, which belong to a Mrs. Elizabeth Wade. Papers and items of interest."

Newcomb looked over his shoulder toward the doors. The two uniformed officers stood there, hands on their belts. Both had ominous deadpan expressions. One nodded toward Hollister and Newcomb.

"They are waiting there to spare you embarrassment in front of your audience before this morning's presentation."

"What in the hell is this about? Who are you?"

"We met in the cab this morning. I moonlight. My name is Hollister. Investigations. We received a call concerning Mrs. Wade's loss. I have called your office. I have not shared the details of our visit here, but your arrest would likely cause a stir at your place of employment. Perhaps we can avert that inconvenience."

"She left them on the train, Mr. Hollister. They are right here, and I didn't know how to contact her. She should have called me."

"She is not able to call, given the anguish of the loss. Ten or fifteen years' writing? We were contacted by her caregivers thirty minutes ago."

"What? Caregivers? She's as fit as anything."

"Mr. Newcomb, her growing alarm and incapacitation will magnify the claims against you." Hollister turned toward the doorway and held out his free hand, and then raised it, as if to stop the officers at the door, for a moment at least. Newcomb looked over his shoulder at the two officers, who seemed about to step forward. Perspiration beaded at his temples and on his upper lip.

"OK, OK. Here. I have to go. I have a presentation to make." He raised the lid to his case. "Here it is." He grasped a sheaf of yellow legal pad paper. "There. Now leave me alone," he hissed.

Hollister grasped the yellow sheets, glanced at the underside. "The white pages too, Newcomb. You are a half step from arrest and another quick call to your office. Your boss. The theft, the train compartment you offered. The presentation you will miss in a few moments. The papers, Newcomb."

Hollister wondered about the man's interest and added, "The papers. And the rest of what you took."

"What?"

"The white papers. And the rest. Open the case, Newcomb. Time's up." Hollister looked up as the two officers waved and left the doorway, one of them pointing to his radio. "A call," his finger and wide smile said. Newcomb began to turn toward the door, and Hollister stopped him.

"The rest of it, now! Or sit in interrogation while your boss decides whether to bail you out. If you dare call him."

"OK, OK." Newcomb drew out another sheaf of legal pad pages, white, same clear handwriting. Some typed. Hollister took the white papers.

"And?" Hollister held out his hand. Newcomb sank in his seat. He could see curious interest on the faces of people at the neighboring tables. They were following the hushed drama.

"Elizabeth's belongings, and now I will begin to talk louder." Newcomb reached into the case and drew out a worn envelope, faded handwriting, old stamps. Hollister spied a piece of gloss as Newcomb tried to fold the lid shut.

"And the photographs, Newcomb."

Newcomb slumped. "There was only the one. That's it. That's all. I swear." He lifted the lid and picked out a bright, grainy photograph of trees and sunlight. Green and bright. Looking closer, Hollister saw rusty train tracks. Weeds and decay. Newcomb held the photograph out. Hollister took it and made a guess.

"And how about the final piece of the puzzle?" He lowered his voice to a whisper. "Open the case, Mr. Newcomb. You've already turned over enough to have you arrested, here and now. Simple theft." His voice gained strength, and Newcomb quickly opened the case and swiveled it on the table for Hollister to look.

"No, Mr. Newcomb. She said there were two letters. Perhaps in your pocket?" Hollister held out his hand.

Newcomb stared for a moment and smiled. "It's not all what it appears to be. I was assisting her with her writing. Here." He reached into his jacket's inner pocket and drew out another worn envelope. Hollister took it. He could see foreign stamps. A faded postmark. The stamp. Danmark.

Hollister stood. "I'll take these to Mrs. Wade. If anything is missing, we'll be back for you, no discussion next time. And I'll call directly to your boss. Probably end your career."

"It's everything." Newcomb sighed. "It's everything. It's a story, but really no story at all. No plot. No nothing. Nothing turns out in the end. And you can go to hell, Hollister."

"I've been there, Newcomb. But I came back. And that's only the beginning of my story." Hollister turned and headed for the lobby, then stopped and returned to Newcomb's table. Newcomb was rearranging the papers in his briefcase. Hollister slid the chair from the table and sat down.

Newcomb looked up in surprise. His eyes were glistening, his face flushed. "What?"

"No more trouble, Newcomb. I promise. I had one other question that bugged me. All the way down here. And I want to take something good back to tell Mrs. Wade. Besides the papers and things."

"What do you mean? I've got to hurry now." He breathed deeply and shook his head. "No. I'm going to skip the conference. I don't feel well," he said. He closed his eyes and shook his head. "What do you want, Hollister?"

"Well, I'm sorry for leaning on you. But I had to get the papers. And I have a question. You gave your card to Mrs. Wade. You put your trade magazines in her writing folder. She figured it was to make up for the weight of the papers you took, so she wouldn't notice."

Newcomb closed his eyes and raised his hand. "Enough, Hollister. I would have called her today, to say there had been a mistake when we were packing up our things to get off in Sacramento. That I had her papers, somehow by mistake." He shook his head. "I would have brought them to her tonight or tomorrow. I needed to look through the papers. Her notes. There was something I needed to know."

"What in the world?" Hollister began, and Newcomb cut him off.

"You have no idea. It's such a crazy coincidence that we met on the train. She knows about most of it. We met once, years and years ago. In Bethlehem. In Pennsylvania. A party. A going-away party for a guy leaving for Europe."

"And? If she knows, so what then?"

Newcomb narrowed his eyes and leaned forward. "You said you have been to hell and back. What did you mean?"

Hollister pushed his seat back and started to get up. Newcomb grasped Hollister's arm and went on. "No! You tell me what you meant by 'hell and back,' and I'll tell you about Elizabeth Wade and the party in Bethlehem. And my own hell and back." He stared at Hollister. "Hell and back?"

"It's personal. My dad. He was a cop. He was the smartest and kindest man in the world. He always told me never to turn from anyone in need. Never. It was our duty. Especially if they were down and out. Or some kind of victim. If they didn't have a chance." Hollister looked down, and then back at Newcomb. "He drilled that into me over and over. Our duty. One day he and his partner were sent out to a house where a strung-out guy was holding his former girlfriend and a couple of kids at gunpoint, something about child support. My dad was shot down as he tried to calm the man down. Could happen to anybody, I guess, but it cost me my dad. All I had in the world."

"I'm sorry," Newcomb said.

"No. I let my rage get out of hand, same time I never forgot my dad's words. About duty. Helping when someone was down. But I stayed angry and struck out at anyone who I believed was pushing the weak ones around. I became the bully and the loser myself. Until a kind lady took me and a couple of my friends under her wing. And so I'm back. On track." He looked at Newcomb. "So. What's your story?"

"It's not as frightful as yours, Hollister." He paused. "I'm sorry. For you. And for your father. I think maybe you will be making up for it. You will find a good way to do that."

"OK. We'll be even, then," Hollister said. "Once you tell me about the party. Bethlehem."

"Yes. I don't think you will understand this, but I've been living in my own hell. Imagine. A party." Suddenly Newcomb looked sheepish. Ashamed. He looked down and shook his head. "It's about a story written a long time ago, about a man who goes into a darkened room and a woman who is in the dark room kisses him, and then she runs away. The man never forgets it, the moment. What might have been."

"Newcomb. Are you putting me on? A darkened room? What are you talking about? What does this have to do with Mrs. Wade's papers?" Hollister leaned back.

A convention official approached Newcomb, pointed to his watch and nodded for him to come along. "Your presentation. Five minutes, please."

Newcomb waved the man away. "Yes. I'm coming." He turned back to Hollister and leaned forward. He breathed heavily, sweat beading on his forehead. He swiped at it with a table napkin. A crumb of toast remained on his eyebrow. Hollister reached out and lightly brushed it off. Newcomb smiled. "I see you are a kind soul." He leaned closer.

"Well. In Bethlehem. The party. Way back. The seventies. I was finishing up my studies at the university in the town. Engineering. I had been in the country several years. From Germany. I was late getting started. But I had one or two good friends, and one of them invited me to this party. It was a going-away party for a faculty member at a nearby small college. He was going to Europe to work. Or study. The party was very dull for me. My friend left, and I was tired. I went into a bedroom in the apartment. To just sit for a bit. In a big chair by the window. I must have fallen asleep."

"What does this have to do with Mrs. Wade's papers, Newcomb?"

"Yes. I am getting to that. I woke up as someone was closing the door. A person sat down on the bed and made this sound that was very much like the sound I must have made when I sat in the chair. Relaxed and bored and wishing the party was over. Something like that, if you can imagine what the sound would be."

"Was this a man or a woman?" Hollister asked.

"I don't know, but from what Elizabeth told me about the party, it was her."

"What? You were there? With her?"

Newcomb brushed the question away, a wave. "Before I could say anything, and I didn't want to scare the person, the door opened, and someone else came in, real quick, and closed the door. In the brief glow of light from the hallway, I could see it probably was a man. Or at least I thought it was a man. He stood at the door, and I heard him turn the lock. Maybe in the door handle. So now I was really in a spot, but before I could think to say anything, he took some shuffling steps backward, toward the bed. And he sat down. I heard some very low words, surprise at first, and then she was telling the person to just be quiet and wait. Then it was very quiet, and I didn't dare make a sound. I could hear that they lay down on the bed. I think she was crying. Or it could have been the other person."

"The papers, Newcomb? What does this have to do with her papers?"

Newcomb sighed, then nodded to the impatient conference official standing near the table. The official tapped his watch. Newcomb waved him away again. "I wanted to look through her notes. She talked about this on the train, and then stopped. There was something important at just this point. I wanted to study her notes today, and then I would call her and tell her I had found I had shuffled her papers and my magazines by mistake as we were packing up."

"That's not enough of an explanation, Newcomb, though I thank you." Hollister looked closely at Newcomb's eyes. He was beaten, worn down.

Newcomb shook his head. "You are right. There is more. Nothing terrible. Simple, really. And I am ashamed." He waited. "Elizabeth and I talked at the party. Just ideas, but important ones for me. On the train out here, we talked about it, our conversation, so many years ago, but also a little bit about the darkened room. She never knew I was there." He scratched at the lock on his attaché. "I wanted to search her notes, or see if maybe she had even written about it as part of her story. I wanted to see if it matched what I knew to be true. In the room that night. The facts. Or if she would gloss over it. Or change it."

"At the party, you never told her you were there? Or when you talked on the train?"

"No. I didn't move or say anything. After what seemed like a long, long time, they left the room. Without turning on the light, real quiet. They slipped out into the hallway. And of course I didn't mention it afterward, when I went back to the party. But I felt I knew so much about her. And I knew what had happened in the room. It wasn't the usual sort of thing." He paused and breathed in several times, straightened up and looked at Hollister.

"Hollister. I have always wanted to be that man in the dark. Not a bystander. It has been my story, always." He waited. "And on the train, as she read from her notes, I wanted to be in her story. Somewhere. Or at least something from that party. I had to search her notes. I wanted to be in her story." He looked down. "Are we even now? You know something of my shame. My night-mare. But also my dream. I was in her story. But no one will know. Not even Elizabeth. That's my hell." He stood up and reached out his hand. "Sorry for all the inconvenience. If you can tone down my confession to Elizabeth, I would appreciate it."

Hollister shook Newcomb's hand, an angular grin. "I will think about it." Hollister hesitated. "Hey, by the way. One more thing. The letter from Denmark. I'm not going to read it, common courtesy. But it was in your pocket, not with the rest of the papers or the letter or photo. What was in that letter? I'll trade you for an even friendlier report to Mrs. Wade, sort of what you would have told her tonight or tomorrow. And anyway, I believe you on that. What was the second letter about? What was so special about the letter?"

Newcomb stared. "You'll tell her my apology?"

"Sure. What was the letter about? Why did you have that in your pocket?"

"It was to Elizabeth. It's a mystery, and I wanted to find out more. It was almost like a form letter, but it was asking a Mrs. Elizabeth Wade to set a pris-oner free. Someone unfairly imprisoned. The letterhead was an international organization for human rights, offices located in Denmark. I really don't know why I pulled it out separate. It was a plea for someone's release from a prison." He hesitated. "Maybe the prison of regret, Hollister. Maybe she'll tell *you*." He picked up his attaché, turned on his heel, and followed the conference organizer toward the door.

Chapter 27

BILLY HER LAUGHTER,
BRIGHT AS THE SUN (2017)

Bodil and Billy drove toward Terndrup, north and west of Hadsund. Søren had remained at home, in his workshop. The morning was brisk. Wind and bright sunshine. Billy felt refreshed, dreamless sleep with no reminders in the night from Elizabeth about her story, about writing or revision. Or Rita. He sensed he would learn some of the mystery surrounding Elizabeth and her past from Rita. Or perhaps there was none. He had received no revelations in Pennsylvania. As he remembered it, the old woman had shared nothing other than some regret. Or fears. The visit there seemed a lifetime ago. And perhaps this would be the same, with Rita supplying no clues.

Bodil hadn't said anything other than "let's go now." Søren had also been very quiet. They were planning a quick drive to København and back the next day, to deliver Søren's carvings and the coat to the shop for sale. They had invited Billy to drive along, but did not raise any question about him possibly heading back to the States once he had met with Rita. They would drive to Arhus and take the catamaran ferry from there instead of Ebeltoft. A little over an hour. Billy wondered if they were worried about the trip or about delivering the things for sale. Søren had told Billy it was all on commission.

Fields and dark forest framed the short drive, the road making angular turns to outline small parcels of farmland and homes, many of which looked much like Bodil's house. Whitewash and tile roofing. Scattered small flocks of sheep and goats. Cows. In the daylight Billy was surprised to see that many homes had solar panels installed. Electric pancls and some he thought were likely thermal hot water. An occasional windmill. Bodil was unusually quiet.

"You OK, Bodil?" he asked.

"Yes. I am. Fine." She closed her eyes for a moment and shook her head, downshifting for a sharp corner. "No. I am not fine. Not OK either. I just don't know."

"What is it?"

Bodil let the car coast to a stop. She turned off the engine and put her forehead on the steering wheel. "This is so crazy. I mean, I am driving you to Rita's house for you to clear up her mystery in your William Story. Your book. So this visit, it is the real thing. Your book, it is not really fiction, but it doesn't feel real. It's like a dream, and I don't know if it is a good one or a bad one." She leaned back and thumped the heel of her hand on the steering wheel. "But that's not what I mean. I mean, what about me? I pick you up as I am leaving my airport, and you come to our little house and tell us stories that bring me and my man clinging to each other in the night. And this is at our house, where my man makes precious gifts for people and I fly away again and again. And I wonder if he will be there when I come home. Home? Where is home? It is where one day he will make a beautiful coat for a woman who will be near him all the time, not running off, and who carries his child on her knee. A true story, William. Where is the Bodil Story that I want? Well, William? Where is the real Bodil Story?"

She leaned back and closed her eyes. "I am so sorry, William. You did not need to hear this. I have been so happy the past two days. And Søren is too. I mean, he is usually very satisfied, and also very quiet. But today and yesterday and the evening before, he is the most wonderful man. Yesterday and today he makes me feel like the most beautiful and desirable woman in the whole world. Telling me little pieces of his day and how my hair shines in the sunlight. It's like, I don't know. Magic. Yes, in a magic story while the real world floats by. I don't know what to do."

Billy had no idea what to say. A tight knot. "Well. I don't know either," he said. "Maybe just ride to Copenhagen tomorrow and let Søren drive. Just watch him while he drives, and see if you know him. Maybe every now and then tell him what you're thinking. Or feeling. Or something about the Bodil Story. And if I'm returning to the airport with you tomorrow, be sure I sit in the back." He shook his head, thinking how childish his words sounded.

"You are not going back yet, are you?" Bodil's voice was anxious. Tight hands on the steering wheel. "You can stay with us a day or two more, maybe?" She took in a deep breath and smiled. "And we need another bedtime story." She laughed and started the car. "Or maybe you will stay with Rita and her family or friends for a while. It will be interesting to meet her. It's not too far now. I think I have the right directions." She looked over her shoulder and steered the car back onto the road. "I am sorry for sounding like a foolish girl, William."

They drove in silence. Past a stand of fir trees. Measured rows. She slowed again. "Here it is." They turned into a short gravel drive that opened onto a wide yard surrounded on three sides by a freshly whitewashed farmhouse with many windows and three entryways.

Bodil answered Billy's question. "It's like ours. A farmhouse, and this one looks like it is also a converted barn and stalls, for living." She turned off the engine and set the brake. They got out and went to the closest door. Several cats and a rooster followed at their heels.

A woman greeted them and invited them in. Bodil introduced Billy, the person from America who was bringing a message for Rita. It seemed to be news for the woman. Bodil assured the woman they had called Rita to be certain sure she was at home. The woman's face lightened. Billy tried to follow the conversation but could understand only that they were delighted he had come. It sounded to him that Rita was not there. Bodil said good-bye to the woman. They went back toward the car.

"She's not here?" Billy asked.

"No, she is here. She lives in her own small house. The *skurvogn*. That's a shed or work shed, actually. Or a small cabin. And for workers it's a small building on wheels, and they take it from job to job. They keep their tools in the shed and eat their lunch and drink coffee there. Or drink beer. This is a collective. That means they all take part, share costs, maybe eat some meals together. Two or three families, or more. And some individuals. Maybe like Rita. We'll see."

"A collective farm? Like in Russia?"

"No. Those are big ones run by the state. This is either rented from an owner, or one of the people here owns the place. Or they all do, as a group. I don't know if they farm or if they have jobs. You can ask Rita. This is her skurvogn. Here."

The small wooden building was on a rise above the driveway, angled away from the farmhouse, the front door and a small brick patio facing south, on the far side of the shed. Bodil and Billy rounded the skurvogn. A thin woman sat in a chair. She was covered with a light wool blanket. She looked up toward their footsteps and beamed a cheerful smile. She had clear blue eyes and long light-brown hair, feathers wisping in the light wind. She put up a hand to gather her hair.

"Is this Bodil and William coming here? I am talking as much English as I know. For William. Come and sit with me while the sun is still warm." She held out her hand. "William?"

"Yes. I am very glad to meet you, Rita." He reached for her hand. "It seems like I should know you, from working on the book. And knowing your mother. She wanted you to have a copy of the book."

"Yes. I have heard about the book, a little bit. From Bodil." She smiled, her hair persisting in the wind, dancing across her face, expectant eyes. She reached up and brushed the hair back again. "Yes. It is easy knowing someone in the book. Maybe I was very young in my mother's story. And Bodil is here?" She held out her hand. Bodil took Rita's hand in both of hers. They talked carefully, in English.

"We spoke on the phone. I am glad to meet you," Bodil said.

"It is very nice. You had such a beautiful voice on the phone, Bodil. And here too, of course. I have made coffee in the kitchen." She laughed. "Which is right next to the living room and bedroom and bathroom, all in one. Lucky it's just me in the skurvogn." She shifted in the chair and started to get up. Bodil put a hand on Rita's shoulder.

"I can get it just as easily as you," she said, and went up the two steps into the tiny house. "This is what I do for a living."

"There is coffee cream and honey right next to the cups, Bodil," Rita called out. "And some biscuits."

"I see it all. Such a pretty house." Bodil came from the house with the cups and coffee, and went back for the rest.

"Yes. My father fixed it up for himself, I think. And then he left it to me. So I moved it here. My own little corner of the world." Billy listened, trying to interpret the messages into points of reference.

"Your father lived here?" he asked.

"No. It was a workroom behind his home. Outside Copenhagen. Where he could go and work in peace." She laughed as Bodil poured coffee for her. "Thank you, Bodil. Oh dear, my poor old dad."

"You were that hard on him?" Billy asked, a friendly jab.

"No. I did not live with him," she said. "I never lived at home."

"Oh. I didn't know." Billy felt a silent wave of ominous information. "And your father lives in Copenhagen?"

"No. He died three years ago. No, four years now."

"Oh my. I am sorry. Again. I didn't know. We didn't know. And then you moved here?"

Rita laughed. "It would be so much easier if I had sent you a small autobiography. Or my memoir. If I was old enough to have one." She laughed again. "It would have saved the confusion." Her smile and laughter were as bright as the sun and wind, Billy thought. The skurvogn was a matching yellow, with clean white trim.

Rita went on, looking at the sky. "I lived at the school where I was in training, and then I had an apartment in Copenhagen with friends who had the same interests. We worked together too. One of them moved here for a while. I had visited a couple of times. So when my father died, I asked if I could move here. They didn't really have room, so I told them I had a skurvogn. And here we are today."

Billy's mind raced with the day's information and questions, clouded by Bodil's fears and the wonder at how things so obvious sometimes unfolded so slowly. He wondered aloud, "Your work?"

"Yes. My group writes letters for a nonprofit— NGO, I think you call them. For a cause we are very much concerned about. Imprisoned dissidents. Never mind if they are actual dissidents, or whether they are falsely accused, which is often the case."

"Everyone here? At the farm?"

"No, no. Nobody here. Here, some have jobs. One takes care of the animals and the hay, and two of them take turns helping with me. I wish they would send letters too. But that is what I do. Ten years now."

Billy felt it would be in order to ask. "Do you get paid to write the letters? I mean, is it your job?"

"Well, I am on a pension, of course. Some people are paid something, I think. But my pension is more than enough. To live in a skurvogn, for sure." She laughed at the thought.

"A pension?" Billy asked, and at the same moment Rita answered, he knew the dreaded words she would say. He was relieved when Rita started with what he did not know.

"Well, yes. I have hidden from you the difficulty I have getting about, even getting up from the chair. There have been times when the thunderclouds sneak up on me, and by the time I understand it is going to rain, before I can get inside, I will be soaked." She laughed. "My joints and my back and my legs and muscles don't work well together. They battle one against the other. It has been my life since I was born." She paused. "And of course you knew I am blind."

"Yes. I mean no, I did not know. And I was very slow to see it," he said. "I can prove I didn't know. I brought a book Elizabeth wrote. Your mother. I am really stupid sometimes. I am very sorry."

"Oh no, William. It is not a problem to be sorry for." She reached for his arm. Carefully, where it might be, and patted him gently. She laughed. "I knew you were there. Not to worry. For the book's pages, I have a scanner hooked to my computer, though it doesn't get all the words right all the time." She sipped at her coffee. "And the voice is too friendly and bland. But at least it reads all the words in the book." She hesitated, then smiled and turned toward his voice. His arm. "William. If you were reading to me my mother's book, would you read me all the words? Even words which might be unkind? Or not all true? Every last one?"

"Yes. Of course I would. Why do you ask?"

"When do you have to return to America?" Rita asked, a smile widening her radiance.

"I might leave for Copenhagen tomorrow. With Bodil and Søren, or I could wait another few days until Bodil goes back to work. It was nice driving to Jutland with her."

Rita interrupted. "I mean, when do you for absolute sure *have* to be back in the States? For your job or school or whatever. For your wife or your lover? Or your kids?"

"Oh. I see. Well, I took a couple weeks off from work, but that's not a problem, it's part time. I finished community college and start college in the fall, another couple months. That's the one thing I can't miss. No kids or girlfriend. Not married."

"And how is Elizabeth? My mother?"

Billy weighed an answer. "She's fragile. But in a tough sort of way."

"I thought so." Rita reached to where Bodil had been sitting, on the opposite side from Billy. She touched Bodil's arm. "Bodil. Can you manage your home without William for a day or two? Or longer, if he is comfortable here? And then come and get him? I will know how he is doing by how fast he is reading. And maybe he will read slowly, with meaning." Rita beamed with pleasure. "Is this all right, Bodil?" She turned toward Billy. "And William? Can you stay and read to me the book?"

Billy and Bodil exchanged silent questions. Bodil's eyes were a frightened stare, but she nodded an OK to Billy, shrugging. He wondered what his face said in return.

"I don't really like it," Bodil said, a sudden sad grin at Billy. "William's bedtime stories from his book have turned my man into a very tender and secret lover. But we will manage. Maybe we will begin to tell our own bedtime stories. Write them. In the night."

"And maybe it would be a good thing for me to stay and read the book," Billy said. "I have never read it all the way through. I mean, only in sentences and paragraphs and chapters. Maybe we can read it as a revision. Some changes or additions we might make. I'm sure we might even find a mistake or two. I did much of the writing. From your mother's notes. Maybe you would help me, Rita. There are some things we could add."

Rita beamed a tight smile and lifted herself forward in the chair, surprising Bodil and Billy. She seemed to fill with energy and resolve. "It is so good that you drove here today, William and Bodil." She patted Billy's arm on the side of his chair. "Yes. Let's go in, William. There is a chill in the air. We can make some supper. And talk. We have time. You can sleep in the loft or over in the house. They have a room. Bodil, good night, and leave the things right where they are. William can come out and get them as soon as I am settled in my chair. In my comfortable and safe and small space. This will be like a familiar vacation."

Rita struggled to get to her feet. Billy stood up to help, lifting Rita under one elbow. They turned and took a step toward the yellow and white frame. Windowpanes reflecting sun and wind and sky. Billy stopped. "Let me carry you, Rita. Just this one time." He grinned at Bodil. "Before the rain." Rita leaned on his arm. He bent forward and lifted beneath her knees. "There, I've got you." He hefted her weight to a comfortable balance. "Nothing can stop us now," he said.

Rita clasped Billy's neck. "No, William. I've got you," she said. "You are right. Nothing can hold us back. Nothing. Not even the story. And what did you call them? The revisions?"

Billy took two steps toward the skurvogn and stopped. He called to Bodil over his shoulder. "Tell Søren his secret is safe with me. About the sawdust and soap." Bodil gave him a puzzled look, a shadow of disappointment, and he softened. "Have a good trip to Copenhagen, Bodil. And remember, Søren must drive." He turned back to the effortless weight in his arms. Two steps into the skurvogn. He leaned toward her question. "Yes, I will read to you every word." He nodded to Bodil and pulled the door shut with his toe.

Chapter 28

OUR STORY—BLESSINGS AND CURSES, AND STORIES OVERLAP (2017)

illy sat at the kitchen table, late evening. The empty coffee cups and spoons were gathered at the edge of the table. Cleanup. It had been a long day, homecoming, and finding out what everyone had been up to, telling about the trip. Elizabeth left the kitchen and prepared for bed. Billy was still tired from the flights home. From Denmark and New York, jet lag, and more.

At least no bus rides, he thought. Hollister had picked him up at the airport. Nearly two months away from home, too much to tell. Stories. Crisscrossing and weaving into simple or magnificent tapestries. Stories crossing stories.

Kathryn picked up the last of the cups, waving Billy away from helping. He thanked her for the evening and got up to leave, wondering how his mother might be doing. He would sleep at her apartment, then begin to rethink and rework his plans in the morning. He took his jacket from the back of the chair and walked to the bedroom doorway. He leaned into the bedroom. Elizabeth was under the covers.

"Can I come in and say good night?" he asked. "Kathryn is out here in the kitchen cleaning up, making another cup of coffee. Her nightcap."

"Sounds so comfortable," Elizabeth said. "Like a home should be, the sounds of cups and spoons. And when Kathryn is humming to herself, she's so wistful. I want to live inside one of her tunes."

Billy went into the bedroom and sat in the bedside chair. Memories of the months of notes and talk and writing. Elizabeth asked him the questions that had been posed so many times around the table, in so many different ways. She did not wait for answers.

"Are you pleased with the book? Your trip?" She looked closely into his eyes, trying to figure a puzzle. "Are you happy?" He looked away, considering how to answer. Elizabeth went on. "What will we do now? Now that we have finished the book? And what will you do?"

"Well, college next month. Start off part-time, until I get settled and figure out the finances. Lots of paperwork, and I haven't done any of that yet."

"The story isn't finished, William. You know that, don't you?" He was surprised by the question. "Our story isn't finished, William, even though my part in it has just about run its course." She whispered. "It's your story too. You're a different person than you were a month or two ago. Or a half a year. Or probably five years. Do you know what I mean? Before our paths crossed. Our stories."

"I guess so. I think I do," he said.

"No," she said. "The story I believed in all those years was about avoiding the fear. The fearful dreams. But your story so far was just proving you could make it, that you could do it. And now you've caught a scent of where the path might lead, and where stories might cross."

Billy could see Elizabeth's eyes in the dark. He wondered if they were illuminated by the reflection of the kitchen light in his own eyes.

Elizabeth smiled, as if she had heard his thought. "Yes," she said, and went on, taking his hand in hers. "It's OK, William. Your story is precious, and it's waiting to show itself. I just hope you won't worry as much as I did, along the way. And that you don't flee happiness. You know, running away just because things aren't perfect."

He caressed her hand and leaned over the edge of the bed, touching his forehead to her arm.

She went on. "I've been so afraid I would end up in one or another of the tragic stories I loved so much. The days after we met, I felt like Robert Frost's poor old hired man, coming in here to take a nap before being told I had to leave. Dying in Kathryn's back room, an unwelcome guest in the end."

Billy looked up and smiled.

She went on. "Or my favorite sad love story. Evangeline finds her lost love dying on a cot in a sick ward. Wasn't it in a monastery, William?" Her longing question echoed. "There's more to a story than just where we came from or where we went. Or where we ended up. More than a plot even, William," she said.

"What do you mean, more?" he asked. "Another chapter? Elizabeth's Story, Book Two?"

She laughed. "No. We could refresh some of the foolish chapters. But we can't go back and re-live them, can we? At least, I can't. This book is enough for me, even without a plot."

"I don't know," he said.

"But I heard you talking about it at the table, William. How you delivered the books, and so much more came to light. I mean, there is so much more, as the stories cross. My mother, for one. Almost sixty years of silence, other than one letter. And Rita. They're parts of your story now. Waiting for a voice. Waiting to be told, but within your story, filling it out. From the inside, out. Rita's voice. I can hear it. And I think even my mother could gather her voice."

"You mean rework your story? What we have written?" he asked, confused.

"No. That's still Elizabeth's Story, whether finished or not," she said. "Whether memoir or fiction, it's still true enough as is. And complete enough. But there is so much hidden treasure. Just out of sight. You have met people in the shadows. And so much is still hidden from view, where the stories overlap. The moments where stories overlap. Where things are added. Or taken away. Blessings. Or curses. And anything in between. Where the stories overlap, William. It's not just my story. In fact, it's not Elizabeth's Story at all."

He looked toward the light in the kitchen. Kathryn's evening song, a hymn to completion and rest. Gentle longing tones, woven in the night.

Elizabeth patted his hand. "Tomorrow, maybe. We can talk," she said, and hesitated. "William. Before you go. Tell me your best story. Tell me a story about a boy and a girl. One that ends happy. Then maybe I can sleep."

Kathryn hummed a low tune in the kitchen. A moment's silence, and began a new one. Whistling softly at first. Then a few words and notes. "Memory Lane."

Billy smiled in the dark. "Van Morrison," he whispered to Elizabeth. "And wherever Kathryn doesn't know the words, or can't recall them, she'll hum through the lapse. Like one of her unfinished poems."

"Tell me the story, William," Elizabeth said again. "About a boy and a girl."

Billy stood and straightened the covers over Elizabeth, smoothing her hair away from her face. He motioned for her to scoot over. Once she was settled, he stretched out beside her, on top of the covers. He inhaled the dim light from the kitchen. Telling a story, sweet night shades and sounds. Soap and salt and sawdust, blessings and muffled whispers. He reached for Elizabeth's right hand and enfolded it in his. He propped a pillow behind his head, made himself comfortable. He smiled for the nighttime tales. Bodil and Søren. And Rita.

He began. "A boy and a girl walked on abandoned railroad tracks. Stepping carefully on the ties. The distance between the ties too wide or too close for an easy step. The lovers' fingers twined loosely. 'Carry me,' the girl said. The boy scooped her in his arms. Held her close. 'I have you now,' he said. 'No stopping us now.' He carried her toward the dusky evening. Solid footsteps. Rough wooden rungs in the weeds. Around the bend. Where the tracks disappeared. Beyond the gathering darkness. Memories of green and light, beyond the bend in the trees. Just out of sight." Billy saw that Elizabeth breathed gently and repeated it. "Just out of sight. Green and light." He waited in the bedroom's silence for several minutes. He released Elizabeth's hand carefully, pulling the covers over her fingers. "Memory Lane" echoed softly among kitchen sounds. He sat up, carefully swung his feet to the floor, and stood at the side of the bed.

Billy reached into his jacket pocket and drew out a tissue-paper packet. He opened it. A small wooden figure. Smoothed carving. Faint aroma of soap and sawdust. And salt. He caressed the soft wood, three pads lifting a strained promise. An improbable blossom. Søren's trinity flower, from the workshop shelf. On the drive to the airport, Søren explained once again the surprising tiny branch budding in the rain, his prized possession. Bodil's hand on Søren's shoulder as he drove. Her prayer. Their gift.

"So unexpected, yet here we are," Søren said, glancing toward Billy in the back seat, "and now also growing within my woman, William. *Velsignelsen.* The blessing."

Bodil beamed embarrassment, even though she had told Billy the news days before. "And wait until he tells you," she had begged, in her excitement. A glow he had not seen before. The Alfetta hummed in fifth gear. "And of course I am returning to Jutland with my man today." She patted Søren's shoulder. "No more flying away from Kærby," she said. "Never ever. A little one. A little twig. And maybe there will be some more of them in our story." She laughed. "I like that. Twigs!"

Billy folded the tissue around the carving. Elizabeth slept soundly, regular breathing. Another song in the kitchen, Kathryn's evening magic. Coffee cups and spoons, shelves and drawers. The yawning chasm of time. A distant echo and a hazy photograph, sunshine shards through a leaning green chapel of trees.

—∞—

"There, I've got you," he whispered. "Two steps up, pull the door shut. Nothing can stop us now." He remembered her words.

"No, I've got you." Laughter like warm raindrops. "Nothing will hold us back. And we will write our stories."